Cameras swung in their direction

Still gripping her hand, Lee held up the black velvet box to the gathered reporters. "Hey, everyone, my girl just returned my ring."

Shocked silence fell over the onlookers. Jules weathered the stares. As long as Lee understood her motives it didn't matter what other people thought.

"This wonderful woman," he continued, "has spent the past nineteen months comforting my family and friends." Jules squirmed and Lee's fingers tightened. "Now she wants to quietly disappear because she doesn't want me feeling pressured. What do you think? Shall I let her walk away?"

"No," the crowd howled.

"I don't think so, either." He dropped to one knee.

Startled, her eyes widened....

Dear Reader,

I never meant to write a "back from the dead" book in my military heroes series. But I became really intrigued by Lee Davis—outgoing, fearless and larger than life— whom I'd killed off in *Here Comes The Groom* (Harlequin Superromance, January 2011).

By the time I started writing *Stand-In Wife* (Harlequin Superromance, August 2011), I was playing with bringing him back, and by book three—*Bring Him Home* (Harlequin Superromance, June 2012)—I'd evolved the setup that allowed me to resurrect him. And I'd also fleshed out his fiancée, Juliet Browne, whose story I always meant to tell.

She was originally going to find a new guy through his army buddies' matchmaking, but Lee proved impossible to replace. So, I thought, why replace him? And I loved the concept of a man coming home to discover the woman who'd rejected his proposal wearing his ring and ensconced in the bosom of his family. What fun.

Of course, once I started thinking and reading about the effects of captivity I realized that the guy who returned wouldn't be the same man who'd left and the story became less comic and more complex. Drop me a line— karina@karinabliss.com—and let me know what you think of the results.

Happy reading,

Karina Bliss

www.karinabliss.com

A Prior
Engagement

KARINA BLISS

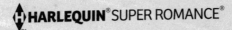

Recycling programs
for this product may
not exist in your area.

ISBN-13: 978-0-373-71849-8

A PRIOR ENGAGEMENT

Printed in U.S.A.

ABOUT THE AUTHOR

New Zealander Karina Bliss has written eleven books for Harlequin Superromance since 2006 when her debut, *Mr. Imperfect,* won an Australian Romantic Book of the Year award. She was also the first Australasian to win the Romance Writers of America's coveted Golden Heart award for unpublished writers. Based on the sunny Hibiscus Coast in New Zealand with her husband and son, Karina keeps contact with her readers through social media. Make contact through her website: www.karinabliss.com or www.facebook.com/KarinaBlissAuthor or www.goodreads.com/karinabliss.

Books by Karina Bliss

HARLEQUIN SUPERROMANCE

Other titles by this author available in ebook format.

To Trevor, who brainstormed revisions through a five-hour drive to Napier and remains the best decision I ever made.

And to my editor, Victoria Curran, book midwife extraordinaire.

Thanks for your patience through a difficult birth.

CHAPTER ONE

SLEEP WAS ALWAYS elusive, the first night in a strange bed.

Juliet Browne plumped the pillow, trying to put more volume into it. It was too soft, the mattress too firm and ambient light emanated through a picture window to her right when she was used to cocooning darkness.

She could close the curtain....

Except what she *did* like about this room was the gnarled pohutukawa branches, spindly as ballerina legs and tufted with leaves dancing in the wind outside the window. Moonlight filtered through them, dappling the stark walls and Spartan-white duvet cover with monochromic graffiti. There was something anarchic about the bony branches that channeled her growing emotion.

Don't be sad.

Rolling on her back, she stared up at the ceiling, shaped like an inverted triangle. This house was pale, stylized and angular, reflecting its architect owner. She liked Mark, liked his steadiness, his creativity, his easy conviction that, gee, life was pretty good, wasn't it?

Tears prickled behind her eyelids and she blinked them away, sidling closer to the edge of the bed, as far away as possible from the man sleeping on the other side. It was normal to feel bewildered, even bereft, under the circumstances. Sex represented the last goodbye in a two-year journey of moving on—it was bound to raise Lee's ghost.

Go to sleep, she sternly ordered herself and his ghost.

But if their short, intense relationship had taught her anything, it was that Lee Davis had never been one to lie down quietly. Tucking the sheet around her, Jules thought about the trust agreement she'd been amending that day. The intricacies of subclauses would soothe her faster than watching branches dance.

A sound startled her awake. Opening blurry eyes, she saw her evening clutch bag vibrating on the nightstand. The realization of where she was returned slowly. Glancing over her bare shoulder at Mark, curled away from her, sound asleep, she turned back in time to see her quivering bag topple onto the floor, spilling its contents.

Mark muttered but didn't wake. Just as well—she'd told him she'd switched off her cell. He'd wanted an intimate dinner with no outside interruptions. Instead, she'd put it on vibrate, unwilling to entirely disconnect from the world.

The low hum stopped as the call went to message. Rolling to the edge of the mattress, Jules shoved her things back into her handbag. A lipstick, comb, a couple of business cards—Juliet Browne, Solicitor, West Harbor Law—a credit card and keys hooked to a miniature tennis ball. Just out of reach, her cell pinged a message, its screen casting a green glow across the white carpet.

She frowned, catching sight of the time. Who would be trying to contact her at six o'clock on a Sunday morning? Pushing aside the covers, she crept out of bed, grabbing her cell en route to the bathroom, where she slid the partition door shut before flicking on the light switch. Ignoring the naked brunette illuminated in the mirror, she checked her messages. Texts from Dan, Ross and Nate…. Surely Lee's surviving army buddies weren't already after a progress report? And two missed calls from Nate. She scanned the text messages first.

From Ross at midnight: Have you talked to Nate yet?

From Dan at 1:00 a.m.: Phone me soon as you've talked to Nate.

Anxiously she listened to Nate's voice messages, the first sent at eleven-thirty the night before. "Jules, I need to talk to you urgently. Good news, incredible news but—" he gulped "—call me, okay?"

His second was the call a few minutes ago. "Where *are* you if you're not at home?"

Then she read a text from him: CALL ME!

In growing alarm, she punched in his number.

He picked up after the first ring. "Jules," he said. "Thank God. Claire and I are bouncing off walls here."

"What's happened?"

"It's good news—the best—but you need someone with you."

"Someone is with me. I'm at Mark's."

There was a moment's silence. "Oh shit, you've slept with him."

"What did you think we'd do when you guys set us up, play tiddlywinks? What's going on?"

"Hang on." A few seconds later, Claire, her best friend and Nate's fiancée, came on.

"This needs to be done in person," Claire said by way of greeting. "Go home and we'll meet you there." She and Nate lived forty minutes east of Whangarei, the small city that acted as a gateway to northern New Zealand.

Jules clutched the cell. "If *you're* up this early on a Sunday it must be bad." Claire was notoriously grumpy in the mornings.

"I swear it's brilliant news…astonishing—" Her voice broke.

Nate came back on the line. "Look, we can't do this over the phone, Jules," he said impatiently. "Just get home."

"Is Claire cry—" The bathroom door opened and Mark

came in, rubbing his face. His hair was ruffled. And he was naked. Resisting the urge to cover her own nudity, Jules cut the conversation short. "Fine. The spare key is under a fake rock to the left of the potted geraniums."

"You *can't* be serious," Nate said, incredulous. She broke the connection before the former celebrity bodyguard could lecture her about security.

"What's going on?" Mark asked.

"That was Nate and Claire." In the mirror, two people stood naked in a confined space under a bank of spotlights. Jules edged past him and into the bedroom. "Good news, apparently, but they want to tell me in person."

"Why would they withhold good news? That doesn't make sense."

"It doesn't, does it?" Anxiously, she started dressing, putting a run in her nylons in her haste. Jules wiggled into her cocktail dress, a fitted sheath in flamingo-pink, and stepped into the matching stilettos. "Zip me up?"

He did, and then dropped her shawl, a fine paisley silk, across her shoulders. "Want me to come with you?"

"No." Mark raised an eyebrow and Jules patted his arm. "Thanks, but I'm sure it's fine." A romance was one thing, letting him into her relationship with Lee's friends something else. Even if the guys had set them up. Mark's brother Richard served with Ross in the SAS and Mark had designed the renovations for Claire and Nate's home.

Her new lover pulled on jeans and walked her to the front door, which he unlocked. "Phone me when you know."

"I will." She waited for him to open it.

"Wait a sec. You forgot something."

Jules tamped down her impatience as he disappeared in the direction of the kitchen. A few minutes later he returned with the enormous bunch of pink peonies he'd given her the night before, still in their cellophane. He'd wrapped the ends in damp newspaper. And as much as Jules wanted to race home and find out what the hell was going on, she took a minute to kiss this thoughtful man.

"I had a great time," she said, then added more truthfully, "I'm glad it was you." Last night had been about more than a physical connection—she'd needed the tenderness. And if the sex hadn't been earth-shattering, it would get better as she practiced letting go.

He grinned, suddenly boyish as he turned the burnished doorknob. "I'm glad it was me, too. Call me."

"I will." When he closed the door, she ran.

THIRTY MINUTES LATER, Jules spun into the quiet cul-de-sac where she lived, the loud rumble of her recent purchase—a 1959 Cadillac de Ville—vying with the dawn chorus of the sparrows nesting in the old oak in her front yard.

Nate's glossy black four-wheel drive was already parked in her driveway and she screeched to a halt behind it. Opening her clutch bag, she pulled out her diamond ring and slid it on, then grabbed her house keys and the flowers. In last night's clothes, with tousled hair, slutty stilettos and kiss-swollen lips, she felt like Cinderella minus the midnight intervention. Which was crazy—her friends wouldn't judge her.

No, she was doing that herself.

The door opened before she could insert the key in the lock and she found herself dragged into a convulsive hug by her best friend.

Jules froze. "Oh God, I *knew* it was bad news."

"No, it's great." Claire loosed her hold. "I'm sorry, I've crushed your flowers." Tugging them from Jules's hands, she nervously smoothed out the cellophane. "Go sit down."

But Jules was looking beyond her to Nate, who was standing by the tiny tiled hearth, his fists jammed in the pockets of his jeans. Her stomach dropped. His dark eyes were red-rimmed. Her attention shot to Claire. Her friend's long blond hair was tied back, revealing her pale face; she'd clearly been crying, too. And her piercing blue gaze reminded Jules of a nurse assessing a patient.

"You're scaring me," she croaked.

"If you'd just sit—"

"Tell me now!"

"It's Lee." Nate sucked in a breath, then his face split in a wide, shaky grin. "Jules, he's alive."

The words made so little sense she couldn't process them. Lee was dead, his body detonated by insurgents after an ambush in Afghanistan nineteen months and three days ago. They'd held a memorial service and his SAS comrades had played the Last Post. She shivered, recalling the echo of that mournful bugle. "I misheard you," she said politely. "What did you say?"

"Lee has been discovered alive." Claire gave a half laugh, half sob and reached out a hand, but Jules fended her off.

"No!" It was fatal to let in a whisper of doubt…or hope… after so many months of fighting to accept the grim reality. But the word *alive* had already found a resonance inside her and was sucking all the oxygen out of her lungs. In front of her, Claire kaleidoscoped to a tiny smiling dot.

Jules returned to consciousness to hear Nate say, "We should have made her sit down."

Something pressed against her left cheek. "Ow!" She fumbled at what felt like a wet plastic bag of marbles and opened her eyes. She was lying on the floral couch, her legs raised on cushions.

"It's okay." Nate replaced a package of frozen peas on her left cheekbone. "Only a bruise."

"What happened?" she said in bewilderment.

Tenderly, Claire pushed strands of hair away from her face. "You fainted and hit your head falling. It was the shock."

Lee's alive. Shoving away the peas, Jules jerked upright, and then swayed under a wave of dizziness.

"Easy." Nate steadied her by grasping her shoulders. "Give yourself time to grasp that Lee's a—"

Jules wrenched free. "Stop *saying* that. It's cruel!" Her teeth began to chatter and she hugged herself, blaming the frozen peas for the shivers.

Sitting on the couch, Nate tugged her into his arms. "I swear to God," he rasped, holding her resistant body tight against his chest. "Lee's alive. He's safe."

The sob burst out of Jules, as graceless as a retch. Then another and another. *Alive.* She was barely aware of Nate rocking her, of Claire wrapping her arms around both of them, laughing and crying. A rush of elation percolated through her bloodstream and she started laughing, too.

"Tell me…how…why?"

Nate launched into an explanation of some setup and a body switch. Clinging to Claire's fingers, Jules nodded but all she could hear was the beating of her heart. Alive. Alive. Alive!

"…and when the Americans raided a remote mountain outpost, they discovered the dugout where they'd been holding him."

Some dark thread in his tone caught her attention. "They?"

"He's been a prisoner of the Taliban."

Nate read her fallen expression and added soothingly, "He's in a military hospital in Bagram. His condition can't be too critical or he'd have been evacuated to better facilities in Germany."

"We have to go to him."

Nate exchanged a glance with Claire, who put her arm around Jules. "The SAS has arranged for the guys to fly out tonight."

For a moment she stared at her friend blankly. "Oh, my God." Jules massaged her temples. "He doesn't know about his dad."

Nate gestured to the rock on Jules's finger. The diamond was big and brash, a powerhouse that seemed to seize all ambient light. "Or that he's engaged."

Knowing Lee had intended to propose, his buddies had given her the engagement ring. They'd found it when they'd packed up his personal effects.

Reality hit her like an oncoming locomotive. Instinctively Jules covered the ring with her other hand.

"Now he can propose in person," Claire said cheerfully, as though a six-week whirlwind romance easily withstood a year-and-a-half's separation. A separation where one of the parties had been presumed dead…and the other was boinking someone else.

And that was the least of her problems.

CHAPTER TWO

LEE WOKE AT first light, habituated by many months of the rhythmic chanting of dawn prayers that his captors began their day with. And found himself in a private room in a military hospital at Bagram.

His prayers had been answered.

He stretched his fever-weakened muscles, relishing the clean, scratchy cotton against his torso and any damn mattress, even this serviceable hospital one, cushioning his body. Frankly, he needed the sensory reminder that he wasn't lying on a dirt floor, scratching fleabites while his belly squirmed with dysentery.

The comfortable bed allowed him to close his eyes, confident he wouldn't be kicked into consciousness, and helped him bypass those terrible waking seconds when he thought, *I have to survive another day.* And later, when he'd given up all hope of rescue—*What am I surviving for?*

Opening his eyes, he scanned the simple prefab hospital room, luxuriating in the peacefulness. Closed his eyes and reveled in the lack of pain.

The Americans who'd found him had been kind, treating him with brisk efficiency. A Special Forces soldier—a Kiwi—found alive. Except none were missing. That information had been enough for Lee to begin to doubt his sanity. Again.

Too hyped to sleep he switched on the light—a light!—and poured himself a glass of water from the jug beside the bed. Because he could drink his fill, he had another. Grateful for the small things. A glass. Being hydrated. Hair clean, if uncut. Lips moistened with lip balm, wounds cared for, fever broken. Particularly thankful that his thigh ached from the drugs they'd pumped into it to treat his viral leishmaniasis.

The condition he'd lived with, untreated, for weeks. Along with his name and his unit, it was the only thing he kept repeating between delirium dreams.

Still taking inventory, Lee ran his fingers across his chin, enjoying the smoothness. Last night a nurse had shaved off his beard in preparation for the big meet with the brass this morning, the first he was capable of since his rescue a few days ago. He traced the ridge of scar tissue on his cheek. Maybe designer stubble would be a better idea.

He paused to examine his hand, ignoring the tube taped to the back that connected to an IV feeding him salts, glucose, amino acids and vitamins. His knuckles were swollen. Above the fresh white bandages on his wrist, the skin was weathered and scarred, ingrained dirt in the calluses. His ragged nails were at various stages of regrowth. Not so pretty.

He wiggled his feet, lifted them off the bed, enjoying the light-as-air sensation after months of wearing leg irons. Under the bandages the raw flesh prickled and burned with the effort so he lowered them again.

All that water had made him need to pee. Grabbing the IV stand, he used it as a support and hobbled painfully into the bathroom. He marveled at the clear stream produced by his hydrated kidneys.

At the sink, Lee turned the tap on and off a few times before lathering up his hands. On impulse he cupped them under his nose and inhaled the sudsy fragrance deeply, though God knows there was nothing special about military-grade soap.

Before returning to bed he dropped to the floor and began laboring through five sit-ups and five push-ups. That was all he could manage in his current state. But it was second nature to force himself through this ritual, to try to retain what muscle he could in the forlorn hope he'd find an opportunity to escape.

It hadn't come.

And yet here he was. Free.

Emotion choked him. Halfway through a push-up, his arms gave way and he collapsed on the floor. Automatically, Lee wiped his face dry with the hospital gown. The innocent do not cry, his captors said, because they do not fear death or God's judgment.

After long months of ironclad self-control, weeping was his greatest luxury.

Exhausted, he dragged himself back to bed and slept.

The next time Lee opened his eyes, two uniformed men sat beside him. The insignia on the elder's beret and the badges on his camos indicated senior rank. Lee struggled to sit up but the man restrained him. "Rest easy, son."

The man's accent, his calm commonsense, felt warm as a breeze from home. "I'm Colonel Lucas Bradford, Senior National Officer and Commander of the New Zealand Defense Forces—and this is Dr. Joseph McKenzie."

Lee inspected the second man. Civilian clothes. A clipboard and an intelligent "trust me" empathy. *A shrink.*

Lee smiled, not an easy task with his cracked lips, no matter how much lip balm he used. "Why is it so hard to believe I'm Lee Davis?" The two men seemed taken aback by his astuteness. "I've been getting looks," he explained. "People pausing at the door to stare at me." Even in and out of fever, he'd noticed.

"It's true we doubted your identity," Colonel Bradford answered. "Perhaps it will help if I tell you why." He pulled a file out of a leather briefcase beside his chair and opened it. "Lee Davis died nineteen months ago in a convoy ambush. His uniformed body was found two days later, strapped with explosives. It was detonated with a trip wire as the recovery crew approached, killing four."

He paused, letting Lee fill in the gaps. The cleanup would have been horrendous, a charred mess of bone chips, fragments of flesh and almost nothing remaining of the booby-trapped corpse. "A fingertip collected for DNA testing confirmed one of the four dead as Lee Davis." Instinctively he glanced at Lee's left hand lying across his chest. Five fingers.

Lee pulled his right hand from under the sheet and held up his middle finger. The tip was missing to the top knuckle. "And I thought they just did this for fun." Realizing he was giving the SNO the bird, he grinned. "No disrespect, sir."

"None taken."

"I'm guessing local allies were part of the cleanup and collection team."

The colonel's gaze narrowed. "An insider would explain the accuracy of the ambush."

"Take a DNA sample from me."

"We already have. The results came in a couple of days ago." The older man grinned. "Welcome home, son."

A lump rose in Lee's throat. Maybe being hydrated wasn't such a great thing. "It's good to be back, sir." Or it would be when this sense of surrealism wore off. "My captors told me there had been an ambush."

"You don't remember?" Dr. McKenzie spoke for the first time, his high voice sounding more like a cartoon character's than a psychiatrist's.

"First thing I recall was coming to trussed up in the back of a Toyota pickup." Bought with opium money, the vehicle was a Taliban favorite.

He paused, reliving the triumph of his captors as they jabbed him with gun butts and laughed while he bounced around the cargo bed, unable to brace himself as the pickup bucked across the dunes. Bewildered as to how he'd got there. The sun had been high, the metal had burned where it touched his bare skin. Blood had obscured his vision.

"You were thrown clear when the improvised explosive device detonated under the Humvee," said the SNO. "You must have nine lives to have survived that and a lengthy captivity."

"I was down to my last, sir," Lee said, and it wasn't a joke.

"What puzzles us is why they kept you alive."

"In a previous deployment I'd saved a baby with septicemia." As the team's advanced medic, Lee had often treated people in the remote villages in the course of patrols. Part of the campaign to win hearts and minds—and vital intel.

"Her grandfather, the headman, initially refused treatment, despite the pleas of the baby's mother. Steve Langford, our unit commander, lost his temper and told him he was a selfish old bastard…." Lee swallowed, remembering his troop mates. Dead. All dead. "The elder finally agreed to treatment if I came alone and unarmed."

He shrugged before continuing. "The headman—Ajmal—showed up at camp to watch my execution." He'd been on his knees, wrists tied behind him, a grip on his hair forcing his head back and a blade pressed against his larynx when their startled gazes met.

Lee smiled grimly. "Ajmal's surprise matched mine." He cleared his throat because in his imagination, he could still feel the blade. "His son was the local Taliban commander and, as it later turned out, the baby's uncle. I demanded nanawatai. Asylum." Amazing how fast the brain can think seconds from death.

The colonel nodded; the doctor looked confused. "Pre-deployment our men study Pashtunwali," the SNO informed the psych. "Nanawatai is one of its tenets."

"I know about Pashtunwali," the other man replied defensively. "It's a two-thousand-year-old code of honor used by the Pashtun tribes and carries the force of law. I haven't heard of nanawatai."

"So you won a reprieve," the SNO said, returning his attention to Lee. "And they were left wondering what to do with you," he added.

Lee rubbed the stiff, starched cotton of the sheet. "Had I known what lay in store I might have opted to have my throat cut," he joked weakly.

"Time to rest," Dr. McKenzie said, taking control. "A debrief can wait. Our immediate priority is restoring your health and reuniting you with family."

The colonel nodded in agreement. "As soon as your identity was verified we updated your file and contacted your next of kin." He glanced at the psychiatrist and Lee's gut clenched, because he knew what was coming.

"I'm sorry to break bad news," Dr. McKenzie began in his cartoonish voice.

"My father died." Lee waited for the other man's nod to impale him. "When?"

"Six months ago. A heart attack." The psych anticipated his next question. "Very quick and an autopsy confirmed nothing could have been done. Our deepest condolences."

"It's not a surprise," Lee finally managed to say. "Dad was eighty-four and had bypass surgery a year before I deployed. I'd half expected..." His voice failed him. He stared at the sheet caught between his fingers; he was like a child clutching a comforter. "You've contacted my siblings?" Thirteen and fifteen years old when Lee was born, their relationship was warm but unessential. Dad had been the rock in his life since their mother's death when Lee was eleven.

"Your brother and sister have been informed, as well as the men in your team," said the SNO, and Lee's head snapped up. "Dan Jansen and Nathan Wyatt have resigned from the SAS, but Ross Coltrane is still serving. In fact, your troop mates are flying here as we speak."

"You'll be in hospital at least another five days before shipping home," the doctor explained.

Lee struggled to find his voice. "They said all my unit died in the ambush."

"Steve Langford was the only SAS fatality. Dan Jansen wasn't on patrol that day."

"For a year and a half I've mourned my brothers. Now you're saying *three* are alive?" A laugh escaped him and it was the strangest sensation, like finding water after a drought. "And they're coming here?"

"They all but hijacked a Hercules," the SNO said drily. "They'll arrive tomorrow. Nathan Wyatt also informed your fiancée."

And just like that Lee's euphoria abated. "I don't have one."

The SNO frowned then read through his notes. "Juliet Browne…okay…this explains why she's not with them." He glanced up, gave a little cough. "Apparently you mentioned that you intended proposing to her. When they found an engagement ring as they cleared out your locker they… ah…gave it to her."

The air wheezed out of his pillows as Lee sank into them. Ten grand it had cost him because only the best would do for Jules. "And she accepted it?"

"I NEED TO TALK to him as soon as possible," Jules told the military representative sitting in her office. "Explain about the ring...about a lot of things." Hyped on twenty-six hours of nervous adrenaline and three morning espressos, tired of waiting for the ax to fall, she stood up from her desk and paced the carpet. "Why can't I phone *him* instead of waiting for his call?"

Her relationship with Lee followed a pattern, Jules had decided at around three in the morning when she was using her treadmill like a hamster on a wheel. He dropped into her world and blew normal to smithereens, inciting giddy elation quickly supplanted by panic.

Corporal "call me Kyra" Wallace had arrived to offer information and discuss Lee's post-release management strategy. Though she'd dressed in mufti to excite less curiosity, the woman's straight back, clipped speech and laser gaze gave away her profession. For now, only family and close friends knew Lee had been found alive.

"I understand your anxiety," said Kyra, "but Sergeant Davis asked to be the first to initiate contact. He's had so little control over his environment it's very important to allow him to set the pace. And given the unusual circumstances of your engagement, he said—"

"Wait." Jules gripped the edge of her desk. "He already *knows* the guys gave me his ring?" She'd hoped to be the one to tell him. "Oh God, no wonder he doesn't want to talk to me!"

"Not at all," Kyra soothed. "I understand his first concern was that it might constitute a problem for *you*."

Jules opened her mouth, closed it. Then tried again. "What?"

"He told Dr. McKenzie and the SNO that he intended to propose and has no issue with his buddies' action. But he also understands that you accepted the engagement ring as a token of remembrance, not as a pledge."

That didn't make sense. Unless… Needing to sit down, Jules skirted her desk and sank into the leather chair ergonomically designed to support and cradle her. "Earlier you said he doesn't remember the ambush," she said. "Post-traumatic…something…amnesia."

"Retrograde," Kyra supplied. "From the head wound sustained during the attack."

"Exactly how far into the past does his memory loss go?"

"We're still determining that. He recalls patrols but they could date back to previous deployments in the same area."

"Could his amnesia extend prior to his deployment?"

"I know of a couple of cases where memories were lost for about a year, but that's unusual. However, Sergeant Davis's head wound wasn't properly treated and he was beaten into unconsciousness at least twice during captivity."

Jules flinched.

"This is difficult to hear," Kyra apologized, "but for both your sakes it's better to be fully briefed. Understanding what he's been through will help you deal with any changes you see in his physical condition or personality."

"Yes, of course," Jules said briskly. "Tell me everything, I can handle it." She dug her fingernails into the curved leather armrest. *Lee.*

"He's lost a lot of weight, through a struggle with untreated leishmaniasis."

"And that is?"

"A parasitic disease, common to the area. The symptoms are similar to malaria—fever, weight loss and anemia. There's also swelling of the spleen. Sometimes the spleen has to be removed but that's been discounted in Corporal Davis's case. After a course of drugs he should make a full recovery."

Should. And suddenly Jules was terrified again. "What else?" she said.

"He's scarred from wearing restraints."

"Restraints," Jules repeated firmly. One of her fingernails pierced the leather through to the rubber foam.

"He wore ankle shackles constantly and was often chained to a wall. He was found in a windowless room within a mud-brick compound and slept on a mat with one blanket. Though it appears he did get some exercise in an outside yard up until three months ago."

And what happened three months ago? Jules wanted to ask, because Kyra's direct gaze had slid away. But grief had taught her to focus on challenges as they arose.

"And his mental state?" she asked instead.

"There will be scars," Kyra answered, "though psychological disorder isn't inevitable. As a Special Forces soldier Sergeant Davis already has stronger physical and psychological resilience than most former hostages. Which is how he survived."

"Bloody-mindedness, you mean." Jules managed a smile. Who'd have thought she'd end up celebrating that particular trait?

Her cell rang, the ordinary sound incongruent with the conversation. Automatically about to pick it up, Jules paused. It could be Lee. If he had amnesia and didn't remember... Her heart beat hard against her ribs. And if he *did* remember, he'd hate her. Conscious of Kyra's scrutiny, she braced herself and took it out of her suit jacket. "Jules Browne."

"You didn't call me," Mark said.

Mark. She'd completely forgotten about him. "No, I..." She couldn't deal with this right now. "But I will," she promised. "Soon as I can." Jules hung up on him.

Kyra was digging in a bag. "Here's some reading material on hostages post release." She handed over a sheath of handouts. "In a nutshell what he needs most initially is uninterrupted time with loved ones. The army's role is as an information resource and to help with practicalities—having Sergeant Davis's death certificate revoked, for example. We'll also act as a gatekeeper with the media."

Dear God, she hadn't considered publicity. "How much attention is Lee's story likely to get?"

"Returned from the dead after nineteen months' captivity by the Taliban…. Interest will be huge."

Maybe she deserved this, Jules thought numbly. *Woman accepts ring she wasn't entitled to*. It was a pebble in the pond and the ripples kept getting bigger and bigger. She must have looked stricken, because the other woman smiled reassuringly. "It's okay," she said. "We'll give you coping strategies."

That would be a fast car and a full tank of gas. "Thank you."

"You've been grieving his loss for nineteen months, and moving on with your life. There will have been changes in his absence, of circumstances, possibly of heart."

There was a question in Kyra's voice.

Jules chose her next words carefully. "We have outstanding issues that make a long-term future unlikely."

"I can organize counseling—"

"I'll keep that in mind." Jules didn't naturally confide in people. Besides, this music could only be faced alone.

"It's natural to focus on the problems associated with reintegration, but many former hostages describe positive benefits…closer relationships, more emotional involvement, stronger personal values, increased assertiveness."

This time, her smile was forced. "Lee never had a problem with assertiveness."

Kyra grinned. "Less then."

The desk phone rang. Would Lee call her office? She needed to work out time zones. Conscious of Kyra's scrutiny, she picked up and managed a brisk "Jules Browne."

"Your ten-thirty has arrived."

"Thanks, Margie." The breath she'd been holding left her lungs in a rush. "Put them in the boardroom. I'll be there in five."

Hanging up, Jules wiped her damp palms on her pencil skirt. "I'm sorry, but I have clients waiting."

"I understand. Better to take a holiday when he's home."

Except Lee wouldn't want her in his life.

Jules walked the other woman to the door. "One more question. Will his complete memory ever return?"

"It depends on the severity of the injury, which is unknown. But given the time that's passed since the original trauma, it's unlikely."

And didn't that just leave Jules with one hell of a dilemma.

CHAPTER THREE

"So I GUESS I should fly over, too, if your friends are?"

Lee appreciated the offer, but the nervousness in his older brother's voice made it easy to turn the suggestion down. Rob's idea of adventure travel was eating pawpaw at a tropical resort; flying to a war zone would give the guy hives.

"Meet me on the tarmac in Auckland next week with the rest of the family," Lee told him. Pushing aside his empty meal tray, he lay down in bed with the borrowed cell. "Tell me about Dad."

"He'd be over the moon right now," Rob burst out, then added soberly, "Six months, mate. You only missed him by six months."

"Yeah, well, shit happens." *State the obvious, why don't you?* "Hopefully somewhere Dad knows I made it. Who knows, maybe he even put in a good word for me."

"Yeah." Rob cleared his throat. "I had his funeral taped if you ever want to see it."

"What?"

"And your memorial service."

"Rob, that's just weird."

"I did it for Uncle Vaughan." Dad's ninety-year-old brother in the U.K. was past the age of long flights. "He requested it."

"Uncle Vaughan was always weird, too," Lee said.

"You'd be surprised how many people who pooh-poohed

the idea have since asked for a copy," Rob said defensively. Clearly he'd got flack for this.

"I guess genealogy requires the chronicling of the bad as well as the good," Lee replied. Genealogy was Rob's hobby.

"I knew you'd understand."

Lee steeled himself. "I hear Dad had a heart attack?"

"Died in his sleep. Jules found him when she went to wake him."

"Wait." He pushed himself higher on the pillows. "*Jules* was with Dad when he died?"

"They were on holiday in Tasmania...doing a road trip. Against my advice, incidentally, but I don't hold her responsible—at least not anymore. To tell the truth, Lee, I was a bit rabid initially. It was the shock, wanting someone to blame. But Jules was terrific to Dad after you died...ha... it's going to take a while to stop saying that. Of course, Connie—" their sister "—got her nose out of joint when Jules supported Dad's move into a retirement home, but only because Con felt guilty not having Dad live with her. Though why she'd think he'd want to when she has a houseful of teenagers is beyond me."

Lee felt his brain starting to spin. "Back up. *Jules* talked Dad into moving to a retirement home?"

"She helped him with all the research. He was really depressed when you died...there I go again...and Jules suggested he cash in, downsize and have some fun."

"Did she," he said flatly. Dad had always hated the idea of an old folks home and, like Rob, wasn't much interested in travel. Jules had met his father once...how had she inveigled her way into his life? And after having dumped Lee, why the hell would she want to?

"You've talked to her, right?" Rob asked.

"I'm working up to it."

His brother picked up the hard inflection. "You're okay

with your buddies giving her the ring, aren't you?" Rob laughed nervously. "Dad was on board with it. Hell, we all were. She's become part of the family."

"I have no problem with Jules being given the ring, Rob." *It's her accepting it that bothers me.* But that was for her to explain.

"Well, that's a relief. Anyway, that's why she and Dad were in Tasmania. They'd done Hawaii the year before. Connie and I were getting twitchy about Dad spending all his savings, so you could have knocked us down with a feather when his estate amounted to two hundred thou." He cleared his throat. "Which brings me to something I need to talk to you about."

"What's that?"

"With you being dead, Dad's estate was split between me and Connie. Obviously we'll reimburse your share...but... it'll take a couple of months to sort. I spent mine on an office upgrade, and Connie and Phil bought a bigger house."

"I'm not in any hurry for Dad's money, Rob." A thought struck Lee. If he'd been confirmed dead through a DNA sample, there would have been no delay in selling and distributing *his* estate. All his toys gone. The paddleboard, the kite surfer and surfboards, his designer clothes. His Harley-Davidson.

Oh. Shit. "I left half of everything to Jules."

Updating his will pre-tour came automatically, and with the ring in his pocket he'd wanted to provide for the woman he loved if he didn't survive Afghanistan. He hadn't anticipated a rejection. Blindsided, brokenhearted and just plain furious, he'd headed straight from her house to the military airbase for his last deployment. Changing his will hadn't even crossed Lee's mind.

"That's when we knew she was a good sort," said Rob.

"When she insisted on giving her share to Dad." Lee's father had been his other beneficiary.

The magnitude of Lee's relief was frightening. He didn't want to hate her. He'd loved this woman, had intended to marry her. "So you and Connie also inherited my estate after his death?" He tried to imagine Rob or one of his sister's sullen teenagers in his Italian leather jackets and winced.

"Well, actually, Lee," Rob said apologetically, "Dad spent the money you left him to pay for the trips with Jules. They did Tasmania, Hawaii and a week in Queenstown. And he treated us to some family trips, as well. But when he died there was one hundred and seven thousand, six dollars and eighty-two cents of your estate." Rob was an accountant. "And Dad bequeathed it to—"

"Jules," Lee finished. "And let me guess," he added bitterly, "this time she took it."

"In his will Dad said that he believed you'd have wanted her to have it. He absolutely forbade her to give it to us." There was no resentment in Rob's tone. "Of course, now she'll have to return it," he added, "but I doubt she could have spent much in the past six months."

Lee resisted the urge to remind his brother that he and Connie hadn't been slow spending their father's estate.

"Besides," Rob said, "if you two are getting married she's just had a head start on 'what's yours is hers' anyway." The confirmed bachelor laughed heartily.

Lee didn't join in. "One question, brother," he said. "Does my sweetie still have the same phone numbers?"

"JULES SPEAKING."

Her husky voice shivered down Lee's spine like a caress in the dark. An onslaught of mixed emotions prevented him from replying and he stared blankly at the view from his window—the shipping containers used as living quarters, American attack helicopters and transport planes.

"Hello," she said, then swallowed audibly. "Lee?" Her voice dropped to a whisper. "Is that you?"

He clutched the borrowed cell phone. Who would have thought his name on her lips could still resonate. "Yeah, it's me…. How are you, Jules?" His instinctive default to small talk amused him. So *that's* what would survive with the cockroaches after Armageddon.

"I'm so glad you're alive…so glad," she stammered, and he didn't doubt her sincerity. Getting himself killed a few weeks after she'd rejected him couldn't have been easy for her. She would have felt guilty, even regretful. Not because of her answer—Lee didn't kid himself on that—but because of her delivery. Maybe she'd even thought she loved him when he was never coming back. That would constitute a perfect relationship for Jules. Love without commitment.

"I hear we're engaged," he said abruptly, because he needed this over with. "You'll have to fill me in on the missing details." He'd had long, lonely hours to review his part in their last meeting and it hadn't been pretty, either. An admission of wrongdoing from her along with an apology for deceiving everybody and he'd seriously consider letting her off the hook. Assuming she reimbursed all his money and hadn't screwed over his dad.

Okay, maybe he wasn't going to forgive her.

"Hang on, I'm in the bank." Her voice faded as he heard her talking to someone else. "Will you…it's my…a couple of minutes privacy…*thank* you. Lee, I'm here." He heard her take a fortifying breath. "I understand you have amnesia and that some memories are hazy."

Not that hazy, sweetheart. And the particular one she referred to was tattooed on his heart. But like the New Zealand Inland Revenue Department's catchy slogan, it was his job to be fair. He hadn't heard her side of the story yet, after all.

It struck him that playing along was the perfect way to test her integrity. "I've also got big gaps before the ambush," he lied. "Which means I'm relying on people I trust to set me straight." And if that wasn't an opening for a confession he didn't know what was.

A second passed, then another. "What's your last memory of us?" she said.

Disappointment made him cruel. "Making love," he said grimly. "Lying in each other's arms afterward. You telling me you were happy." All true of their final night together. Before his morning proposal. "What's the last thing *you* remember?"

"The same," she said and his bitterness dissolved every flickering regret he had. She was going to try to brazen this out.

"But obviously," she added, "I can't hold you to any kind of commitment after what you've been through. I'll return the ring."

Yeah, you'd like this to be easy, wouldn't you? "And what if I want there to be an 'us,' Jules?" he challenged. "What if I want to take up where we left off?"

Silence had echoes; Lee had discovered that in captivity.

"You think we might have a future?" she said.

All credit to her acting skills, she almost sounded hopeful. "I still have strong feelings for you," he said through gritted teeth. Anger. Disillusionment. Disgust. "I'm being discharged from the hospital in four days, and fly in Sunday New Zealand time. Come meet me."

"At the aerodrome?" She hesitated. "I'd rather our first meet be private."

I bet you would. Except that wouldn't suit his purpose nearly as well. "I can organize privacy," he reassured her. *I can, but I won't*. Lee layered some sensitivity into his tone, the sensitivity she'd once accused him of lacking. "Please… I need you there, Jules."

Another hesitation. "Of course, I'll be there."

After they finalized details for Sunday, she said, "And Lee, I'm so sorry about your dad. We spent a lot of time together and—"

"I understand he left you my estate."

"You'll get it all back, every penny."

"That's good to hear."

"Only…not quite yet."

This just got better and better. "Are you saying you spent all my money, honey?" he said mildly.

"Not spent…invested. But don't worry, I'll reimburse you within a few weeks. And in the meantime, I'll spot you."

It took all Lee's self-control to keep his tone even. "Kind of like paying interest?"

"Yes." Jules sounded relieved. "Let's think of it as interest."

Oh, baby, you have no idea what interest I'll charge. Unable to stand another minute of this bullshit he cut the conversation short. "Listen, Jules, I've gotta go…the doctor's here," he lied. "I'll see you soon."

"Will you call—"

The click of the line as Lee cut the connection was akin to losing him all over again. "Goodbye," Jules whispered. Replacing the cell in her purse, she dropped her face into her hands in the loan officer's partitioned open-plan office and released her shock at this first contact with Lee in smothered sobs.

Now that she'd heard his voice she could truly believe he was alive. And instead of confrontation, she'd been offered tenderness and a second chance. She couldn't think about that, because Lee deserved the truth and she was going to give it to him. But not over the phone.

She'd spent last night downloading all the studies she could find on hostages. Common post-release challenges included insecurity, feeling misunderstood, difficulty relating to loved ones and readapting to social conventions.

Less common but entirely possible were post-traumatic stress disorder (PTSD), withdrawal and attempted suicide. All the studies stressed that the key to successful reintegration was a secure environment and the support of a close network of family and friends. Chirruping, "Hi, honey, you don't remember this, but I rejected your marriage proposal," couldn't be construed as helpful.

She'd have to wait to see him in person before could she gauge his ability to handle the truth.

The loan officer returned as she was dabbing away her tears with a tissue she'd dug out of her handbag. The other woman took one look at Jules's face and faltered.

"It's okay." Briskly, Jules blew her nose. "This is good news crying." She encouraged her with a watery smile. "I'm hoping you'll continue the theme."

"Sorry." Awkwardly the vibrant blonde returned to her desk. "I've double-checked with my manager. As good as your income is, it only just sustains your existing mortgage payments. Borrowing an additional one hundred and ten thousand against the house, well, the numbers simply don't stack up."

Jules dropped the tissue into the trash can beside her. "I knew it was a long shot."

The woman checked the documents in front of her. "If you'd taken in renters over the past year and a half you'd have enough collateral in the house to borrow against. That was the plan, wasn't it, when you applied for a mortgage?"

"Plans change." After Lee's death, Jules hadn't wanted

witnesses to her meltdown. Glancing at her watch, she stood. Running out of time seemed to be the current theme of her life. "Thanks for your help, but I've gotta dash."

She'd stalled Mark long enough.

"So let me see if I've got this straight."

Mark placed the glass of water Jules had asked for on the white marble breakfast bar in front of her. "You're certain you won't resume your relationship with Lee, but you're ending ours anyway."

It was a lovely space, his open-plan kitchen, all granite counters and metallic appliances.

Threading her legs around the bar stool, Jules took a sip of water. Her throat was dry from so many apologies and explanations. "I can't deal with Lee's return and dating. It's too much." If she couldn't be honest with Lee—yet—at least she could be honest with Mark.

"I get that," he said. "And I'm willing to give you space until everything settles down. Because I like you, Jules." He smiled at her, a shy smile that was incredibly attractive from such an assured man. "A lot. I think you like me."

"I do, very much." He was exactly the right guy for the evolutionary step into mature love. The kind of love that allowed a woman to keep her emotional independence. Lee had not been that man.

"You're scared," Lee had replied when she'd told him she wasn't ready for a commitment. "I haven't been here before, either, and it's terrifying. But there's no guarantee that waiting will increase our odds of a successful marriage. It's right…you and me. I believe that. So forget the rationalizations and trust your feelings."

How could she trust feelings that were so new and disjointed she didn't know up from down?

"If you trusted *my* feelings you wouldn't try to rush it,"

she'd countered. "Which means you're worried we won't last, either."

"Either," he'd said slowly. "You mean in conjunction with you?"

"So TELL LEE you're seeing someone."

Mark's modulated baritone drew her out of the past and refocused her on the architect. She took another sip of water, chilled from the fridge filter. "He's had a bad time, worse than we could imagine. I have to tread carefully." Being honest hadn't worked out when Lee had been healthy, full strength. "And I don't want to hurt him if I can help it."

"You know what this is," Mark said. "You're feeling guilty because while he's been a prisoner in some Afghanistan hellhole you've been happy."

"Happy?" she repeated incredulously. But, of course, Mark had only known her a month, hadn't seen her through the first dark year after the ambush.

"Wrong word?" He took her empty glass and refilled it. "Moved on, then."

Only when she'd made a confession would she be free to move on. "And now Lee and I have to move on again." Jules accepted the full glass, only realizing that her hand trembled when water spilled over the rim.

Mark steadied the glass by cupping his hand over hers. "I can be patient," he said.

Once she'd badly needed Lee to say that. But his miraculous reappearance had confirmed one thing. She wasn't over him. And that wasn't fair on Mark. "For how long?" she asked. "A week? A month?" She was curious to see when he'd remove his hand. "Six months?" Ah, there was the physical withdrawal. Her mouth curved in a rueful smile. "I'd rather part friends than leave you dangling for however long it takes me to get my head straight."

He picked up a dishcloth and mopped up the water on the white counter. "Head or heart?"

"Both," Jules admitted.

"Here's the deal." He tossed the cloth into the shiny sink. "If you sort this out within two months, I'll probably still be available."

Relieved by his understanding, she laughed. "I'll keep that in mind."

Of course, whether Mark returned her call would depend on whether Lee chose to make her confession public.

CHAPTER FOUR

LEE WAS ON the floor in his hospital gown, bare ass flapping in the breeze as he sweated through the seventh of ten push-ups when he heard a burst of male laughter behind him.

His heart swelled.

"This wasn't how we pictured the reunion," Nate drawled behind him.

He pushed up on shaky arms for one more push-up. "Two hundred and six…"

He heard Dan's familiar snort. "Still the bullshit artist."

"Quit waving that scrawny butt in the air and turn around." Clearly, Ross hadn't lost his impatience. "I need to see your ugly mug and make sure it's really you."

Lee eased himself to the floor, taking his time because the sweet familiarity of their banter had bought tears to his eyes. Screw hydration. It was more trouble than it was worth. "I wasn't expecting visitors at three in the morning." He'd had to start exercising surreptitiously since the nurse caught him. Grinning, he rolled over on his back.

His first impression was of smooth jaws—he hadn't got used to beardless men—his second of bulk. The three men seemed to fill the small room with muscular vitality.

Momentarily their expressions registered shock. But Lee had braced himself for that. "What the hell are you doing here at this hour anyway?"

"Well, you know. We just happened to be passing Afghanistan, and figured we'd drop by." Dan reached out a hand to help him up. Sun-streaked hair, his blue eyes appeared lighter because of his tan. At thirty-four, Afghan fighters' faces were already deeply lined. If they'd survived to that age.

Limping over, Ross—Ice—grabbed Lee's other hand. "For me, it's a nostalgia trip. I had such good times in this hospital." Leaner than Dan, irises a sandblasted gray, Ross was the only one sporting a military haircut.

Further debriefings had brought Lee up to speed. Ross had been seriously wounded in the ambush and Nate had carried him to safety. And the limp was permanent. His friend was now an SAS instructor instead of a combatant.

The two men swung him to his feet as easily as if Lee was a child and he experienced a momentary sense of helplessness. Though he was twenty pounds lighter than before the ambush he'd still considered himself the biggest, most physically powerful of his unit.

He didn't have time to process the new reality before he was jerked into a hug that bracketed him between two walls of muscle.

"This is because you saw my ass, isn't it?" he said before they all started bawling. Assuming they didn't collapse his ribs first. Neither man responded, except to tighten his grip, which made it even harder for Lee to breathe, given his lungs were already expanded with emotion.

"God, it's good to see you," Dan said hoarsely.

Ross sniffed. "And I'm frickin' crying over you *again*."

"Yeah, well, I believed you were all dead, too." His throat closed. Who would have thought happiness could be so gut-wrenching?

Lee also felt a growing claustrophobia. Being held and being held down for a beating were still too closely linked for him to be comfortable with all this hugging. Suddenly panicking, Lee began to struggle.

Immediately they released him. Already there were questions in their eyes, like probes. Lee looked beyond them to Nate, standing in the doorway. Tears streamed down his buddy's cheeks channeling into the creases made by his wide grin.

Oh shit. That did it. His vision blurred. Stepping forward, he grabbed the other man in a bear hug.

"I still can't believe it." Nate's grip on him tightened convulsively.

Again, Lee felt that terrifying sense of constriction. With an attempt at casualness, he broke the embrace. "Go easy. I'm finely boned these days."

His mate's brown hair was civilian-long now, as was Dan's. Narrowing his gaze incredulously, Lee reached out and tweaked a strand. "You're using *product!*"

Nate flung back his head and laughed. "And the pretty one's home."

His mouth twitched in a smile and then Lee laughed, too. He'd always been fastidious in his grooming off duty, a little vain even. And these guys had all given him shit for it.

"Of all the things to notice!" Dan hooted and all four of them were roaring. Ross bent over double, while Nate slid helplessly down the wall. Dan clutched his sides.

"Sh...shh-shush," Lee managed to hiccup. "The duty nurse will chuck you out." They stuffed fists into their mouths to stifle the noise they were making, which only caused everyone to laugh harder. They ended up sitting on the floor, passing around Lee's bedsheet to wipe their streaming eyes.

"So," Lee said when they'd regained control. "What's with the hair gel, princess?"

"Nate was a Hollywood bodyguard until last month," Ross supplied. "Ask him about rock star Zander Freedman's man-scaping." And then Ross cracked up again.

"Give me a break," Nate replied, feigning hurt. "I haven't had a manicure for months. Look." He held out his nails for inspection. Short, clean—he turned his hands over—a few calluses on the palms.

"Yeah, mine need tending, too." Grinning, Lee held up his own hands. His buddies' smiles faded as they surveyed the missing fingertip, the nails growing at different rates, the battered and bruised flesh. A chill fell over the room. Suddenly, he was flanked by elite soldiers, each with death in his gaze. Lee dropped his hands. "The ones who did this are all dead," he said curtly. "It's over."

It needed to be over. Grabbing the sheet he hobbled to the bed and got in, sliding his misshapen fingers under the cover.

The other guys stood. "Who put that scar on your jaw?" Ross said. Ice wasn't one to let things go.

Might as well spell it out. "We're not talking about what happened during my captivity. Ever."

Dan made a gesture of protest. "But—"

"I'm not bringing any of that shit home." Under the sheet, he fisted his hands. He didn't want his friends' eyes becoming mirrors, reflecting his experiences. Something in his life had to be pure, untainted. "I'll talk to professionals if I have to," he said. "Not to you."

His buddies exchanged glances.

"And no going behind my back, either, finding out stuff. I mean it!"

He only realized his voice had risen when Dan said quietly, "Okay, mate. We get it."

Lee unclenched his fists. Maybe that's why he was so angry with Jules. She'd tainted his old life with lies, taken it over as hers. He was ashamed that he'd spent months planning how to win her back. Ashamed of his resolution that if he survived he'd turn himself into the man she deserved.

Actually, he thought grimly, he could still keep that vow.

He shoved thoughts of Jules aside in favor of something far more important. "How did Steve die?" Instinctively Dan and Ross looked at Nate. That made sense. Dan hadn't been on patrol because of a tooth abscess that needed treatment. And Ross had been unconscious, critically injured.

Nate took a moment to meet his gaze, his dark eyes bright. "He didn't suffer. When you're fully recovered…" He swallowed. "I'll fill you in on the rest."

Lee sighed. "The shrink told you to go carefully with me, didn't he?"

"It was suggested," Nate admitted.

"Plenty of time to talk about the hard stuff, mate." Dan came to sit on the edge of the bed. "Let's get you healthy first." Always Shep, the good shepherd. Overseeing his flock.

Yesterday Lee might have insisted. But reentering the world after captivity was akin to walking into a rave party. His body could finally rest but his mind, unaccustomed to stimulus, was in overload. And he needed to conserve his strength for Jules. "Fine, let's concentrate on the good stuff."

"I got married," Dan said. Almost shyly, he flashed a gold wedding band. "To Jo."

"Well, yeah." Lee settled against his pillows. Jo was Dan's best friend from childhood. "Who didn't see that coming?"

"Me and Jo," Dan said drily. "You could have dropped a clue."

"You weren't ready, grasshopper…. The SNO said you've quit the service?"

"Taken over the family farm."

Lee had spent time on the Jansen farm. They all had. "I'd like to visit you there," he said, recalling the patchwork of green paddocks and gently rolling hills. God, he'd missed home.

Casually Dan laid a hand on his shoulder. "As long as you want, mate. I have other news but I wanted all of us together again before I spilled the beans."

All of us together again.

"And so here we are." Dan's fingers on Lee's shoulder tightened as he said, "Jo's pregnant."

Lee rested his hand on Dan's, leaving the other two to vocalize exuberant congratulations. My family, he thought, my brothers. "You'll make a great dad," he managed to say at last.

"Enough about me." Dan pulled them all back from the emotional precipice with an easy grin. "Ice is marrying Viv."

That actually startled Lee. "Jeez. And you're *okay* with that?" Viv was Dan's little sister.

"I'm right here," Ross reminded him.

"I wanted a year's probation first," Dan responded seriously. "God knows, Ice has a poor track record with commitment."

Ross frowned. "Still right here."

"And he countermanded your orders." Lee laughed. "I'm amazed."

"I've changed." Ross laid a hand over his heart, gray eyes wide. "I'm a card-carrying proponent of coupledom."

Lee snorted. "Yeah, right."

"I didn't believe it, either," Nate said. "But Viv can handle Ice in her sleep. They're darling together—like King Kong and Fay Wray."

"Screw you, Nate." Ross kicked him with his good leg. "You're the goo-goo-eyed one these days."

Not all three of them. Lee groaned. "You're in *lurrrve,* too? Who is she?"

"Viv said yes a couple of weeks ago," Ross continued smoothly, ignoring Lee's question. "The wedding's in just over four."

"What's the hurry?" Lee noticed he'd been stonewalled but let it pass. "Do we have *two* pregnancies to celebrate?"

"No." Ross caught his future brother-in-law's eye and repeated firmly, "No!"

"Ice is rushing Viv to the altar because he's shit-scared she'll change her mind," Nate said cheerfully.

Ross scowled. "We're scheduling around Viv's work commitments in New York. Lee, we need to get you measured up for a groomsman suit, soon as you're home."

"Well, okay then." Grinning, he shook his head in disbelief. None of these three had been anywhere near ready for commitment when he'd last seen them. He'd been the fool who'd led with his heart. "So if you're not a Hollywood bodyguard anymore," he asked Nate, "what *are* you doing now?"

"Restoring *Heaven Sent* and launching a game-fishing business with Claire."

"No kidding, good for you." Steve's wife and Nate had gone halves on the old boat three years earlier in a restoration project that everyone else—especially her husband—had considered crazy. He added quietly, "How's Claire coping with raising Lewis alone?"

To his surprise Nate's cheeks colored. Beyond him, Ross and Dan exchanged a complicit look.

Secrets. Lee hated them. His captors had told him only what they wanted him to know. "No censorship," he warned.

"We got engaged last month," Nate said.

Lee felt like Alice falling down the rabbit hole. Nate had been Steve's best friend. He barely controlled an outburst of anger. He hadn't been here, didn't know the details. "Congratulations," he finally said.

Nate's gaze met his. "Steve will never be forgotten."

"Of course not." But some of the joy had gone out of this reunion. "So Dan's married and you're both engaged. I'm guessing you gave Jules my ring because you didn't want me feeling left out."

"Please tell us we got it right," Ross said.

In the two weeks between her kiss-off and the ambush, he hadn't told anyone about Jules's rejection. He'd been shell-shocked, he guessed.

"You told me you were going to propose," Nate insisted when Lee didn't respond. "Remember? I teased you about Jules being Miss Congeniality and you said, 'That's my future wife you're talking about.'"

"You didn't like her," Lee recalled. Good instincts, as it turned out.

"I didn't know her," Nate corrected him. "I do now. She played a role in getting Claire and I together. I owe her a lot."

Was there any pie his interfering fiancée hadn't stuck her finger into? "My, she's been busy during my death." He thought he'd kept his tone light but his friends exchanged worried looks.

"Obviously, you and Jules need time to sort out how you feel about each other," said Dan. "But we watched her mourn you. She loved you."

"Hell, she still loves you," Nate supplied. "If you'd seen her face when Claire and I told her you were alive."

"I'll bet." Clearly she'd fooled everybody.

"Mate, if you have to let her down," Ross pleaded, "do it gently."

Whose side were these guys on? For a moment Lee toyed

with telling them the truth...but he wanted to be the one to punish her. "Honestly, I can't wait to see her."

He was alive and Jules was so dead.

"I SEE YOU'RE not wearing Lee's ring," Claire said.

Curling her bare finger farther around the steering wheel, Jules kept her gaze steady on the highway. "Nope."

"Still set on returning it then?"

"Uh-huh." She'd hoped to avoid this particular discussion.

They were halfway through a ninety-minute drive south to Whenuapai airbase for her reunion with Lee. And that was plenty to be dealing with, thank you very much.

In her peripheral vision she glimpsed Claire frowning and tried not to tense. Until today, she'd managed to dodge a heart-to-heart with her best friend, who was fortunately too busy getting her game-fishing venture ready for launch to demand one, particularly with Nate dropping everything to fly to Afghanistan. Jules had expected Claire's thirteen-year-old to accompany them today, which would have saved her from this conversation, but right now Lewis was sitting in an English exam.

"Even though Lee wants you to keep the ring?" Jules glanced at her, startled, and Claire added, "Lee told Nate."

Bloody Nate. Passing on information to his fiancée. "Even if we'd actually got engaged before Lee left," Jules reasoned mildly, "it's been nineteen months since we saw each other. And we only dated six weeks." At the memorial service, well-meaning people had offered her that argument as a comfort. And she'd imagined the ghost of Lee laughing his ass off because it had been one of her reasons for turning him down. *We've only known each other six weeks.*

"Don't give me that," Claire said sharply. "We grieved our men together. I know how you suffered."

How would Claire react once she knew the truth? How would the guys, Lee's family? She'd never told her best friend that she'd rejected Lee's proposal. Claire had had enough on her plate after losing her husband. Jules concentrated on the road. "I'm not the priority here."

"It's not like you to give up without a fight."

I'm not usually the one in the wrong. The lawyer with a reputation for honesty was about to be revealed as a fraud. "And who am I fighting, Claire?" she challenged. "Someone probably battling PTSD."

Accelerating, Jules pulled into the fast lane, overtaking the beetling VW they'd been following for the past five miles. "Lee is in no state to make decisions about us." The '59 Cadillac started rattling her disapproval of the speed. Until a month ago, Claire had owned this pink Coupe de Ville and Jules wished to God she still did. *Never buy anything for sentimental reasons.*

"I get that you're protecting him." Claire opened her bag, grabbed a roll of mints and offered her the packet. "But don't throw yourself on your sword, Zena, unless you have to. Give equal weight to hope, okay?"

"Okay." But her agreement was perfunctory. Hope was a sentiment Jules couldn't afford. "How's our time?"

"We've got plenty."

The wail of a siren drew her attention to the side mirror, and she returned to the slow lane. A minute later a police car passed in a blur of flashing lights. Lucky they couldn't ticket a racing pulse. "What time is it?" Jules said before remembering she'd just asked.

"Nerves kicking in?"

"Forget butterflies, I have bungee jumpers rebounding up my throat."

"If it helps, you look gorgeous."

"Thanks." Jules had changed clothes six times in the attempt to create the effect of pretty but penitent. Eventually she'd settled on a simple black-and-white jersey dress with three-quarter sleeves. The pretty came from a gathered center-front detail that lent her breasts the same generous curves as her hips and accentuated her waist.

Time to distract Claire. "I listed my house with a real estate agent yesterday."

"What? I still can't understand why you won't tell Lee you bought a shareholding in the law firm first. He may be happy with a repayment plan."

The distraction hadn't quite worked the way she'd hoped. "He's lived in limbo for nineteen months. I'm not asking him to put his new life on hold." In the meantime, she had a thousand dollars in her purse to give him, thanks to a cash advance on her credit card. Racking up twenty-four percent interest wasn't how Jules liked to run her finances but hopefully it wouldn't be for long. The house was priced for a quick sale.

"So what do you want from today?" Claire wasn't distractible.

"To see Lee, to make sure he's okay, to do whatever I can to assist his recovery. I can't think beyond that."

"Does your reluctance to consider romance have anything to do with Mark?"

It would be so much easier to lie. But look where the lie of accepting Lee's ring had landed her. "No. Mark and I are done."

"Misplaced guilt then, about sleeping with another guy?"

"No, I don't feel guilty." At least not about that. "You can't cheat on a dead man." A thought occurred to her. "I'm guessing the guys do, though?" Campaigning to find your dead buddy's fiancée a new love because you've figured he'd want her to be happy was an awkward disclosure. Not as awkward as hers, but still.

"Squirming," Claire admitted. "But Mark is your news, not theirs."

"Assuming I tell Lee about him." It wouldn't have any relevance after her primary confession.

"You'll tell him," Claire said. "But…pick your moment, Jules."

"What do you mean?" She shot her an anxious glance. "What do you know?"

"Nate said to be prepared for a difference in his appearance."

"Kyra already told me that."

Her friend said carefully, "A big difference, Jules."

And Nate was a battle-hardened veteran. Her throat went dry. "Okay."

"Apparently Lee's refusing to talk about his captivity to anyone but professionals."

"I can understand that," Jules said. Keep the good and the bad separate.

"Do you? The guys are finding it frustrating because they have to guess what his triggers are."

"Triggers?"

"For example, hugs. They've worked out he can only cope with brief embraces. He does push-ups and sit-ups several times a day and balks when they suggest he rest. He wants company and within ten minutes makes excuses to be alone."

"None of this was mentioned in Kyra's briefing."

"The professionals don't know him like his friends do."

"Thanks for telling me." Confession might be good for the soul but hers was clearly going to have to suffer until Lee was well enough to hear it. Another siren sounded behind her, then a second squad car raced by. Jules said reflexively, "What time is it?"

"Relax, we'll make it with an hour to spare."

Ten kilometers farther, they hit a traffic jam. A truck had lost an insecure load, closing the highway.

CHAPTER FIVE

THEY CAREENED INTO the aerodrome fifteen minutes after the plane's scheduled arrival, by which time Claire had taken the wheel so Jules could concentrate on biting her nails. She had begun to sweat under her armpits, and every tousled curl, so carefully styled this morning, she'd raked flat in her nervousness.

Encircled by chain-link fences topped with barbed-wire coils, the military airbase proved a vast space of runways and rangy grass, surrounded by a maze of parking lots, hangars, sheds and outbuildings. Which meant she and Claire still weren't technically there yet.

By the third military checkpoint Jules was hanging out the window flashing the pass to try and speed things along and almost desperate enough to flash her boobs. Finally the Caddy squealed to a halt beside a corrugated hangar where Kyra waited, looking as crisp and cool as only military personnel can manage.

"Go," Claire encouraged her. "I'll park."

Halfway through scrambling out of the car, Jules turned. "What if I say the wrong thing? Do the wrong thing?"

Claire leaned over and squeezed her forearm. "This is you and Lee. Trust your instincts and remember he'll probably be as nervous as you are."

And therefore depending on her. Jules took a deep breath. "You're absolutely right. Wish me luck."

"Luck."

Despite her calm appearance, Kyra overenthusiastically seized her arm the moment she stepped onto the curb. "The plane landed ten minutes ago." The corporal hurried her the length of the hangar, which was so large it was like walking in the shadow of the moon.

The hot wind, redolent of pasture and tarmac and the salty marsh of the nearby estuary, whipped under Jules's dress. She clamped it to her thighs as she matched Kyra's stride.

At the end of the hangar they stepped into a buffet of noise from a Hercules's powerful engines. Lee's plane was an ungainly aircraft, dark gray with a bulbous nose and big tail bearing the insignia of the Royal New Zealand Air Force. The thundering rumble abated and the blur of movement on the wings resolved into four spinning propellers as they slowed to a stop.

Some twenty people milled behind a guard of honor-soldiers in full military uniform. "Are those TV cameras?" Jules fumbled on the top of her head for her sunglasses. Damn, she'd left them in the car. "I thought the media were being left out of this?" She spotted three cameras.

"Only the two major networks and three dailies—Lee opted for controlled publicity."

"That's controlled?"

"Jules!" Lee's older sister, Connie, waved frantically from the crowd. Flanked by her three lanky teenage sons and equally lanky husband, Phil, she was a small excitable blonde who verbalized thoughts as randomly as shrapnel. "Look, there's Lee's fiancée!"

A telephoto lens swung in her direction and Jules ducked round the corner of the hangar. "I'm supposed to meet Lee privately."

"Really?" Kyra's brow wrinkled and she checked her clipboard. "That's not what was requested."

A shout went up—they must have opened the aircraft's door. Oh, God. Jules steadied herself with a palm against the sun-warmed metal. "I'm requesting it now."

"Follow me." Swiveling on her heel, Kyra strode to the nearest building, an unprepossessing bungalow with a wide weathered deck, and flashed her ID. She led Jules into a lounge area and pointed to the picture window. "It's reflective glass. You'll be able to see everything but they won't see you. I'd better advise of the change of plan…it may be a while before you see him. There's a press conference organized." She paused at the doorway, smiled. "Good luck."

"Kyra, wait." Jules had to be sure. "Do I fill in the gaps… where Lee has lost his memory?"

"If it's pleasant, yes, if not…?" She waited.

"We had a fight, a bad one. He doesn't remember."

Kyra hesitated. "Reestablishing intimacy requires honesty but…also time and place."

"That's what I thought."

"I can hook you up with a therapist if you need—"

"I'll keep you posted."

At a ragged cheer outside, Jules sped to the window, barely acknowledging Kyra's farewell. Lee had already descended the ramp stairs, which was clear from the row of poker-backed soldiers standing in salute. Reporters jostled for a better view, obscuring hers.

Heart in her throat, Jules flattened her palms against the windowpane and stood on tiptoe, straining for a glimpse of Lee. But all she saw was a cluster of sand-colored berets with the flaming sword emblem that distinguished the SAS moving past the guard. Maybe when they got to the end… but no… Lee's relatives surged forward, like ants around a dollop of honey. En masse, the group moved out of sight.

Disappointed, Jules unstuck her hands from the window

and then sat on the L-shaped brown couch and put her head between her knees.

Not long now.

She smoothed her dress. Stood up. Sat down. Crossed her legs. Uncrossed them. The air-conditioning whirred softly above her and a cool sweep of air from the vent ruffled her hair. Her hands grew cold, then icy. Jules started to shiver.

No one came.

She adjusted the thermostat then walked the room until she'd warmed up. How long did a press conference take? Restlessly, Jules picked up a magazine, *Aviation Today,* from the functional brown coffee table. Putting it down again, she wandered to the window, where she could see the Hercules was being unloaded with military efficiency. After a couple of minutes, the nervous energy sizzling along her nerve endings propelled her to pace.

Claire had set them up on a blind date, luring Jules with the promise of a six-three blond god. Caught up at work, she'd arrived late then, too, and spotted Mr. Fun Times, leaning his elbow on the bar and flirting with a bunch of tipsy women.

Ugh. Indisputably gorgeous, but with a lazy self-assurance and a self-congratulatory whiff of "lay-dees' man" that had set Jules's teeth on edge.

Backing up to leave, she'd been hit on the rump as someone pushed their way in through the swinging doors. Lee had loped over as she was brushing off her assailant's apology. She'd shaken Lee's hand firmly, commended him on finding a happy hunting ground and bade him adieu, only to find herself being steered toward the bar to buy him a drink.

By way of apology, he'd explained, for both her tardiness and the assumption that he was a crass, dumb-as-a-rock asshole that hooked up with other women while waiting for his date.

Turned out the tipsy women had ditched husbands and kids for a girls' night out and the flirting was strictly in fun. Jules had bought him that drink; in fact, she'd bought them all one.

He'd asked if she believed in love at first sight that very night. "Hell, no!" had been her stance then, and was still her stance now.

She could hear his reply as if he'd said it yesterday. "Then remember that this was our beginning."

Somewhere a door slammed. Jules glanced at the clock. Twenty minutes had passed. Licking her dry lips, she walked to the water cooler and fumbled for a plastic cup, knocking half a dozen to the floor. *Calm down, deep breaths.* She crouched to retrieve them and carefully replaced them in the holder before filling her cup, watching the oxygen bubble rise with a deep gurgle. Raising the cup to her mouth, she turned.

Lee stood in the doorway.

Jules started, splashing icy water onto the industrial-grade carpet. She ignored it.

He wore the SAS's dress uniform—olive military-style jacket, brass buttons shining. Sunglasses covered half his gaunt face. Lee took off his beret. "Hello, Jules."

Carefully, she put down the cup. "Hello, Lee."

A minute ago if she'd been asked to describe him in one word she would have used *dazzling*. His smile, his looks, his charming personality. He reminded her of summer. Except there was nothing of summer about him now. If she'd seen him on the street she wouldn't have recognized him.

More frame than flesh, his hair had darkened in captivity to a light brown. The military uniform juxtaposed oddly with the thick stubble covering his jaw. He could have been a pirate after six months at sea, desiccated, hollow cheeked, the bones of his face bladed. His nose had been broken and mended badly. He wore reflective sunglasses that hid his reaction to her.

Jules could feel the muscles around her mouth twitch and spasm as she struggled to match his composure.

Be strong. Be brave. Except… Her face crumpled, like a clay cliff weakened by incessant rain. "Oh, Lee." He sucked in a breath as she went to hug him and his hands shot out and caught her by the elbows. Jules hesitated. "Am I hurting you?"

"No." But his voice was hoarse.

"I'll be careful but let me…" Stepping forward, she leaned her forehead against his jacket, gently, blindly. "I have to make you real."

With a muffled oath, he released her elbows, his arms clamped around her shoulders and he bowed his head over hers. For long seconds they stood there. He smelled of dry-cleaning chemicals, exhaustion and himself.

Jules closed her eyes, conscious that she could break herself on this man still. The thought galvanized her into action.

He clearly wasn't up to hearing the truth today. But for both their sakes, there was something she had to do.

Pulling free, she got her bag, scrambling through the contents until she found the small velvet box zipped into the side pocket. "This belongs to you."

Lee took the box and opened it almost perfunctorily. Under the sunglasses, his full mouth twisted. "I'd forgotten how big and shiny it was."

"I had it cleaned," she said awkwardly. "And insured…. I'll forward the papers when you have a permanent address." He was staying with Rob in the short term.

"How much did you insure it for?"

"Ten thousand."

"Quite a sum. Sure you want to return it?"

"Yes.... Do you have to wear sunglasses for an eye problem?"

"No." He snapped the box closed. "Remind me why you're returning it?"

"I don't want you feeling any sense of obligation," she said, reaching up to his shades. "Can we take these—"

He caught her fingers. "Or is it that *you* don't want to feel obligated to *me?*"

Her stomach lurched. "This isn't rejection, it's about giving you a clean slate." His palm was rough. She glanced down and gasped at seeing the missing fingertip.

Lee released his hold. Mortified, Jules grabbed his right hand before he could hide it in his pocket, and clasped it tightly. His fingers trembled. Or hers did.

"I'm not rejecting you," she repeated.

"So you love me." The cynicism, the doubt, the bitterness in his voice stripped her bare.

"Yes." Ironically she loved him more now than she had when she'd turned him down. But that didn't make him any more right for her.

Lee smiled. "You are *incredible,*" he said. Jules frowned because the smile didn't match his sharp tone. He strode to the window and her vision blurred, watching that familiar loping stride. All she'd had for nineteen months were freeze-frames of memory. "The guys are very protective of you, say you've been through a lot. And Rob and Connie consider you part of the family."

"None of that matters," she said. "Only what you want."

He opened the box again and the sun caught the diamond, and refracted its light off his shades. "Yeah," he said harshly. "Let's give me what I want."

In two strides he was beside her, catching her by the wrist and tugging her through the door, down a passage and outside where soldiers milled with relatives and camera crew. A military man, someone senior, Jules guessed by the brass on his uniform, was being interviewed on camera. "Great to have one of our own returned to us, and I'd ask you to respect his privacy while he reintegrates—" Catching sight of them, he paused. Cameras swung in their direction.

One hand still gripping her wrist, Lee held up the black velvet box. "Hey, everyone, my girl just returned my ring."

The conversation trickled into silence. Jules weathered the stares. As long as Lee understood her motives it didn't matter what other people thought.

"This wonderful woman has spent the past nineteen months comforting my family and friends." Jules squirmed but his fingers tightened. "Now she's suggesting she quietly disappear so I won't feel pressured by a proposal my friends made on my behalf. What do you think? Shall I let her walk away?"

"No," the crowd howled.

"I don't think so, either." He dropped to one knee and she saw her face, wide-eyed and startled, reflected in his upturned sunglasses. The wind ruffled his hair, revealing a jagged scar across his scalp. As if she needed another reminder of what he'd been through.

"Juliet…what's your middle name?"

"Carmen." Jules dropped her voice to a whisper, conscious of their audience. "What are you doing?"

"Juliet Carmen Browne, who *loves* me." The box opened with a snap and the big diamond glittered. It seemed almost gaudy. Lee lifted his shades and for the first time in twenty months she looked into eyes the extravagant green of a tropical rain forest. Glittering like the diamond he lifted out of the box's white satin interior. Feverish. "Will you marry me?"

Appalled, she looked beyond him to the expectant expressions of her friends. Claire was smiling and nodding through brimming tears, the guys were grinning, Lee's brother and sister beaming.

She looked back at his upturned face.

"Or you can end this right now," he said. Sunlight illuminated every hollow, every scar, every suffering-etched line of his. The diamond sparkled.

Swallowing hard, Jules held out her hand, watched as he slid the ring onto her finger.

"Kiss her," Connie shouted. Lee pushed to his feet. Cupping the nape of her neck, he pressed his mouth to hers, hard. A stranger's kiss.

"So," he said. "Let's go home."

CHAPTER SIX

HE'D LET ANGER get the better of him. Lee splashed water on his face in the men's room of the airbase thirty minutes later, then studied his scowl in the mirror. *You think?* With a growl he reached for a paper towel.

"Don't resist the emotions that come up," the shrink had advised. "Let them wash over you like waves and they'll pass." He hadn't mentioned waves the size of tsunamis.

Trouble was, he'd been blindsided by the upsurge of longing when Jules had pressed her forehead into his jacket. *I have to make you real.* Through long months of captivity, he'd never expected to see her again, hold her. Breathe her in. Fall into those brown eyes with the gravitational pull of Jupiter.

Crushing the paper towel, he torpedoed it into the bin.

How dare this goddamned liar still make him feel something for her. With a straight face, tell him she loved him. *You want to make this real, Jules? Then let's get real in front of witnesses.* He'd expected her to crack and confess when he'd put her on the spot with a proposal. Hey, it wasn't as if she didn't have practice saying no to him.

He'd seen the hesitation, her brief—too brief—struggle with the truth. Before she'd squared her shoulders and coolly accepted the ring. No doubt she figured she'd quietly dump him when the media spotlight passed on to the next novelty news item—a weather-forecasting goat maybe.

A public denouncement would hurt his family and

friends, monkey in the middle of all this. The resulting publicity would also make it more difficult for him to sink into anonymity. He'd torture Jules's conscience for a while before he dropped the "I know what you did last summer" bomb. Who knows, he might even win a confession. He needed her to own up to what she'd done, to take responsibility. Dammit, he deserved that much.

Grimly, Lee checked his watch, did a time conversion and popped a tablet of miltefosine. He washed it down with water straight from the faucet and tried not to gag. Determined not to sit around in a hospital, he'd insisted on oral drugs. Unfortunately, nausea was a side effect for the first few days, but he was doing his best to hide it. He'd had enough of being treated with kid gloves.

He stripped off his new, smaller uniform—his old size had made him look like a teen in his dad's borrowed suit—and hauled on a T-shirt he'd borrowed from Ross and new jeans, which he still had to tighten around his lean hips with a belt. Then he inspected the weakling in the mirror. Clearly, he was months from combat fitness even if the idea didn't send him into a cold sweat.

"There are noncombat options," the C.O. had said privately. "Talk to Ross about them."

Staying in the military didn't appeal to Lee, but then again, nothing did. Now that the initial euphoria of his release had worn off, Lee found himself exhausted and strangely rudderless.

"Rebuild your health, rest, play, spend time with your loved ones," the boss had ordered. "Then we'll talk about your future with the service. And in the meantime you're on full pay. I'm also chasing back pay, though red tape means it's a couple of months away." He grinned. "There isn't a form for resurrection."

Lee hadn't been expecting that. "Thank you, sir."

"We look after our own," said the C.O. Lee had had to struggle to hide his skepticism. "I'll see you in Auckland next week, now go home with your fiancée."

His fiancée.

Savagely Lee replaced his shades. He wouldn't tell Jules about the money. Not when there was interest to collect. Striding out of the men's room, he told himself there was an upside to his impulsive gesture. He got to torture her longer.

Besides, he didn't have to stay with his siblings. Both had expressed hurt when Lee hinted at staying with one of his buddies, but they couldn't pull rank over a fiancée. Lee wasn't sure he could do normal yet and with Jules he felt no compulsion to try.

He embraced this anger at Jules; it gave him purpose and soothed his uncertainty.

Guess he did have a purpose. Teaching his erstwhile fiancée that karma was a bitch.

He'd already said goodbye to his siblings so he was surprised to find his sister still there, waiting for him.

"Phil's parked outside with the kids," Connie said. "But I had a thought. Why don't you and Jules come stay with us tonight? It doesn't seem right parting so quickly."

His relatives weren't as good as his buddies at hiding their shock over his changed appearance. Harder to accept was Connie's attempt to take his arm.

"Thanks but, as I said earlier, Jules has to work tomorrow." Evading his sister's help, he hitched up his loose jeans. "While I remember, did you keep any of my leather jackets for the boys to grow into?"

"Hardly, that would have been macabre.... Dad took them. Then after he passed—" Her green eyes filled. She regarded him helplessly.

Throat tightening, Lee tucked her into a comforting embrace.

"I'm supposed to be consoling you," she wailed into his chest as he rested his chin on the top of her head. So little, his big sis. "It's okay," he rasped.

Patting his bicep, Connie pulled away and wiped her eyes with the heel of her hand. "Anyway," she said shakily, "I think your clothes ended up at a thrift shop."

A thrift shop. Great. They'd given them away.

"Jules will know."

All roads led to Jules.

They stepped outside. The sky was overcast. Lee lifted his face and breathed deeply. He could smell rain in the air. After months in a dank, dark cell he yearned for it. Misreading his hesitation, Connie guided him down the steps. Meekly he accepted her help. Thank God, he was leaving town.

"Won't you reconsider?" she wheedled. "I made a welcome-home cake and the Jacksons were coming over specially to see you." Lee frowned. How the hell did his brother-in-law's parents constitute immediate family?

"We've talked about this," he said patiently. "Give me a few weeks to settle in then we'll do the homecoming re-union."

He'd found he could only handle thirty, forty minutes of company before he flamed out. So his minders, both official and self-appointed, had kept this initial meet short. Fifteen minutes with the press, an hour with his nearest and dearest and then home with Rob. In Auckland. Near the resources of the NZSAS headquarters. It had all been carefully managed until he'd done the unexpected by proposing to Jules.

The proposal had changed plans substantially. The maverick in him liked the disruption he'd caused. The realist wondered what the hell he was doing. All he knew was he had to reassert his independence, his freedom. Scary as that was.

They reached Connie's people-mover. Engine idling, Phil sat behind the wheel with the stoic expression of a man used to waiting for his wife. The three boys were iPodded to the max in the backseat. "I told her you'd say no," Phil commented as Lee opened Connie's passenger door. "You and Jules will want to be alone for a bit." He winked.

"You betcha." *Only not for the reason you're thinking.* God. Sex.

"No harm in asking," Connie retorted, then visibly brightened. "We'll celebrate your engagement at the homecoming party, too."

"Great." Lee dropped a kiss on her cheek. *Just great.*

As she secured her seat belt he noticed his three nephews staring at him as if he were some kind of alien. "Boo!" They jumped.

"For heaven's sake!" Connie clutched her chest. "You nearly gave me a heart attack."

"Sorry, sis." He and his brother-in-law shared a grin as the boys' faces cracked into wide smiles. "Still the fun uncle," Lee reminded them. *Fake it until you make it.* "I'm relying on you guys to bring me up to date with technology, too."

"Jules and the guys are waiting for you in the parking lot." Phil pointed over his shoulder.

"Thanks." Lee held his smile despite a sudden wave of nausea. "See you all soon." As soon as the vehicle disappeared, he leaned against the building, kneading his roiling stomach. He waited it out and straightened his shoulders. Unfortunately, there was still one set of gatekeepers between him and freedom.

He found the gang waiting next to Nate's new four-wheel drive—the flight home had been spent discussing Lee's vehicle purchase options. Pro-Ford Dan was driving south to Beacon Bay; pro-Holden Nate and Claire were heading north to a beachside settlement thirty-five minutes east of Lee and Jules's destination, Whangarei. Only Ross, who'd nearly been jettisoned for insisting real men bought Land Rovers, lived here in Auckland.

Lee's tribe circled Jules like a protective wagon. *It should have been so different. Yeah, well, get over it.*

Dan spotted him first. "We were just saying that your capital with the press will have gone sky-high with the on-camera proposal. If it becomes too much we'll find you a bolt-hole."

"I finally have freedom of movement and you're suggesting hiding again? After the Taliban, I think I can handle a few journalists."

"You're underestimating—"

"Then I'll call for backup." Lee reached in his pocket and pulled out his new cell. "You programmed every number personally, remember, Shep?"

His buddies looked at Jules. "I'll phone if we need you," she promised. It was a changing of the guard, and Lee didn't like it.

Ross leaned against Nate's Holden, taking the weight off his lame leg, which had stiffened through the long flight. "Feed him up, won't you, Jules?"

"I will," she promised nervously. His sweetie was a soup-and-salad queen.

"I'll courier some protein powder and bars," Ross reassured her. "Along with the meal plan I used through rehab."

But Lee didn't want Jules reassured. "I can't wait to exchange these ugly nurses for a pretty one." He hooked an arm around her shoulder and squeezed. "Love's the best medicine isn't it, darling?"

She responded with the blank smile she'd defaulted to

since she'd accepted his proposal. "I'll go fetch the car," she said, and hurried off. His gaze followed her, pulled like a dog on a leash, he thought disgustedly. He hadn't factored libido into his scheme because it had been dormant for nineteen months. Would Jules maintain this charade as far as sex? Would he? His body suggested it might consider the idea.

"You look beat," Nate said. "Stretch out in the backseat on the way home, take a nap."

"Next you'll be asking if I've used the little boys' room before my big drive."

"I already know you have."

Everyone laughed but when Nate put his arm around Claire, Lee glanced away. He'd never get used to seeing his buddy loved up with Steve's widow.

"Come for dinner when you feel up to it." Flicking her blond ponytail off her shoulder, Claire smiled at him. "My son is longing to see you. And if you need us at anytime—"

"Yeah…. A few quiet days first, hey?" Lee let his weariness show in his answering smile because it made everyone back off.

"Of course." There were new layers of wisdom in the way she looked at him, as though she understood what he was doing—and why. He blinked. Then she kissed his cheek before hooking an arm around Nate's waist. "Ready to go home, Wyatt?"

"Home sounds good."

Grief hit Lee in an avalanche. He had no home. His unit had disbanded, his father had died and the love of his life was a liar and a fraud.

"See you and Jules at the farm next weekend, mate." Dan gave him a light hug. Distracted, Lee hadn't steeled himself for it and instinctively shoved his friend away. There was an uncomfortable silence as everyone scrambled to put a game face on.

Trying to make a joke of it, Lee managed a weak smile. "Since we're in New Zealand how about we default to a Kiwi bloke's farewell. See ya." *Don't make a big deal of this. Please don't make a bi—*

Ross grabbed his jaw between his two large hands and smacked a loud kiss on his forehead. "See ya."

Everyone laughed and the tension broke. Lee swatted the Iceman away. "I know you need practice but save it for your wedding night." *Where was Jules with the damn car?*

Then he heard the rumble of a powerful engine and Steve's 1959 Cadillac pulled up alongside, Jules behind the wheel.

And Lee fell down another rabbit hole.

"So what made you buy the Caddy?" Lee asked as they cruised the country roads after leaving the airbase. Experimentally, he laid his arm across the back of Jules's seat and watched her shoulders tighten. Tension, he liked that. He wasn't going to give her a moment to relax.

It was his first real chance to study her, to notice her pallor, the faint circles under her eyes. Guess she hadn't got much sleep since Lazarus rose from the dead.

"Claire decided to sell it. Don't you remember…?" She paused, no doubt winding through the logistics of his "amnesia." What he could and couldn't remember.

While he waited, he studied her once-beloved features. Her determined chin offset by the soft curve of her cheek with a biteable roundness when she smiled. Long lashes. He'd teased her once by saying they undermined her authority and she'd tortured him with butterfly kisses.

"…Claire always thought of this car as Steve's mistress," Jules finished. Becoming aware of his scrutiny, she tucked her hair behind her ear, a sure sign of anxiety. Usually she was careful to cover the left ear because she thought it stuck out. It did, but in a cute way. Nerves weren't something he associated with this toughie, but then she was living one hell of a lie.

Lee turned his attention to the scenery. It was easier watching the countryside transform into suburbia. "And now Claire's engaged to her husband's best friend."

Her sideways glance was troubled. "She mourned Steve. She still mourns Steve. So does Nate. Keep an open mind."

"Sure. They're my friends, after all." He wasn't going to discuss this with her. He returned his attention to her profile. "So how about you? You mourn me for long?"

They were merging into the highway heading north. Jules checked her side mirrors and accelerated. "The day I heard you were alive was the happiest day of my life."

"That isn't an answer."

Again she considered her reply. Once he'd found that lawyerly trait to weigh her words before speaking endearing. But now, it meant that obtaining a confession wasn't going to be easy.

"I've been told you don't want to talk about the past nineteen months."

That was the thing with Jules. He could never second-guess what she'd say next. "You heard right." He wound down his window, needing the breeze to dispel the sensual lure of her perfume.

"I feel the same way."

He snorted. "You think our experiences are comparable?"

"Hardly. But, like you, I don't like to dwell on the bad times. You have the right to decide what to disclose and to whom. How you want to deal with this." She gave him another incisive glance. "When you're building a new life, constantly picking the scab can be self-defeating. That's something these past months have taught me, for what it's worth."

"Wipe the slate clean and start again?" So that's how she justified her deceit.

"If it's possible. Yes."

Well, it's not possible, Jules. He opened his mouth to reply and then closed it, overcome by a rush of nausea.

"You've gone white. Here." She passed him the water bottle from the console between them. "Hydrate. There's a blanket in the backseat if you want to fold it up for a pillow."

He accepted the bottle but didn't speak, wholly focused on not losing his breakfast. Sweat popped on his forehead.

"Lee, do I need to stop?"

Desperately he nodded.

Lee used all his willpower not to throw up as she took a couple of minutes to pull over, easing into the wide verge at the side of the highway.

As soon as the vehicle pulled over, he flung open the door, stumbled a few paces, then bent double and hurled into the bushes. Cars whizzed by at a hundred kilometers, buffeting him with gas fumes.

He heard the crunch of gravel and then felt her hand between his shoulder blades, cool and steady through the thin cotton of his T-shirt. Finally the paroxysms passed.

Some tissues appeared before his blurred vision. Shakily, Lee wiped his mouth and straightened. Jules caught him by the arm and steadied him. "I'm fine," he gasped, but took a couple of seconds to extricate himself.

"Wait here," she said gently.

She returned to the car for the water bottle he'd dropped.

Lee rinsed his mouth, splashed his face then used more wipes to dry off.

"It's not as bad as it looks," he said as they got back to the car.

Jules slid behind the wheel. "I'm taking you to the nearest Emergency."

"Nausea's an early side effect of the meds I'm taking," he explained. "It'll wear off in another day or so."

"I can't believe the army doctor didn't insist you stay in Auckland for observation."

He probably would have—if Lee had shared his symptoms. "I'm an advanced paramedic," he argued. "I can gauge when I need medical attention and I know all the warning signs to watch for."

She kept shaking her head.

"If I'm still not well in a couple of days I'll seek treatment, I promise."

"Lee—"

"C'mon, Jules, why would I stay in Auckland when I can go home with my brand-spanking-new fiancée?" If his sweetie was hoping for an out, she was outta luck.

He replaced the water bottle in the console and picked up one of her business cards "Hey, new cards…. Wow, you're a partner."

She flicked the card out of his fingers. "Nice try, mate. Okay, here's the deal. We'll keep going if you try to rest." Reaching into the backseat, she got the blanket, rolled it into a pillow and handed it to him. "Tomorrow morning you're visiting the doctor."

"You're the boss." Until he regained his strength.

"There are mints in my bag." He found them.

She turned the ignition. "Oh, and take the cash, too. A thousand dollars." She smiled. "Your first interest payment."

Lee opened his mouth to tell her to keep it. But how would that teach her about consequences? He pocketed the wad. "Thanks."

LEE SLEPT AND finally Jules could process the past few hours. *Well, you've done it now, girl.*

No point in beating herself up. The circumstances, Lee's condition, hadn't given her a choice. When he was healthier, stronger, she'd tell him the truth. Until then… Her hands tightened on the steering wheel. Oh God, what was she going to do until then?

She stole a glance at him, trying to find the big, angry man who'd walked out on her, slamming the door behind him. All she could see was someone she loved—ill, exhausted and stubbornly fighting it. But angry. Yes, still angry, though now it was targeted at his weakness, his exhaustion and, she suspected, at people trying to get him to let time do the healing. He'd always been impatient for results.

But if Lee imagined she'd meekly stand by and let him have his own way—if it wasn't good for him—then he hadn't just lost his memory, he'd lost his mind.

Her lips curved in a pained smile. *There you go, find humor in this.*

One thing *was* clear. He hadn't changed into a man who'd easily forgive her once—*if*—he recalled the memory of her rejecting his proposal. Jules could barely understand her own motives for accepting the ring she'd earlier refused.

When Nate and Dan had called her to Ross's hospital bed, she'd thought it was to say another goodbye. Ice's injuries from the ambush had been that horrendous. Instead they'd presented her with the ring. Taking comfort, she realized numbly, from the belief they were fulfilling their dead buddy's wish.

And she'd put it on with trembling fingers, not saying a word. Not one.

CHAPTER SEVEN

THE HIGHWAY ENDED and became State Highway 1, a mostly two-lane road north, cutting through countryside interspersed with towns. The trees in early November fluttered late spring's new leaves and the grass was a lush green. The warm air through Lee's open window was positively flirtatious, though she could also smell rain. Overhead, the clouds were gray.

Jules drove mechanically. She kept her eyes on the road but every other sense was attuned to the silent rise and fall of the chest of the man sleeping beside her. She had to resist the need to touch him, to keep substantiating that he was real.

When her first grief had passed, she'd consoled herself with the thought that somewhere, with the benefit of heaven-sight, Lee understood her impulsive decision to accept his ring from the guys. Earthly Lee had never been one for saintly forbearance and the new Lee beside her, scarred, damaged and edgy... Only a fool would hope he'd understand.

It started spitting as they crossed the Brynderwyn Hills and Jules pulled off the highway, angling the vehicle so the raindrops didn't hit Lee's sleeping face. Engine idling, she unclipped her seat belt and carefully leaned past him to wind up his window. He didn't stir, out cold after his long flight.

His face had softened in sleep, which made it easier to

find the vestiges of his once-extraordinary looks. Good bones were good bones—except where they'd been broken. He breathed heavily through his crooked nose and rage made her own breathing harsh.

He had not deserved this. None of them had.

But he was alive and that was a miracle she'd never cease giving thanks for.

She stared at the face so close to hers and murmured, "I accepted the ring because everyone needed me to and because I so badly wanted us to have parted on better terms than we did."

Lee grunted, settled his head more firmly on the makeshift pillow and sighed, his breath stirring the loose strands of her hair.

Jules closed her eyes. She was afraid of her response to him, always had been.

She'd been fourteen when she'd decided that the most self-destructive thing a woman could do was follow her heart. Like her mother had repeatedly done. Maturity had given Jules a more balanced view, but everyone started a relationship on their best behavior. Seeing a person's true colors took time and until then you held something back. It seemed a simple enough precaution. And then she'd met Lee and realized she wasn't smarter than other women, she was simply Napoleon before Waterloo.

"That's settled then," she whispered. His "death" had burned away any bitterness about how they'd parted but she wasn't going to bleed out for him again, this ill-fated love of hers. Not again. She had too strong a sense of self-preservation for that.

The decision steadied Jules, gave her purpose. She smoothed away a lock of hair that had fallen over his eyes and resolutely sat back.

He was troubled, of course he was—no one could come

through what he had unscathed. He needed love, patience and support; and she had atonement to make. She would take care of him until he was well enough to hear the truth. Maybe helping him into a new life would act as compensation in some way.

Flicking on the windshield wipers she pulled onto the highway. The left blade dragged, reminding her that she needed to replace it. But spending U.S. $87.50 plus postage to import a wiper blade wasn't a priority when you were scrambling to find one hundred and ten thousand dollars.

Jules had let her heart rule her head when she'd bought this car from Claire and was living to regret it. The Pink Lady had very quickly become the Pink Elephant under the strain of daily use. She'd sold her practical Volvo to afford the purchase. She could sell it, buy a cheap import and free up fifteen to twenty thousand for Lee. Jules sighed. That only left ninety-five thousand dollars to repay.

The wipers made a faint squeal as they ran out of rain and she switched them off. Whichever way you looked at it, she had a hell-busy week ahead.

Jules reassigned clients in her head while the Caddy swept along the wet roads, darkened to a slick black. The sun pierced the clouds periodically, spotlighting tableaux of passing scenery. A field, a stand of trees, a patch of blacktop. She'd have to work half days—there were some clients she couldn't pass on.

The Carpenters, on the verge of finalizing separation papers, wouldn't want another lawyer. Neither would Mrs. Potter who was coming in to sign over Enduring Power of Attorney. Cedric was in the middle of his asset planning—it would take her more time to brief someone than finish it herself.

Lee jerked upright with a hoarse shout, startling Jules into slamming on the brakes. The Caddy's wheels locked, and the vehicle slid across the wet road and squealed to a stop in the oncoming lane.

Lee sat up, dazed. "What happened?"

Some ninety meters ahead lay a blind corner. "Hang on." Jules forgot the clutch as she tried to change into Reverse. The engine jumped and stalled. "Damn it!"

She turned the key, pumping the accelerator in her haste to get them out of trouble, then belatedly realized she was flooding the engine and eased off the pedal. Too late. The engine coughed and died. Once, twice she tried the ignition. No go. In frustration she hit the steering wheel. "We'll have to push it out of this lane."

Lee was already unfastening his seat belt. "Put the gear stick in Neutral."

They scrambled out of the car. "Thank God it's a quiet road," she said. "I took a shortcut to bypass Wellsford's bottleneck."

Lee braced against the bonnet. "Once we've got her moving, you steer and I'll push."

"You shouldn't be exerting yourself. Let's change places."

He gave her a male look and she shut up and planted her hands against the door frame. "On three," he said. "One… two…*three*." They both heaved on the car. Nothing happened.

"Is the hand brake on?"

Jules checked. It was. Shamefacedly she released it. "Thank God," Lee muttered. They pushed again, and this time the Pink Lady groaned and started to move at a snail's pace.

"What happened to the law of momentum?" Jules panted.

"It came across a couple of tons of pink metal…. Why'd you buy this heap again?"

But another sound caught her attention. Among the comfortable country noises, she picked out the faint squeal of air brakes.

Lee heard it, too. "Playtime's over." Arms wide across the bonnet, he bent his head, long thin muscles cording as he shoved. High heels sliding on the loose stones, Jules heaved against the door frame, reaching one hand to steer the vehicle. The Pink Lady picked up speed.

Glancing forward, Jules caught a flash of sun on metal as a milk tanker came into view through the trees, then disappeared approaching the corner. Their corner. "Get ready to run!"

"C'mon!" Lee yelled above the approaching truck. "You've played chicken before, haven't you?"

"This is crazy!" She shoved harder, wrenching the steering wheel. Lee grimaced in effort. The Pink Lady glided into the correct lane as the tanker barreled around the corner…swinging wide. Air brakes squealed as the driver wrestled with the steering wheel to adjust his line, his mouth open in surprise.

The blast of his horn was deafening as it rolled past with two feet to spare, the backdraft lifting her dress and swirling it around her thighs. Furious, she raised her fists. "You bloody idiot!"

Next minute she was jostled aside. Lee leaped through the open door of the driver's side and slammed on the brakes as the Pink Lady overshot the verge. The car stopped inches short of a ditch.

Aghast, Jules stared at him through the windscreen, leaning against the hood for support. "I could have got you killed on your first day home," she gasped.

He grinned. It was his old grin, dazzling and devilish, and her erratic pulse jumped even further out of regular tempo. He'd been holding out on her.

"Why'd you buy this heap again?" he demanded through the open side window.

"Because you loved it."

And just like that, his face fell. "You say all the right things," he muttered. He climbed out of the driver's seat. "I hate to tell you, but she was a passing phase."

"A passing…" Jules sucked in a deep, unsteady breath and started to laugh increasingly hysterical laughter. She'd read more into his enjoyment of Steve's car than was there. "Oh, Lee," she managed to get out weakly. It didn't matter how many myths he exploded, she'd take the real man any day. Unable to articulate her wellspring of emotions, she stepped forward and hugged him. "Oh, Lee."

He stiffened. "Jules, I'm sweaty."

"And you stink. I don't care."

"I care." Carefully he loosened her hold and she remembered Claire's comment that he found hugs difficult.

"So, what happened to cause the skid anyway?" Lee bent to inspect the tires. "Did you hit an oil slick?"

"You yelled." Recalling the anguish in his tone, Jules shivered. "Ajmal?"

He straightened. "I'm sorry," he said curtly.

She knew better than to ask if he wanted to talk about it. A drop of rain fell on her bare arm, then another, surprisingly cold. "It's going to pour," she said. *Who was Ajmal?* "And you've just burned up all your reserves helping me save the Pink Lady." Sweat dampened his hair from the recent exertion. His skin was the color of wood ash and a blue pulse beat erratically under the thin skin at his temples. "Let's get you in the car."

"I'm fine," he grumbled.

"You will be fine," she replied pleasantly, "when you're rested and fed and medicated." She deliberately stressed the last word and was rewarded with the hint of a smile.

"I'll join you in a minute." He turned and leaned against the door, rolling his head back to feel the drops on his face. The rain gathered mass. What on earth was he doing? Jules ducked into the car, grabbed a red umbrella from the backseat. When she reemerged, Lee had walked away a few paces, spread his arms, face still lifted to the sky.

While she could only see his back, his posture suggested a yearning that silenced her.

The shower became a downpour. Raindrops bounced off the road surface, and quickly formed puddles. Arms outstretched, Lee surrendered to it, celebrated it.

Jules stood under the umbrella and waited.

When at last he climbed into the car, water had plastered his hair to his skull and the sodden T-shirt clung to his body, revealing every rib, every sinew of lean, wasted muscle. But his green eyes were luminous, as though the rain had filled him to the brim and spilled over. He looked at her warily.

She passed him the blanket. "I don't expect you've had much chance to enjoy rain lately."

"Not much." He wrapped the blanket around his shoulders, dragging off the T-shirt underneath it.

"You make it look fun."

He smiled. "Try it."

"Rain check. Want me to get a change of clothes out of the trunk?"

"Thanks."

Reopening the umbrella, Jules got out and rummaged through his bag. He'd left owning a house, a Harley, an old ute, boys' toys and an extensive wardrobe. He'd returned to nothing, his only belongings this duffel bag holding a few changes of clothes and basic toiletries. They'd have to remedy that.

Clutching the dry clothes against her chest to protect

them from the squally droplets blowing under the umbrella, she got back in, catching a flash of skin before Lee hauled the blanket over his shoulders.

Covered, he accepted her bundle and finished dressing under the blanket. Jules busied herself wringing the worst of the water from his discarded clothes before dumping them on the backseat. She fought the urge to weep.

In the six-week whirlwind that was their relationship she'd experienced the world afresh with him. One weekend they'd taken a road trip on his Harley, buffeted by a coastal breeze, gone skinny-dipping on an isolated beach and made love under a waterfall in the bush, laughing so hard they'd nearly drowned. He'd coaxed her into walking barefoot, like a couple of kids, to the campground store for an ice cream. This man, so at ease with the elements, with himself, had spent the past fourteen months in a dank, dark cell.

Heartbroken, she smiled at him. "Let's get you home."

LEE HAD HIS first real chuckle when Jules pulled into her garage. Vintage 1930s, like her Art Deco cottage, it hadn't been built for an American car the size of a '59 Caddy.

"Go ahead, make a wisecrack," she invited as she threw a cover over the protruding rear end with the ease of long practice, then slid the roller door down to a protective pad she'd placed over each Jetson taillight. "I've had everything from 'Does my bum look big in this?' to 'Surely you measured the garage before you bought the car?'"

"Your insurance premiums must be huge—anyone could come and open the garage."

"They could but…" Triumphantly, Jules produced a wheel lock.

And despite his exhaustion, Lee laughed. He turned to the house. "I thought you'd have finished the renovations."

The outside looked as dilapidated as ever, still in need of a repaint, particularly the wooden window frames.

"Nope," she said cheerfully.

Slinging the duffel bag over a shoulder, he followed her up the broken path to the curved front steps, where the paint was worn to bare concrete in patches from sixty years of foot traffic.

And stalled on the second step. "Are your flatmates going to be okay with this?" Until now he'd forgotten she shared the place with a couple whose rent helped repay her mortgage.

"I live alone these days." The frosted glass above the front door needed new beading and rattled loosely in the frame as she turned the key and opened it. "Come on in."

Last time Lee had crossed this threshold he'd been leaving, a ring in his pocket and righteous anger shielding his devastation. Suddenly so weary he could barely put one step in front of the other, he followed her into the tiny hall and turned right into the living room he'd helped paint a light brown.

On the stripped floorboards, pastel coffee mugs sprouted around the base of the couch and armchair like ceramic mushrooms. Both the coffee table and fireplace mantel were stacked with papers. He scanned the title on the top of the nearest pile and his jaw tightened. *Common Problems with Post-release Hostages.*

Jules dropped her bag over it. "If I'd known you were coming home with me I would have cleaned up," she apologized.

"It's a palace compared to what I've come from," he reminded her.

Dropping the keys on the coffee table, Jules went to close the curtains across the bay window and Lee took the opportunity to pick up another report from the mantel, brushing off petals from a vase of wilting pink flowers next to it. "Different types of amnesia," he said drily. "I'm touched by your concern."

"Anything that helps…. Let me tidy that away."

Embarrassed, she held out a hand for it; Lee tucked the folder under his arm. "Bedtime reading. I might learn something." Given that most of his amnesia was feigned, he sure as hell hoped he did. "So what does all this stuff say about the odds of my memory returning?"

"Every case is different, but given the length of time that's passed…probably low." Collecting the dirty coffee mugs, she added casually, "Have you had any flashbacks?"

"No, but there's something about this house that makes me feel…" he frowned "…uneasy? Uncomfortable?"

She darted a nervous glance at him.

Lee waited a couple of beats. "I think it's the beige of these walls."

Jules's tension subsided like a soufflé. "You never appreciated mocha. Remem—you tried to talk me into white."

"Guess I prefer things simple."

"And yet you chose me," she said lightly.

He beamed a loving smile. "We chose each other."

The mugs clunked together as she escaped into the adjacent kitchen. "So what can I get you? A cup of tea, some food?" Dumping the mugs, she opened the fridge. "I have chicken noodle soup…not homemade but organic. I'll stock up with something heartier tomorrow."

His stomach lurched at the mention of food. Lee swallowed hard. "Before anything else, I need a shower."

"Of course, you've been traveling, what…a day and a half?" She led the way to the bathroom, passing her bedroom. Her bed was covered with discarded dresses. That was odd. Blushing, she closed the door in passing. "As I said, I would have cleaned up."

Yeah, but then there'd be no evidence. Lee said nothing. Nervously, Jules rummaged for fresh towels in the bathroom cupboard. "If you want to use my razor, there are fresh blades in here, too."

He thought of the scar on his cheek. "Thanks, but I'm going for rugged."

"You start feeling faint...just yell."

Which meant he looked like shit. A glance in the mirror confirmed it. He saw a pale, glassy-eyed skinny guy clearly about to throw up.

Leaving the bathroom, Jules hesitated. "Maybe you shouldn't lock the door."

"In case you want to join me?" But she was off the hook for a few days at least and they both knew it.

"You don't have to put on a brave front for me, Lee."

So much for striking terror into her guilty heart. The door clicked shut. He turned on the shower and under cover of the noisy spray, threw up in the toilet as quietly as he could. The cure was almost worse than the disease.

There was mouthwash beside the sink. Lee used half a bottle, then drank thirstily from the tap. Better. Digging in his bag he pulled out a new toothbrush still in its wrapper and brushed his teeth three times. Visiting a dentist was on his list of things to do and he wasn't looking forward to it.

He stripped off his clothes and stepped into the old-fashioned shower, groaning aloud at the pleasure of hot water. With the luxury of staying in as long as he wanted—not an option in a base hospital—he lowered himself to the floor and leaned against the tiles, letting the cascade pour over him, steamy and hot, easing the aches in his muscles, the kinks in his mind.

And tried to ignore the passion-fruit scent of Jules's soap and shampoo entwining his senses with unwelcome tendrils of memory.

He must have dozed because next thing he knew, Jules's silhouette hovered anxiously on the other side of the semi-transparent shower curtain. "Lee, are you okay in there?" His hand shot out to hold the curtain closed. He had no desire to show Jules his scars.

"I fell asleep," he admitted. "I guess it's being…" *Safe.* "Jet-lagged. I'll be right out."

When she'd left, he stepped out and toweled dry, noticing that she'd refolded his clothes on the chair. Very wifely. He dressed and then followed the smell of chicken soup to the kitchen.

Jules was at the stove, stirring a pot. "Think you can keep some of this down?"

All Lee wanted was a bed, but his medication needed to be taken with food. "I'll try it." He noticed she'd lined up the vitamins and minerals in his duffel along the countertop with a tall glass of water and added begrudgingly. "Thanks."

He sat at the table, watching Jules move around the kitchen, retrieving bowls and spoons, buttering toast. Her movements tended toward brisk and purposeful in keeping with her personality. But it was her curves he was watching…. She had curves that a Formula One racetrack designer would envy. Lee looked away before his bitterness curdled the soup.

Black-framed photos hanging on the wall caught his attention. Before he was even aware of it, he'd pushed back his chair and was standing before one.

Lee's breathing hitched painfully. Holding a flashlight and wearing a day pack over a green anorak, his father peered over his spectacles at the ugliest animal Lee had ever seen.

Jules came to stand beside him. "Our Tasmania trip.…

That strange little marsupial is a Tasmanian devil. We were on a night walk...they're nocturnal."

"So was Dad." He wanted to touch that beloved face, but not in front of Jules.

"You're telling me." There was a smile in her voice. "I'd fade out at nine-thirty while he stayed up planning the next day."

Except one morning he didn't wake up. *Tell me he didn't suffer. Tell me he coped okay after my death. Tell me he died happy.* But Lee couldn't go there yet. "How did you become such good friends?" They'd previously met once over dinner at a restaurant. He couldn't recall an instantaneous bond being struck. If anything, Jules had been reserved.

"After your memorial service, Rob and Connie asked me if I'd keep an eye on him—since we both lived in Whangarei." She added, "Both of us were on our own and somehow we ended up having dinner once a week."

Gregarious and open, Dad had always collected friends easily.

"One night when we were talking about regrets Ian said he'd had dreams of traveling with your mother which he'd put aside when she died."

Lee folded his arms. "First I've heard of it."

"I had to practically drag him on the initial trip, but then he got the travel bug. The other trips were his idea. And like his son, he could be persuasive." She smiled.

"Neither of us like to take no for an answer." He'd hoped to make her squirm; instead, Jules moved to the next picture.

"Your dad wasn't a quitter."

What the hell was that supposed to mean? Her tone was so neutral as to be accusatory.

"This is a volcano on the Big Island in Hawaii." His father grinned against a backdrop of lava. Same hat, same jacket. He did enjoy getting good wear out of clothes. Briefly Lee closed his eyes. Oh, Dad.

"Because of my work our trips were short," Jules continued. "Never more than a week, but that suited Ian. He didn't like to leave his garden for too long."

"And yet he gave it up for an apartment in a retirement home." Lee struggled to keep accusation out of his voice.

"Rob and Connie saw his decision as being out of character. Maybe it was, I didn't know your dad well before the ambush." She hesitated. "After your death, he found it very hard living in the house he'd raised you."

"And you helped him pick up the pieces."

"We helped each other." The frame was askew and she straightened it, her fingers lingering. "I think I got the best of the deal."

That's what worries me.

"But to answer your question, the retirement home had a communal vegetable garden. Ian could be involved without doing the digging…. This last picture was taken in Queenstown."

It was the only shot of Jules with his dad. They stood on the deck of the vintage steamship *TSS Earnslaw,* arms threaded affectionately, smiling. While he'd been in a hellhole in Afghanistan.

Jealousy, relief, gratitude, grief…they all churned inside him. He'd tethered these emotions for nineteen months; the idea of giving them free rein was terrifying.

"I have a holiday album if you want to see it," Jules said.

"Some other day." He returned abruptly to the table. The kitchen was tidier than the rest of the house, which suggested she didn't use it much. "What happened to your flatmates?"

"I needed my own space." Jules finished preparing the meal. "I turned the third bedroom into a home office."

"You're still a workaholic?"

"I refuse to answer on the grounds that it may be incriminating…. Here you go." She placed a bowl of soup and a plate of toast in front of him, before returning to the counter for her own.

Lee sipped his first spoonful and cursed.

"Be careful," Jules warned as she returned. "It's—"

"Hot, yeah." Picking up his glass, he swilled cold water. "I'm still not used to it."

He caught her eye and got burned again, this time by her sympathy. Something else he wasn't used to. She must have seen his recoil because she got busy, pouring tea from a teapot already on the table, adding milk and two sugars to each mug.

"I don't take sugar," he reminded her.

"You do tonight…it's good for shock."

He raised a brow. "As a paramedic I can tell you that's a myth." He didn't like that she'd picked up on his reaction to seeing his father. "Plus you're being bossy."

"Surely you didn't forget that about me." With a warm smile, she slid a mug over.

"No." He returned her smile. "But we took turns being on top." Shock flared in her eyes, and she stopped stirring her tea. *Hey, baby,* he thought, *and that's on one sip of wholesome soup. Imagine what I might do on a whole bowl.*

Jules started stirring again. "And tonight it's *my* turn on top."

His groin tightened. Definitely still in working order. "When I get my strength back—" he smiled across the table "—you're in trouble."

"Finish your soup since our shared priority is making you healthy."

He managed half a bowl, eating it slowly, giving his stomach time to digest it. The spoon seemed to get heavier and heavier, as did his head. He propped it in one hand. Next thing Jules was pulling his arm over her shoulder. Sliding a hand round his waist, she helped him to his feet. "Let's get you to bed."

"I'm awake," he mumbled.

He did wake up when she led him into her bedroom. Jules must have felt his muscles tense. "It's closer to the bathroom.... I'll take the spare room."

She released him to pull back the covers. She must have cleared away the clothes when he'd been in the shower. Lee collapsed face forward on the fresh sheets, fully clothed. "Ah, God, this is good."

"There's a basin on the nightstand if you need to throw up."

"Spoil the moment, why don't you," he complained into her pillow, and she laughed.

"Sleep in. I have to go to work but I'll be home by lunchtime. We'll go to the doctor—"

He rolled onto his back and opened his eyes. She'd already turned out the light, but the beam from a streetlight sliced through a gap in the curtains, illuminating her silhouette.

"And I want to join a gym." *Start rebuilding muscle.*

"It's too soon, Lee."

"Jules," he said evenly, "you don't have a vote."

"Asking me to marry you suggests otherwise."

But I didn't mean it. And you only said yes to avoid exposure as a bullshitter.

"Speaking of which, aren't going to kiss me goodnight?" *Don't get too comfortable, sweetie.*

Her shadow stilled. "Of course." She came over, and her hair closed out the light as she bent forward. Warm lips brushed against his in a quick kiss. Lee detected a tremor in them. She had to be wondering how the hell she'd avoid sex while she lived this lie. He had no intention of sleeping with her, but he was sure going to have some fun pretending he wanted to.

Briefly he considered suggesting sharing her bed until he got his strength back but dismissed it. His sleep was fitful, restless with bad dreams, and he didn't want her seeing that. There were other ways of being naked and he wasn't doing any of them with Jules.

She straightened, tentatively stroked her fingers through his hair. "I'm glad you're here."

As Lee drifted into sleep he thought, *You won't be saying that tomorrow.*

CHAPTER EIGHT

JULES SHUT LEE'S DOOR, walked down the passage and then closed the living room door behind her to avoid disturbing him.

She caught herself touching her mouth where the brush of his lips still tingled and dropped her hand, frowning. Don't go there, girl. Not having to make excuses to avoid intimacy is the *only* thing going your way.

Despite Lee's bravado, the kiss they'd just shared was clearly more about his proving he could handle physical contact than real desire. Claire was right to have mentioned the guys' concern. Lee was far from the demonstrative friend, brother or lover who'd left nineteen months ago.

But it was the man who'd returned Jules had to make amends to.

Taking in the mess in the living room, she frowned again. She wasn't about to let him exchange one hovel for another. After carting all the papers to her office, she ditched the pink peonies, vacuumed, dusted and scrubbed.

There was little in the fridge for breakfast so Jules baked a batch of muffins. Periodically she paused to check on Lee, very quietly opening his door. His breathing was heavy and regular, and the basin remained unused on the nightstand.

It was midnight before she fell into her own bed, leaving all the doors ajar so she'd hear Lee if he got up in the night. She rose at five, checking him again before she left for work. He lay almost in the same position. Returning to the kitchen, she placed a plate of muffins on the counter along with a list of emergency phone numbers and her direct work line. Scrawled her cell number, too, in case he'd lost it.

Dawn tinged the eastern sky as she parked under her six-story glass office tower, adjacent to the inner-city shopping district. Jules shook off her exhaustion like a wet dog as she disarmed the alarm system. She made a coffee while she waited for her laptop to boot up, then settled in to work.

By the time colleagues starting arriving at eight forty-five she'd written detailed rescheduling instructions for her legal secretary, finalized power-of-attorney documents and tweaked a separation agreement.

Through the narrow gap in the vertical blinds more shadows passed and the hum of conversation rose loud enough to distract her. Her thoughts went to Lee. Would he be awake yet?

Her hand hovered over the phone. Or would she wake him? *Don't get invested, he's on loan...with payment due.*

Speaking of... Sticking her head out of her office, Jules scanned the open-plan central area for the senior partner, saw him huddled with several others around the receptionist's computer, all engrossed in watching something on the screen. "Morning, everyone. Ted, can we talk?"

Six heads swiveled, six pairs of eyes stared. Instinctively Jules's hands went to her blouse. She'd been barely awake when she'd dressed. But it was buttoned.

"What are you doing here?" Ted demanded.

"I work here."

"Why aren't you home with Lee?"

"I will be soon as I've... Wait, how do you know about Lee?"

"She's wearing the ring again." Margie, her legal secretary, rushed over to hug her. "It's the most romantic story I ever heard."

"Honestly, I choke up every time I watch it." The receptionist flapped her hands in front of her eyes, to stop brimming tears from ruining her mascara.

Jules's stomach sank. "It's on the news already?"

"You mean you haven't seen it? Jules, it's the lead story." Margie tugged her over to the computer and reset the link. Onscreen, a news segment started rolling under a title: The Lazarus Proposal. Hostage Soldier Returns to Happy Ending.

"Oh, God." Jules tuned into the commentary to hear "…a fairy tale that is sparking international interest."

Ted dropped a paternal arm around her shoulder. "When did you hear he was alive?"

"Five days ago." She watched as Lee stepped out of the plane. "I needed a few days to get my head around it before I told anybody."

The item cut to him down on one knee in the airport lounge. "Jules Browne, who still loves me…" She appeared in close-up, looking like a stunned trout. And there was a spark of hope in the trout's eyes. Abruptly Jules turned away from it. "Okay, seen enough."

"There was a message on the reception voice mail when I cleared it." Margie handed over a piece of paper. "Some TV network in the States, asking you to contact them."

"Not interested." Crumbling the Post-it note, she dropped it in the bin. Thank God for an unlisted private number. "Anyone else phones, tell them that, will you? Ted, can we talk?"

"Absolutely." They walked toward her office. "Take whatever leave you need, Jules. Oli can quit the bloody golf course for a couple of weeks to cover." Oli was the retired partner whose shareholding she'd bought out.

She suppressed a spike of panic. "I can probably manage half days." Work had saved her sanity for too many months to cut the cord now.

"Do whatever works for you. Oli will only be too happy to do his bit."

"There's something else." No point beating around the bush. "My deposit for the buy-in was a legacy from Lee and I need to return it. How would you feel about my approaching Nick?" Nick had been in close contention with her for the partnership.

Ted's brows rose. "That's drastic. Have you talked to Lee about a repayment schedule?"

She shook her head. "He needs a lump sum to set up a new life—buy a car, put a deposit on a house, possibly invest in a business of his own."

"What's wrong with your house?"

She deliberately misunderstood him. "What isn't?"

"But we only just finalized the legal documents, sent out press releases and printed new business cards."

"I know, and I'll cover any changeover costs." Somehow. "Maybe it won't be necessary. I listed my house with an estate agent earlier this week. It's priced for a quick sale." If the house sold, she could keep her stake.

"And where will you two live then?"

I'll be in a cardboard box in the park. I expect Lee will be as far away as he can get. "We'll sort something out. What's important now is making life as easy as possible for Lee."

Ted took off his glasses and started cleaning them with a hankie, the way he always did when he was thinking things through. "He looks like he's been through hell…?"

Jules breathed a sigh of relief. Ted understood. "Yes."

"Okay, sound Nick out…but with one proviso." Ted put

on his glasses. "If he's harboring resentment about our choosing you, I don't want him."

"Fair enough." Jules glanced at her watch. "I'll put in another couple hours of work now. I imagine Lee will sleep until noon."

Ted looked at her strangely. "You do know your house is under siege by the press, don't you? I saw a live broadcast on TV earlier."

THE FIRST REPORTER KNOCKED on the door at seven. Thinking Jules had forgotten her keys, Lee hauled on jeans and opened it, smothering a yawn. A camera flashed in his face.

"What the—"

"Sergeant Davis, I'm Jessica Forrester of the *New Zealand Chronicle*." Reaching past the smiling blonde's shoulder, Lee covered the lens behind her before the photographer could peel off another shot. "I wonder if I could come in and talk to you and your fiancée about the first day home."

"No, you may not." He returned her smile. "Please leave the property." Removing his hand from the camera lens, he closed the door.

Shit.

"Just to be clear—" the reporter's voice echoed through the mail slot "—we're prepared to pay for an exclusive interview."

"Just to be clearer, having been asked to leave, you're now officially trespassing." Crossing to the window, he tweaked the blinds for a view of the street. A TV van was pulling up to the curb. *And so it begins.*

Locking all the doors, Lee returned to bed and read up on amnesia, ignoring the succession of knocks and doorbell rings as other reporters tried their luck.

Then he dressed, stealing some of Jules's hair gel to man

up his hair. In hospital he'd told the barber to keep some length to help hide his face's gauntness. Used to brandishing clippers, the guy had left Lee with a kind of bob. "My God, you're an ugly bastard," he told his reflection.

He labored through push-ups and sit-ups, then brewed coffee, plated two muffins and pulled an armchair into Jules's home office, where he adjusted the blinds for a better view of the street and settled in. These people didn't realize how low he'd been on entertainment. Biting into a muffin, he grimaced. Dry as an Afghani desert. Lee dropped it into the trash and settled for coffee.

By eight-thirty there were three TV crews milling outside the gate and an elderly neighbor was being interviewed. Lee amused himself by providing the dialogue. "I wish to hell she'd paint the front of her house."

Hunger pangs drove him to the kitchen, where he ate a banana, then rummaged for a recipe book and baked a fresh batch of muffins. So many bowls and spoons and stuff to play with. When the batter was mixed he spooned half into the muffin pan and ate the remainder raw, relishing the crunch of sugar. Which reminded him—he found a phone directory and booked an appointment with a local dentist.

His cell rang as he was sliding the tray of muffins out of the oven. Checking the number, he saw it was Jules and switched the phone off.

Last night, he'd dreamed of having sex with her, in images so vivid they were still imprinted on his brain. The slow, sensual mapping of her delectable body, the tight warm clasp of her around his cock…and the deep intimacy of two people meant to be together.

He couldn't have remembered one of the lusty, fun times in the sack. Oh no, he had to recall the time she'd cried making love and his tenderness for her had flayed him.

The continual knocking became annoying so he borrowed the iPod on her bedside table. Scanning the content, he discovered she labeled music under tasks. *Jogging*.

Curious, he checked the playlist. Michael Jackson's *Thriller* album.

Housework. Lee grinned. Metallica.

Work. Vivaldi. No lyrics to distract her.

Lee. He stared at the screen. All his favorites—Pink Floyd, The Civil Wars, White Stripes, Farnham. She must have compiled it after they'd met. He stuck in the earbuds and went outside to check the backyard for escape routes.

Behind the fruit trees at the end of the garden an old fence bowed under the weight of a rambling rosebush. Beyond it, a gate led to a service alley full of trash cans. Perfect. Next to it was a vegetable garden overgrown with weeds.

In the rusty corrugated garden shed Lee picked up a spade and started digging in the garden. The earth turned easily, loamy and soft, unlike the barren, rocky Afghanistan soil.

Something touched his shoulder, and instinctively he struck out. Jules went sprawling. Ripping out the earbuds, he dropped to his knees beside her. "I'm so sorry...you okay?"

Dazed, she touched her cheek. "I guess you didn't hear me coming... I did call but..."

Lee pulled her fingers away. "I bruised you." On second glance it was too dark to be fresh. He had an intimate acquaintance with the life cycle of bruises.

"It's old. I forgot to cover it with concealer this morning."

Still upset, he helped her up, running his hands down her arms, ascertaining she was okay. "Next time throw a stone to get my attention." The joke came out all wrong, harsh and self-recriminatory. He wanted to torment her, but not for her to be physically afraid of him.

Jules bent to pick up a clod of dirt, weighing it in her palm. "About this size?"

Tension uncoiled inside him. "Funny girl. Speaking of funny, I'm guessing the press got a few laughs when you parked the Caddy in the garage."

"It caused some amusement," she admitted, laying cool fingers on his forehead. "How are you feeling?"

"Before or after eating your banana muffins?" Restless under her touch, he moved away.

"Funny boy." She picked up her briefcase, brushed off the dirt. "I see you made a new batch."

"Something to do with my hands." Their gazes connected, shied away. "The nausea's passed," he added. His body had adjusted to the meds.

"I tried phoning," she said. "Your cell kept going to message."

Lee retrieved the spade. "I switched it off."

"In case the press got hold of the number? That's unlikely."

With a noncommittal shrug, he returned to digging.

"I've fielded calls from Nate, Ross and Dan, not to mention Rob and Connie. Everyone's panicking because they can't get hold of you."

Dammit, he thought he'd dispensed with minders.

"Even if you could send a group text saying, 'Still alive,' it would—"

"Don't *manage* me, Jules, I've had enough of being told—" He jabbed the spade in the earth. "All I want is a couple of days to do what *I* want!"

"And we all understand that," she said. "But with the media staking the house, your family and friends need to hear you're okay."

He'd forgotten what it was like to be cared about. The doorbell rang. They both ignored it. He might resent Jules's intimacy with his family and friends, but these days she could predict their reactions better than he could. Reluctantly, Lee took his cell out of his jean pocket and switched it on.

"Thank you," she said. "And I have something for you." She opened her briefcase and presented an official-looking document.

"What is it?"

"I'm acknowledging your right to the return of your estate. It saves you filing through the courts."

He looked at the sum, his current total worth after his assets were sold, his mortgage discharged and his bills paid. *Half* his total worth since Dad had spent most of his portion.

"Over the page—" Jules turned it for him "—you'll see I'm also reimbursing my travel costs for the trips with your dad. And that figure there—" one slender finger pointed "—is the sum total of interest accrued."

Apparently, four percent interest on $120,000 for two months came to $800. "Isn't the interest covered by the bank, when the term deposit matures?"

She paused, so slightly he nearly missed it. "Just spelling out what you'll be receiving."

He looked at her, trying to work out her game. "Why are you reimbursing travel?"

"Just because we're engaged doesn't mean I feel any sense of entitlement," she said.

"Okay." Given her intention to dump him as soon as she could justify it, this was a clever move. It presented her in a positive light to their friends, his family. Come to think of it, media attention lifted the stakes for someone whose professional reputation relied on goodwill from the Whangarei community. She really couldn't afford to put a step wrong.

Rolling the document, Lee tapped it against his thigh. "You know what I love most about you, Jules?" he said. "Your integrity. It's cockamamy in this case—hell, we're engaged and I trust you. But given how much you like to dot *i*'s and cross *t*'s, I respectfully accept." No point in looking a gift horse in the mouth, and she was correct. This did make the legalities easier. "One thing puzzles me. Why didn't you accept the legacy when *I* left it to you?"

"I felt your father had more right to it." Her earnestness was a nice touch.

"It must have come as a big surprise when he bequeathed it to you again in his will."

"Yes." Her brow creased. "Especially when I thought I'd talked him out of it."

Lee blinked. She *knew* Dad wanted to bequeath it to her? "You could have said no."

"I could have. Only your siblings weren't going to benefit…did Rob tell you?"

"Yeah."

"And your father left it to me unconditionally." Her gaze softened, turned inward.

"And 'unconditionally' was the magic word?" Again, he was confused.

"Yes." She added passionately, "And that's how I'm returning it to you."

Was anything as sharp as regret? Or as meaningless? "You're all heart," he said.

However fond she'd been of Dad, her relationship with him and her acceptance of Lee's money were predicated on a lie. There was no excuse for that, and wishing for one only made him pathetic.

The doorbell rang again. Jules pivoted. "I'll go make a sign for the fence, No Media Past This Point. It should stop the harassment until we leave for the doctor's."

Organizing him again. "I'm not wasting my first day home on another medical. Today's therapy is retail. I've got a grand in my pocket and we're going to spend it. I'll make those calls and then you and I are breaking out of here."

ESCAPING THE PRESS proved child's play. Through the gate in the back fence, down the service alley, cut through the corner of a neighbor's yard and climb into the cab he'd organized to wait a block away.

Jules was silent on the taxi journey into the city center, no doubt scheming how to steer him toward the doctor's office. Maybe Lee was still a little queasy but the symptoms were abating, exactly as they should. She didn't appreciate how accustomed he was to living in a state of discomfort. This was normal.

"I don't think you should overdo it today," Jules said. "A couple of hours, tops."

"My turn on top today, darling," he reminded her. "You had your turn yesterday."

"As long as we stop for food," she said, oblivious to the cab driver's gaze in the mirror. "You need to eat regularly."

Whatever outrageous thing Lee said or did in public, she never lost her composure. He'd always liked that about her. The only thing that seemed to unsettle her was... Lee dropped a casual hand on her thigh and felt her tense. "I fancy fries and steak at the Ballymore," he said. The pub where they'd first met. "They still sell Guinness?"

The contract suggested she felt guilty about her lies. But he needed her guilty enough to confess.

"I don't know. I haven't been able to go in there since your death." She removed his hand from her thigh and squeezed it. "Which makes it the perfect place to celebrate your resurrection."

The warmth in her smile blindsided him. He managed

a weak response then looked out the window at the passing landscape. After a moment, he released her hand and clenched his in his lap. "The city hasn't changed much."

Typical of provincial New Zealand, low-rise offices rose from brightly lit, ground-floor retail. Historic hotels presided on major corners not occupied by a gas station. Corporate uniforms of black or navy dotted the crowds of casually dressed shoppers, many already wearing flip-flops in the optimistic thrall of late spring. The sky was a dense blue between flotillas of long white clouds. Easier to watch their shadows drift over the pavement and buildings than acknowledge the feelings her smile provoked.

"Does it make it easier coming home, seeing that nothing's changed?"

Everything has changed. Lee leaned forward to tap the driver's shoulder. "Pull over here, mate." The taxi stopped outside the leisure center Lee used when he visited Whangarei.

Jules frowned. "Lee, no. It's too soon."

"Jules, yes." He gave her a banknote and jumped out of the cab. "Pay the fare, I won't be long."

Before she could argue, he'd pushed through the gym's glass doors and joined the queue. The ceiling vibrated with some fifty bodies jumping in unison. Faintly he heard the music, overlaid with the muffled calls of the instructor. The weight room was at the end of a hall leading off the reception area, glass-walled because the people who came here liked to see and be seen.

Reception was busy. Judging by all the women holding rolled-up mats, a yoga class was about to start. A group blocked his route to the counter. "Excuse me."

The women's gazes skated over him; they moved to let him past.

That came as a shock. His looks had attracted female attention since puberty. Lee had taken it for granted. Slightly shaken, he queued behind a couple of jocks signing in at the counter, gym bags slung over shoulders and Y-back tank tops making the most of biceps, trapeziums and deltoids. Lee recognized one. "Hey, buddy." He tapped JD on the shoulder. "How the hell are you?"

The personal trainer regarded him blankly. "Sorry, mate, give me a clue. I meet so many people."

He hadn't changed that much...had he? Lee needed to think about this. "My mistake, I thought you were some-one else."

"No worries." JD pivoted to face the counter.

A big man joined the line behind Lee, standing too close. The hairs on the back of Lee's neck rose. "Yo, JD," the new arrival called. The two began a conversation over Lee's shoulder and he had to concentrate on remaining calm, shifting position to catch the gust of an overhead fan. The ceiling shook harder under a vigorous dance number, and the muffled beat of the music found an answering throb in his temple.

More women arrived for the yoga class, increasing the volume of chatter. Their perfume mingled with the fresh sweat of the men sandwiching him in. Lee fought the urge to gag. The guy behind him pushed into him, said, "Sorry, mate," then did a double take. Any second he'd remember where he'd seen Lee's face.

He had to get out. "Excuse me.... Excuse me." He shoved past those who didn't move out of way fast enough.

"Hey!"

Outside he steadied himself against the building and sucked in great gulps of air. He closed his eyes.

"Lee?" Jules's arm circled his waist, and her fragrance, natural and familiar, anchored him. "Are you okay?"

"Never better." Loverlike, he slid an arm across her

shoulders, hiding the fact that he was using her as support. "But I've decided to rent a home gym. Take a low-key approach."

"You're pale."

"Blood sugar's low. Let's hit the shops via McD's. A double chocolate shake will fix it."

If this had been a real engagement he would have ended it now, let Jules off the hook. No woman should have to deal with the sorry-ass screwup he'd become. He didn't owe her that consideration so he dropped his arm from her shoulder and grabbed her hand.

On shaky legs, Lee started down the street.

Jules tugged him to a stop. "Maybe we should get you to the doc—"

A horn blasted and he jerked her out of the path of a mobility scooter driven by a dour old man whose sparse gray comb-over glistened with Brylcreem. The stylish black leather jacket encasing his bulky frame added to his geriatric menace.

As the guy passed, Lee's gaze sharpened. "Wait a minute. That looks like *my* jacket."

Jules shaded her eyes to check. "It could be," she admitted. "When your dad moved to the retirement unit, we donated bags of your clothes to the local thrift store."

"Yeah, Connie told me but..." That particular jacket was his favorite. "Hey, mate!" Lee hurried to catch up to the scooter. *And* he'd spent twelve hundred bucks on it. "Any chance you'd sell your jacket?"

The old guy didn't spare him a glance. "You wouldn't believe how often I get asked that." His craggy profile was all furrows of slumped flesh. Wiry gray eyebrows added a touch of softness to a prowlike forehead.

Lee walked alongside. "Yeah, well it used to be mine."

The scooter slowed; pale blue eyes raked over him. "It's twice your size."

"I'm growing into it."

"You're well past puberty, sonny." They drew abreast of a zebra crossing. "And if you still wanted it, you shouldn't have donated it to the thrift store." Without checking for traffic, the pensioner barreled off the curb, forcing an oncoming driver to slam on his brakes.

Raising his hands in mute apology to several disgruntled drivers, Lee followed. "I didn't give it away." He beckoned at Jules, who had caught up to them. "She did."

"Because he was dead," she explained.

The old bloke glowered. "You think it's fun to taunt the infirm?" They reached the opposite pavement and fell in behind a young mother pushing a double stroller. "Come on, girlie!" he bellowed. "Consider other pedestrians."

The startled woman yanked her stroller to one side.

Lee lengthened his stride to keep up with the grinch. Close up he could see the jacket's collar had darkened thanks to hair oil and was roughened on the elbows from the armrests. So he'd have it cleaned. It was his; he wanted it back. "I'll double what you paid for it."

The pensioner eased his carpet slipper off the accelerator and onto the brake. "A hundred bucks."

"Done." He got out his wallet.

"Do you have another jacket, sir?" Jules inquired.

The grinch ignored her. Lee became aware of the sharp wind and the sharper odor of the old man, as sour as his disposition. It was like smelling himself a week ago. Unkempt and uncared-for.

He slid two fifties out of his wallet.

"I've changed my mind," he said. "It looks better on you. Here…" Lee held out the money "Buy yourself a shirt to go with it."

CHAPTER NINE

AN HOUR LATER, Jules stole away to the women's powder room of Whangarei's premier department store and made an emergency call to the credit department at Visa.

"We wrote offering to increase your limit last month," the representative commented. "You requested no further offers unless advised."

"And now I'm advising," Jules said. "Can it take effect immediately?"

He'd spent five hundred dollars in the first store they'd visited. On shoes. Lord knows what he was doing in menswear.

"Taken care of that for you, ma'am."

"Thank you." Her next call was to the estate agent.

"Hey, I'm just on my way to put up a for-sale sign."

"Don't," Jules said. "Lee's living with me and I don't want him to know it's on the market." Paying him back was her problem, not his. "Also, the house is currently under siege from the press." She explained the situation to Chloe. "Hold off all viewings for a couple of days until the fuss dies down, then we'll show buyers when he's out." Maybe she should encourage him to join the gym after all.

"Just to tell ya. As fantastic as I am at my job, it's pretty hard to get a quick sale on a property I can't show or advertise."

Chloe was a friend, such a good friend that she'd tried to talk Jules out of putting the house on the market. "You'll be lucky to get what you paid for it five years ago," she'd said. "And that's with all the improvements you've made inside. At least paint the exterior and tame the garden first."

"Market it as a handyman's dream," Jules had countered. "Use lots of exclamation marks. They won me over."

Now she massaged her temples. "Do your best. I'll think of something and get back to you. Gotta go." She hung up, then called her colleague. *You're just sounding him out,* she told herself as she waited for Nick to pick up. *Selling your shareholding is a last resort.* "Nick? Jules… Thanks, yes, I'm over the moon. Listen, can you spare me thirty minutes tomorrow morning? Ten, your office? Great, see you then."

By the time she reentered the menswear department, thirty minutes had passed. The salesmen recognized her. "Your man's in the changing rooms." He led the way through the dimly lit interior with its burgundies and forest-green decor, its artfully spotlit suits and jackets. Her heels sank into the plush carpets. "He's having trouble with sizes." The young guy hesitated before pointing to a black velvet curtain. "I'll leave you to it. Holler if you need anything."

"Thanks."

The obvious relief in the salesman's departure gave Jules pause. Maybe Lee didn't want help? Through a gap in the curtain she caught movement and stepped closer to ask. The question died on her lips.

His mirrored expression stony, Lee shrugged off a shirt miles too big for him and let it drop to the growing pile on the floor then reached for another from a hook on the cubicle wall. But Jules's attention was riveted to his upper back and shoulders. Both were crisscrossed with scars, some whitened, some still bright red.

Lee half turned as he put on the shirt and she saw one side of his torso was similarly marked. His body was bone and sinew, the cords of remaining muscle mimicking the ridged scars. The contrast of smooth, unmarked skin between scar tissue only heightened the horror of what had been done to him.

Blindly, she stepped away—one pace, two—struggling for composure. Then she pivoted on her heel and, gesturing to the salesman, started rummaging through the shelves and racks. "He suits warm tones," she said when he joined her. "Or light clean greens and crisp blues." She grabbed a couple of shirts sized medium slim.

"He insists on large."

"Get the size he needs, I'll sell it. Do the same with jeans…and we'll need belts."

With a nod he bustled off. Steeling herself, Jules returned to the changing room, arriving to hear a muffled curse.

"Lee?"

"Hang on." When he opened the curtain, he was dressed in his make-do clothes. "Nothing fits."

With a studied casualness, she glanced at the pile on the floor. "If you're buying your old size, no wonder. Here, try these on."

He checked the labels and scowled. "I'm not buying clothes I'll grow out of within a month."

It would take longer than that to rebuild his former frame. "So we'll give them to the thrift store. Maintain a fine tradition."

He smiled but his expression was still bleak. "I didn't realize what a scarecrow I'd become."

Jules ached to tell him he was still beautiful to those who cared about him. "Look on the bright side. At least you'll have the consolation of never seeing these smaller sizes on the grinch."

Lee laughed. "There is that. Pass them here, then."

The salesman joined them with an armful of jeans and belts and Jules glimpsed a dangling price tag. Her increased credit limit wasn't going to last long.

Too bad.

He needed this.

"YOU FIND US A SEAT, I'll order," Lee suggested to Jules when they entered the dimly lit Ballymore pub. Styled Old English with dark wood paneling, the yeasty smell of beer sat comfortably with the fragrant waft of beef and pastry pies for which the pub was renowned. "What can I get you?"

"Orange juice." She gazed around the bar. "I didn't expect ever to come in here again…. It's…" She gave him a tremulous smile. Despite the unholy mess she'd created, Jules was happy he was alive.

With an abrupt nod, Lee threaded his way through the tables, mostly full with the lunchtime crowd, toward the solid curved bar, where beer mugs hanging on a row of hooks glinted like fairy lights.

The bartender was drawing ale and filling a tray with six tankards. "Be with you in a jiffy, mate."

"No hurry." Lee turned to locate Jules and saw she'd found a table in the corner. When Claire set them up on a blind date she'd told Lee that he and Jules were perfect for each other. "She isn't used to saying yes and you're not used to hearing no." He should have taken the warning then.

It had intrigued him to date someone who thought her intelligence rendered her immune to "guys like you." When he'd asked for clarification she'd realized her mistake and, using flattery, tried to wiggle out of the hole she'd dug. "Gorgeous, charming and macho." But her wry grin had given her away.

He'd suggested even "women like her" had primal in-

stincts that responded to a hulk capable of fending off a
T. rex.

Even now, Lee grinned recalling her reply. "Only to provide it with a meal while I escape."

"At least I offer more to chew on than the nerd who invented the wheel."

"Assuming it was invented by a guy. More likely it was
a woman who needed a more reliable load-carrier since all
the he-men kept getting themselves eaten."

He'd stared at her, experiencing a sensation similar to
free-fall parachuting.

"What can I get you, mate?"

Lee stared blankly at the bartender and then reoriented
himself. "One orange juice, one Guinness." When he'd em-
barked on his project of torturing Jules's conscience he
hadn't anticipated suffering right along with her. "On second thought, hold the Guinness, I'll have a Scotch."

CELL TO HER EAR, Jules listened to a message from her
mother. "I missed your call. Now who's impulsive in love,
recommitting to a dead guy you haven't seen for nearly
two years. Seriously, I'm so, so happy for you, sweetie,
and can't wait to meet my future son-in-law. I'm heading
out so will try again later. I'm dying to hear how the family cynic was swept off her feet. Love you!"

A flute of champagne landed on the table in front of her.
"I figure we should officially celebrate our engagement."
Lee sat down with a Scotch and the open half bottle of
champagne. He glanced at her face. "Bad news?"

"Not at all." She managed to smile. "My mother sends
her congratulations." Much as she'd have preferred to keep
this temporary engagement off her mother's radar the press
coverage made that impossible.

"She still with that guy she was dating when I left?"

During their six-week affair, Lee had never met Helen, and Jules had pitched her upbringing as a situation comedy. Precocious only child bringing up a twice-divorced mother always optimistically searching for Mr. Right.

Jules's father had fallen into the Mr. Wrong category, disappearing when she was an infant. However, given her mother's poor judgment when it came to men, she doubted she'd missed much.

She had loved her stepfather—husband number two—but then he'd cheated on her mother when Jules was twelve, and Helen had severed all visitation rights to punish him. "Yes, she found her happy ever after. She and Gus married shortly after your much-exaggerated death."

"Speaking of which." Jules raised her champagne flute. "To you," she toasted. After shopping they'd visited a salon to fix what Lee called "his god-awful cut." The stylist had layered his hair so it fell softer around his stark bone structure. The contrast gave him a poet's quality and accentuated the intensity of his light green eyes. Light only in color, the inner light was missing. Every time Jules was tempted to blurt out the truth she looked at that shuttered gaze.

"To us," Lee amended, chinking his tumbler against her flute.

"To us." The champagne was pub brand and cheap, the bubbles sour. Jules gulped it anyway. *Toughen up, Browne, you knew this would be difficult.* It didn't help that the attraction was always there—a trail of gunpowder waiting for a spark.

"Any idea what you might do as a job when you're fit again?" she asked.

"None," he said shortly. "But enough about my career prospects—yours are clearly on the rise."

She didn't want to talk about the partnership since it had tied up his money. "I've done okay," she said, after another sip. How ironic that getting her life and career back on track was now causing her grief. "Will you stay with the SAS?"

"Haven't decided." He drained his Scotch.

Her fingers tightened on the stem. "Not a combat unit," she insisted, because this might be her only opportunity to have this conversation. "None of us can go through this again." She only realized how shrilly she'd spoken when a couple at the next table glanced over. Jules lowered her voice. "Please."

Silently, Lee refilled her drink from the half bottle and, when Jules shook her head, picked it up himself and took a gulp. *"Wizard of Oz,"* he said. "The scarecrow wanted a brain, who wanted courage?"

She understood him perfectly. "You're still a lion, Lee."

"Maybe. Any of them need a stomach? Because I've lost mine for conflict. And faith, I'm outta faith. No man left behind." He quoted the SAS creed, drank again. "That worked real well."

Jules sat stricken. "All the evidence pointed to your death."

He seemed to recollect himself. "You're right, it's the alcohol talking." With a grimace Lee pushed her champagne away from him. "Guess I've lost my head for it. Wonder where our food is?" He twisted to scan the busy kitchen, visible through a service hatch.

She was about to follow his gaze when Mark's profile came into view in front of her, where he sat at a corner table lunching with colleagues. Too late Jules recalled the many times she'd refused an invitation to meet him here. His architectural practice was around the corner.

Lee turned back, obscuring Mark from sight. With an immense effort, Jules refocused. "In *The Wizard of Oz,* Dorothy just wanted to get home…. You're home."

"Dad was home to me." He forced a smile, but it couldn't

cover the vastness of his grief. "And now I have you. Ah, the food." He smiled at the waitress delivering it. "Looks delicious, thank you." Then he got busy unrolling the cutlery from a paper napkin.

Jules waited for the waitress to leave. "How can I help you?"

He didn't look up from his meal. "Eat," he said. "Before it gets cold."

"Lee." Leaning forward, she put her hand over his. "You are not alone."

He made no effort to return her clasp. "And the tin woman needed a heart, right?"

"What?"

"My mistake. It was the tin man." Turning his palm up, he lifted her hand to his lips. There was a dark thread through this conversational turn. Frowning, Jules tried to unravel it, but at that moment Mark appeared behind Lee.

"Excuse me for interrupting, Sergeant Davis, but I wanted to say welcome home." He thrust out a hand. "I'm Mark Holloway, Rich's older brother."

Lee released her hand to shake Mark's. "I saw Rich yesterday, he was in the welcoming guard. We only had time to exchange a few words."

"Yeah, he phoned last night and mentioned your homecoming was pretty spectacular."

Jules could have kicked herself. She should have phoned him, let him know about the engagement.

He turned to her with a polite smile and hard eyes. "Hi, Jules." Definitely pissed. "Great photo in the paper this morning. Is that the ring? Can I take a closer look?"

Reluctantly, she held it out.

"You know each other?" Lee asked.

"Through your army buddies." Mark examined Jules's

ring. Odd for a guy to be so interested, but maybe he was a jeweler. "A barbecue at Nate and Claire's."

Lee frowned. Nate and Claire, that sounded so wrong.

"Mark's an architect." Jules freed her hand. "He's drawing plans to extend Claire's house at Stingray Bay."

"If you really want a remodeling challenge you should take a look at Jules's place." Unable to wait, Lee picked up one of his fries and bit into it. Ah, God that was good. He'd missed fat.

"I've seen Jules's house," said Mark. "I thought it had a lot of potential." Something in his tone fixed Lee's attention.

"I can't afford you," Jules said lightly. She was nervous and trying to hide it. Swallowing his fry, Lee glanced at her pale face, raised to the man towering over her.

"Mates' rates," Mark said. "You can't have forgotten."

Lee ate another fry. This one wasn't as good.

"My priorities have changed with Lee home." She was spinning his ring around her finger like a mouse on a wheel. "I'm sure I mentioned that."

They both jumped as Lee's chair scraped the floor. He stood, proffered a hand and a smile. "Great meeting you, Mark. Tell Rich we'll catch up in a month or so when the dust settles."

"I will. And again…welcome home." His eyes bright with the anger of a disappointed man, Mark returned the handshake. "Good luck to you both."

After he left, the unspoken "you'll need it" hung in the air like cordite.

Cursing his stupidity, Lee sat down. The blows from this woman just kept coming.

He picked up his knife and fork and started eating.

"Ask me," Jules said.

Lee added salt. "I don't have to."

"We dated four times," she said. "It wasn't serious."

Did you sleep with him? He stifled the question because it wasn't important. He would not *make* it important. Once he'd won a confession they were through with this sham engagement. Besides, she'd already dumped him; she owed him nothing. "Don't let your meal get cold." Lee tucked in with gusto, though he could have been shoveling sawdust into his mouth. "Delicious."

"Would you like me to tell you about it?" she said quietly.

"No." The first bite of steak caught in his throat and he washed it down with the rest of her champagne. "You dating another guy doesn't matter in the scheme of things, honey. Not after I've spent nineteen months dicing daily with the big issues like mortality, whether there's a God and what the hell I was going to use for toilet paper."

"You *are* angry."

He stopped sawing at his steak. Stupid to think he could handle a lump of fried meat anyway on his stomach. "You thought I was dead. Really, this is no different than Claire falling for Nate, right? And everyone's cool with *that*." Lee painted a reassuring smile over his resentment. "And yesterday you said yes to marrying me, so *clearly* I'm the winner here."

Jules started to speak, but he laid a finger on her lips. Such warm, soft lips. Reunion fantasies with this woman had kept him alive. And he kept caring, he kept damn well caring. "We agreed on the way home yesterday that neither of us wants to revisit the past." This explained why Jules didn't want to talk about what—or who—she'd been doing. "All that matters is the future."

And a little frontier justice. For his own sake he had to speed this up, tighten the screws on her conscience. And he knew just the way to do it.

CHAPTER TEN

BY THE TIME the cab dropped them off, weighted down with shopping bags, a block from her house, Jules was mentally and emotionally exhausted. Through the rest of their lunch Lee had been charming, attentive and relentless in discussing their future.

When he'd asked how she felt about Tahiti as a honeymoon destination she'd mentioned he'd missed news of a major cyclone in French Polynesia, then segued to current events for ten minutes, ending with a potted history of infighting within the UN.

Propping his elbows on the table, he'd gazed into her eyes. "I hope our kids get on together. You do want a few, don't you?"

"That reminds me," she'd continued doggedly, "the Commonwealth family celebrated the Queen's Jubilee last year."

"Sixty years on the throne, amazing." Lee tucked a loose strand of hair behind her ear, casually caressing the lobe with his thumb. "Where shall *we* retire to?"

If he didn't look as exhausted as she felt, Jules would have worried about being alone with him.

He turned from paying the taxi driver. "I forgot to tell you, we're out of milk."

"Are you sure?" She could have sworn she'd seen some in the fridge.

"Positive." He confiscated the shopping bags she carried

and added them to his own. "You nip to the corner store and I'll take these home."

"Okay," she said to his departing back. Come to think of it, she could do with the respite. Slowly, Jules walked to the store, pausing outside to pat the owner's snuffly Pekingese. It was doing her head in trying to filter her words and actions through how Lee would review them once she told him the truth.

Her cell rang and she checked the display before answering. "Hi, Nate."

"Hi, Jules. Listen, the guys and I were talking. How about I organize some security outside your house for a couple of days to hold off the press?"

"That's thoughtful, but—"

"On us, if it's the money stopping you."

His concern touched her. Except she needed to wean herself off friendships gained under false pretences. "Let's see how the No Press sign works first...but thanks."

"How are you doing keeping Lee in bed?" he asked, then chuckled. "That wasn't meant the way it sounded."

"We just spent the afternoon shopping," she admitted guiltily. The Peke barked; she crouched to pat her again.

"You went to the doctor though?"

"He won't see one. I'll insist if his condition changes, but he's got some color and—"

"And laying down the law doesn't work with him. I'm not blaming you, Jules. Remember I spent five days with that stubborn bastard. If he hadn't been a captive, I'd suggest locking him in his room."

She fondled the dog's ears. "On the upside he changed his mind about rejoining the gym. He's rented equipment for home instead."

"He shouldn't be bloody exercising at all," Nate said in frustration. "If you think he's pushing himself too hard, phone me." She was silent. "Jules, it's not disloyal to Lee to ask for backup. We're all on the same side."

Until the truth came out. Upon Lee's death, she'd needed to connect with his family and friends. She'd ended up part of their tribe, almost despite herself.

"Okay," she conceded, standing. "So is Claire handy?" She needed her best friend's advice on the Mark/Lee debacle.

"She's taken Lewis to soccer practice. Um, anything I can help with?" His male reluctance made Jules smile and brought a lump to her throat. She was going to miss them so much.

"No, it's fine." To her horror, her voice caught in her throat. "I'm fine," she finished strongly. She wouldn't tell Lee she'd met Mark through these guys matchmaking—it was the least she could do for them. Come to think of it, if she discussed the situation with Claire, Claire would tell Nate and he'd feel compelled to fess up. Better to keep today's encounter to herself.

"I could get her to phone later," Nate suggested.

"No, don't worry. It's not important." She bent to give the dog a final pat and was rewarded with a lick. "I'd better go.... Lee's waiting."

"I was thinking," Nate said casually. "How about we bring dinner over Thursday? And yeah, I know we're giving Lee space, but that's a moot point with the press camped outside."

Oh, God. Yes. Please. "But the boat launch is coming up and—"

"Great," Nate said. "Expect us at six."

Her local grocery store owner, Rajesh, applauded when she walked in. He pointed proudly to the diminishing pile of newspapers on the newsstand. The kiss photo covered half the front page. It took Jules ten minutes to break away from his congratulations and that was because an incoming text gave her an excuse.

Outside again, she checked it. I'm sorry. Acted like dick. Got jealous. Mark

"You think?" With a disgusted snort, Jules started walking, the two-liter plastic milk jug chill against her fingers. Halfway home, her sense of natural justice prompted her to send a reply. Sorry, too. Should have phoned re: engagement.

Jules pocketed her cell. It was sunny, Lee was alive and she'd helped him today. It was enough. She paused to sniff a hedge of flowering jasmine and smiled at a schoolkid who pedaled by, his skinny legs turning like windmills.

Her neighborhood seemed a foreign country during the weekday hours. Chattering kids piled out of the local school, dragging bags behind them, and doors slammed on four-wheel drives as mothers did pickups.

As a child, she'd always arrived to an empty house, if she was lucky and Mum was single. There'd be a chore list on the counter, which she'd work through before doing homework. Mum would arrive at seven from her job as a supervisor at the local supermarket and they'd eat together. Those were the happy times.

In the alley, she wrinkled her nose at the stench of a neighbor's bin and unlatched her gate. Next door's cat was sunning itself on her back step and, tucking the milk bottle under one arm, she scooped it up for a pat.

Were those voices inside the house? Jules frowned. If the press had muscled their way in... Dumping the milk on the counter, she followed the sound to the living room and came to a dead halt in the doorway.

Cables crisscrossed the living room carpet and furniture had been moved to make room for the dozen or so people milling with TV and digital cameras, notepads and micro-phones. "What the hell's going on?" she demanded.

Lee looked up from the seat in the bay window. Under the hot lights, the blond in his hair glinted and the hollows of his cheeks stood out despite his facial growth. He smiled. "Here's my girl!"

LEE WATCHED AS the tabby in Jules's arms scrabbled and dashed for freedom. His fiancée looked as if she wanted to follow. Excellent.

"What's going on?" she repeated, ducking to evade a boom. "Why are these reporters inside?"

Rising from the couch, Lee steered Jules into the hall. "I decided to give a press conference. A one-off in return for being left in peace. Maybe there'll still be the odd free-lancer snapping pictures but we can live with that."

"I *guess* that makes sense," she said doubtfully.

"Great." He tugged her forward.

"Wait!" Jules balked. "This is about you, not me."

"I don't want to discuss my captivity so I figured we'd focus on the happily ever after part."

"But…"

"But?" He could see her scrambling for excuses, which was exactly why he'd decided to spring this on her. So she didn't have time to find any. Lee looked into her eyes, read her conflict. "You are with me, aren't you, Jules?"

"O-of course."

"Then let's get this over with so we can get on with our lives." He steered her toward the couch.

"At least let me freshen up my makeup, brush my hair."

Lee maintained his grip on her elbow. "You look per-fect." He kissed her forehead. A camera flashed.

"Actually, she is a little shiny through the lens," a cam-eraman called.

Guilt, Lee suspected. Jules shrugged away from his hold. "Won't be a sec," she said, and escaped.

Lee returned to his seat in the bay window. The room was getting stuffy under the hot lights and he threw open the sash window to find a breeze. The faint buzz of a neighbor's lawn mower carried across the street. Inhaling deeply won him the tantalizing scent of freshly cut grass.

"I'm picking up background noise," said one of the cameramen. "We're going to have to close it, sorry."

Reluctantly Lee complied and turned to look into a sea of inquisitive faces. *C'mon, Jules, I need you.*

"Let's start with a few questions for you, Sergeant Davis," said a middle-aged newscaster whose lipstick perfectly matched her nails.

Wait, he *needed* Jules?

"Go ahead," he said.

"What's the best thing about being in New Zealand, apart from seeing family and friends?"

He didn't even have to think about it. "Colors. The variety of hues and landscape, the moderate temperatures."

"Pretty hot over there." The newscaster smiled, a pro putting him at ease.

"And cold." Lee returned her smile, appreciating her skill. "Afghanistan is a country of extremes."

"And extremists," a male reporter interjected impatiently. Young, Lee noted, and probably keen to prove himself. "Did you form any kind or relationship with your captors?"

He had a vision of Ajmal laughing, a gap in his front teeth like that of a seven-year-old's, tears running down his cheeks, hands slapping skinny thighs. He'd just learned that Jules was a lawyer.

"I'm afraid I can't discuss my captivity." The SAS had

prepped him for this. "Too much sensitive military information." He glanced toward the hall. What was keeping Jules?

A third journalist spoke, an older man with grizzled gray sideburns. "But you clearly lived in hardship under terrible conditions."

"And here I am thinking that I'd scrubbed up pretty well."

Everyone laughed. He resisted the urge to hide his hands. The freshly healed scars on his wrists itched.

"Is there a food you're particularly enjoying now you're home?" asked the first newscaster.

"Anything hot is a novelty." Lee concentrated on her. "So is clean water. Electricity is good, moving around freely even better. Which is why we're doing this interview." He grinned. "So you guys go away and leave us in peace."

"The SAS is known as the elite military," said the young gun. "Did your training keep you alive?"

Hell, yeah. "It helped…but we're not discussing my captivity," he reminded him.

"Will you receive a military decoration?" the old guy asked.

"For what…? Staying alive? Not a lot of valor in that."

"Did you expect to be rescued?" The nice lady pro had moved on from breaking the ice.

Every second, every minute. "The day the Americans raided was the happiest of my life. So moving on from the rescue—"

Suddenly the bombardment came from every direction.

"Did you ever attempt to escape?"

"How often were you beaten?"

"Why didn't they kill you?"

Lee tried to smile. "You guys are about as good at accepting 'no comment' for an answer as my captors."

"Excuse me." Jules nudged a path through to him, her

makeup perfect, her hair combed smooth and wearing her highest heels. She'd once told him that as a shortish person she found it disappointing that the ability to eyeball people often improved their manners.

"So you *were* tortured?" persisted young gun, then yelped and grabbed his left foot.

"I am *so* sorry," Jules said. "It's the heels."

Lee smothered a grin as she joined him on the window seat. Her hand sought his and tightened. He wished that simple gesture didn't make him feel better.

"Now here's someone who deserves a medal," he said. "Jules stood in for me with my late father, my siblings and my friends. She even tried to return my ring because she wanted to give me freedom of choice. As though I had a choice when I discovered all she'd done in my absence." As he'd hoped, attention diverted to Jules.

"Were you expecting the proposal?"

"What was it like hearing he was alive?"

"What did you think seeing each other again?"

"What was the first thing he said to you?"

"Hello," Jules replied to the last, and everyone laughed. "I wasn't expecting the proposal.... Lee hadn't planned it, either. It just...happened, I guess." It was her turn to look to him for support.

He tried to resist the call. "Considering I'd settled on this woman within a few hours of meeting her it shouldn't have come as *that* much of a surprise," he said drily.

"Really?" Young gun smirked. "Are we talking love at first sight?"

"For me, anyway."

Jules's fingers twitched in his. Love at first sight, soul mates, she hated this stuff. Lee had thought he'd made her a believer until she refused to take that final leap of faith.

Questions flew. He sketched in the blind date, the whirlwind courtship, his decision to buy the ring. Beside him, Jules squirmed. "It was an impulse buy before deployment," he finished. "When it's right, it's right."

Dropping Jules's hand, he pulled her closer. "I'm guessing that's why she accepted the ring from my army buddies. Because it felt as if it was already hers." *Careful, you're starting to sound cynical.* "I will say one thing about my captivity." Lee finished with a bitter truth. "Jules was my talisman, my reason to stay alive."

Under his arm, her shoulders tensed.

Yeah, my feelings lasted, he thought wearily. *The ones you doubted when you rejected my proposal.* Nothing like long months of isolation and torture to put hurt pride into its proper perspective. And to crystallize what was important. Until he came home to another betrayal.

"How does it feel hearing all this?" a reporter asked Jules.

"Indescribable," she croaked. She was practically wearing his encircling arm as earmuffs, her shoulders were so tight.

"So when's the wedding?"

"We're still getting used to being engaged," she hedged.

Lee stroked her upper arm, rubbing in the guilt with each tender caress. "Soon," he said. "I'm pinning her down real soon."

From the interview they moved to photographs, using the overgrown back garden as a jungle-green backdrop.

By then, Jules needed this over so badly that she let herself be moved into position like an animated puppet. Smiling, smiling, smiling.

"Sit on his lap under the apple tree. Lean against his body—yes, that's it. Unfold your arms. Bring yours around to clasp her hands, Lee. Turn your head, Jules, and look up into his eyes."

The low sun blinded her. Lee adjusted his angle to shade her face. "Better?" His voice was hoarse, from talking, from tiredness. Nodding, Jules focused on the bridge of his nose, because otherwise she'd lose it.

Jules was my talisman, my reason to stay alive.

Maybe she'd lose it anyway. Her cheeks ached from smiling.

Jules was my talisman, my reason to stay alive.

"How about a kiss?" said the photographer. She thought, almost with relief, *Well, this is it. This is where I fall on the ground crying and confessing and begging forgiveness.*

"I hardly know you," Lee told him, and her moment of hysteria passed. Somehow she managed to chuckle with everyone else. "Anyway," Lee added, "you got the kiss shot yesterday at the airport."

He lifted her ring finger instead, and the two of them admired every glittering facet of that diamond for the photographer.

In the initial months after his death, she'd wished she'd said yes, with all her heart she'd wished she'd said yes. But when the initial shock lessened she accepted it wouldn't have worked. And as it turned out, she'd been right to have concerns about his commitment.

Lee had walked away at the first hurdle, severed their relationship with surgical precision. It was important to keep reminding herself of that.

CHAPTER ELEVEN

"So THAT'S IT," Jules told her colleague Nick two days later. "I need cash to repay Lee and I want to know if you're still interested in buying in. As a backup plan," she stressed. "Only if the house doesn't sell.

With a silent whistle, Nick sat back in his swivel chair, stretched out his long legs and used them to spin the seat side to side. "I wasn't expecting this."

He eyed her across his desk, his expression behind his fashion-forward glasses conflicted—the new normal for him since she'd bought into the firm. Affectionate, irritated, wary. Then he found the poker face that served him so well in court. "I assume you've run this by Ted?"

"His only concern is that you might be carrying a grudge because they chose me." She'd given him space these past couple months to deal with his disappointment privately. But they were good enough friends to be frank with each other. "Are you?"

"I was gutted when the decision went your way," he admitted. "I felt— Hell, I still think Ted's choice wasn't made solely on merit."

She'd suspected as much. "You think being a woman gave me an advantage."

"*Positive* discrimination, I believe it's called."

"You really are resentful, aren't you?"

"I'm trying not to be, because you're as good a lawyer as I am—"

"Thank you," she said drily.

"But Oli and Ted chose you because a female partner makes them look liberal and progressive." The firm was a Whangarei bastion, set up by Ted's father sixty years earlier and built from banking, farming, golf and Rotary club contacts. His son had solidified the firm's reputation as solid, reliable and conservative through partnering with another scion of a founder family.

"No, they hired me five years ago to look liberal and progressive," she corrected Nick. "And turning that into more than lip service was bloody hard work. I had to put on my big-girl pants and get over the fact that I had to work longer and harder than you did for the same respect. So if being a woman nudged their decision in my favor, well, I damn well earned that edge."

"Why did you bother?" he said curiously. "Other firms don't live in the Dark Ages."

"Because I wanted to work with the best. Besides, Ted and Oli were just carrying some old boys' baggage. They both travel much lighter now."

"So you're suggesting it's my turn to put on the big-girl pants and get over it?"

"If the opportunity arises to buy me out, you won't have to," she pointed out.

He picked up a paperweight, a crystal hexagon that reminded Jules of Lee's diamond. Instinctively she twisted the ring on her finger—it was forever sliding sideways and digging into her pinkie because she'd never had it fitted properly—and glanced at her watch. Noon.

Lee would have finished his morning workout and started preparing lunch for her return at one. Since he'd described cooking as a luxury, she'd learned to shut up and simply enjoy the feasts he prepared.

Nor could she dissuade him from taming her overgrown

garden, so they pruned and weeded together in the afternoon. By eight he was in bed, exhausted. It was downright scary how easily they were falling into a routine.

Well," she said abruptly, "are you interested in buying me out?"

"I've been job hunting," he said equally abruptly. "Successfully."

"Oh." Jules hadn't considered that possibility. "But you love working here as much as I do."

"I don't want to be perceived as second choice, second-best." She began to protest, but he raised a hand. "I don't want to feel that way, either." The chair creaked as he leaned forward. "I'll accept the opportunity to buy you out and stay. I'll even give you what you paid for it. But it's unsettling for everyone if both of us remain here."

Jules sat stunned. So she wouldn't just lose her shareholding, Nick was asking her to lose her job?

"I don't have to give the other firm an answer for two and a half weeks," he said. "That gives you time to think about it. And like you said, I'm only Plan B if the house doesn't sell. Hell, I hope it does."

She accepted his outstretched hand, manicured and soft, quite unlike Lee's. "Me, too."

The moment she left Nick's office Jules phoned her estate agent and authorized an auction. "A month's lead-up might be customary but it won't work for me," she told Chloe when her friend protested the short notice. "Schedule one for two weeks from now. We already have open houses all weekend with Lee away."

Along with Nate and Ross he was visiting Dan and Jo's farm down country—the location of Ross and Viv's pending wedding reception—to finalize groomsman suits and nuptial planning. Jules had excused herself by pleading outstanding work commitments.

At the farm she and Lee would be expected to share a bed.

Her fiancé hadn't protested; she suspected he was relieved. Which should have relieved *her*.

"How about we also run a full-page ad in the local paper Saturday since Lee won't be around to see it. And use that phrase estate agents have to signal a desperate vendor."

"Motivated seller," said Chloe.

"*Highly* motivated seller," Jules amended.

AT NIGHT IT WAS hardest to fight memories of his captivity.

In the dark space became infinite, stretching out in all directions to the past and to the future Lee couldn't make solid. And that scared him.

He'd learned to evade his nightmares by sleeping in brief snatches. Never too deeply. Occasionally, though, one caught him unawares. Which was how he found himself tumbling through a vast black void, his mouth open in a silent scream.

He struggled awake and fumbled for the lamp switch, desperate for the familiar walls of Jules's bedroom, her nightstand, her paintings and photographs.

Pressing his nose into the linen pillowcase, he inhaled the violet-scented fabric conditioner she used and his panic subsided to a manageable level. This was why, even after four nights, he hadn't suggested moving to the spare room.

As his breathing calmed, he noticed he'd left his door ajar. Afraid the light would wake her, he crawled out of bed to close it.

"Lee?" Her muffled voice prompted him to grab a T-shirt off the floor. As the door opened, he yanked it on over his boxers. Tousled, blinking against the light, Jules said sleepily, "Do you need something?"

"Just thirsty."

She wore pajamas, a green tank over patterned cotton boxers, sensible, sporty, except they clung to the womanly curves of her breasts and hips. And she smelled like Jules, all sleepy and warm and soft—if soft had a smell, which it didn't. He was going mad.

"I'll get you a glass of water."

"I can get it!"

She hugged herself at his harsh tone, inadvertently accentuating her cleavage.

"Sorry." Lee raked a hand through his hair. "I mean, no, thank you."

A tentative smile curved her mouth. Such a luscious mouth. "Good night, then."

"Good night."

She padded down the hall toward the spare bedroom and he tortured himself by watching her long, smooth legs, the sweet curve of her bottom and the rounded sway of her hips.

Why was he doing this? And forget the bullshit about making her pay, because he was paying, too. Why did it matter so damn much that she tell him the truth? There was no justification for what she'd done. And yet he couldn't, even now, douse the flame completely.

He suspected he still had hope. The irrepressible spark that had kept him alive in captivity was now holding him in a torturous limbo with Jules.

In the kitchen he filled a glass from the faucet, then cupped his hands and splashed his face. Cold water and lots of it suddenly seemed like a good idea. He dried off using the hem of his T-shirt. For a long moment he stood pressing the cotton against his eyelids.

Nothing fit him anymore, least of all his old self. His unit had disbanded, his friends were invested in new lives, his house and possessions were gone, his father was dead and the love of his life was a fraud.

"Falling in love is the easy part," she'd said. "Staying in love—"

"Requires a real commitment." Impatiently he'd snapped open the small velvet box again. "I can't make more of a commitment than this. It isn't complicated, Jules. Do you believe in us or not?"

"I believe in the potential of us."

"Yes. Or no?"

"I don't believe, not yet."

A sound made him straighten—Jules stood in the doorway. "I'm thirsty, too."

Silently he gave her his full glass, spilling some as she took it. Jules watched him over the rim as she took a couple of sips, her gaze anxious, assessing. Turning his back, Lee mopped up the spill with a dishcloth.

She rinsed and refilled the glass for him, but he waved it away. "I'm done." He switched off the kitchen light and together they walked along the hall, light from their respective rooms showing the way. He paused at his door, glanced at her without seeing. "Well, good night."

"Lee, wait." Her sympathetic hug caught him by surprise. He froze.

Instantly Jules released him, clasping her hands behind her back. "I'm sorry, I forgot you don't like…" Her voice trailed off.

"Don't like what?"

"Nothing. Good night." She started down the hall.

He frowned. She couldn't know about his reaction to the guys' hugs because she hadn't been there…. "Who told you?" he demanded flatly.

Cautiously, she turned. "Claire mentioned you had a prob… Issue with—"

"Oh, that's right." His laugh sounded bitter in his ears. "Claire and Nate exchange pillow talk now." Lee had tensed under Jules's touch for reasons altogether different from claustrophobia.

"She only told me to make things easier for you."

"Easier for…" His fiancée's hypocrisy was breathtaking. "So the only reason you're keeping your distance is out of consideration for my *phobia*."

Jules folded her arms, and her breasts rounded under the pressure. "I want you to recover fully before we move on to the next stage." She was picking her words as carefully as Lee used to sweep minefields.

Well, guess what, sweet pea, the one you think you're sidestepping is remotely detonated. "I hate to think of you suffering on my account," he said. "Come here."

Her brown eyes widened slightly, and she didn't move.

"Come here," he repeated softly. "If only to convince you that I don't have a phobia."

Biting her lower lip, she stepped forward. Catching her around the waist, he encouraged her closer. "See? No panic attack."

Her palms on his shoulders trembled; he became aware of it as his body attuned to hers. But then he was downright irresistible these days.

Wanting to shock her, Lee skimmed his hands over the swell of her bottom and tugged her hips against his so she could feel the iron hardness of his cock.

Jules seized a silent, indrawn breath. Held it.

He waited for her to pull away. Her eyes met his and her pupils flared with—his hold tightened—desire? Then her lashes fell, hiding her expression. She was conflicted? Well, so was he. There was nothing honest about this interaction.

As he went to release her, she surprised him by sliding her fingers from his shoulders, down his arms, warm where skin met skin. He shivered. They came to rest on his waist.

She let out the breath she'd been holding in a rush and her breasts bumped his chest.

All of Lee jumped.

Immediately she stepped back. "I'm sorry, I—"

He closed the gap. Nudging her body against the wall with his, he bent his head and kissed her.

Jules's muffled groan vibrated through his lips before her mouth opened to him, her tongue seeking his.

Yesterday…it could have been yesterday. They fit together so easily; she opened to him—responded to him— so passionately. How could this not be real?

God help him, he still burned for her. And the futility of his longing—the despair of it—made Lee mean, made him dangerous.

How far would she go?

He cupped a breast, teasing the nipple through the cotton. She pressed against his palm. Oh, sweet Jesus.

Her hands slid under his T-shirt, skimming the waistband of his boxers and moving higher to bare skin.

Lee stopped her before they reached the first ridge of scar tissue.

"This is about you," he said.

"No."

"Yes." He wanted this power, needed it. Lee spun her around so she couldn't reach him. With her spine pressed against his torso, he wrapped one arm around her ribs and nuzzled her neck, pushing away her silky hair to find the soft spot. God, her muscles were tight. Her smooth skin was gooseflesh as she shivered voluptuously.

The scent of her hair, of *her,* affected him on some primal level. It was the only sense he hadn't been able to conjure in his dank, dark, fetid prison. Lee sucked in a deep, heady breath and then had to blink hard as tears sprung unexpectedly to his eyes.

"Lee." Jules started to turn but he nipped her earlobe, causing her to squirm. That sent all kinds of sensations shooting to his groin. "I need to touch you," she pleaded.

His arm tightened around her. "Too bad."

She turned her head and he stymied her next protest with a kiss that made Jules catch his forearm to steady herself.

Lee pushed down the straps of her tank and kissed her shoulders. His cock throbbed.

"I need to touch—"

He kissed her again, harder, shoving the bunched tank to her waist and baring her beautiful breasts. His fingers slid over the boxers to tease her soft, yielding cleft and circle the hard nub of her clitoris.

Jules started to pant. "No," she gasped. "Together. It has to be together." Her hands reached behind, seeking him, and Lee splayed his palm against her belly to stop her.

She retaliated by wriggling her bottom against his erection, creating an exquisite friction. Looking down at her nipples, rosy and peaked, at his hand splayed at the juncture of her thighs over the dampened green boxers, his control frayed.

All he had to do was yank down her boxers to take her. He could already imagine Jules bent over the bed, open to him, surrendered to him, her breasts filling his palms as he thrust into her.

In sex at least he could make her give up control. He could win. And then a prick of conscience pierced his lust. *She doesn't deserve this, no matter what she's done.*

"Don't stop," Jules begged when he stilled. She rubbed her ass against him. Light spilled into the hall from the master bedroom and gleamed in her hair and in her eyes, heavy lidded with desire.

Lee kissed her again feverishly. She *owed* him.

Is this your victory? His goddamned conscience wouldn't shut up.

She'd lost control like this when they'd gone to bed on their first date. Her body overruling the clever brain telling her to be cautious. Lee had used sex then to lure her into a relationship. Because they were meant to be together. In his bones, he knew that.

But he knew differently now.

It didn't matter that their flesh was willing. The other bonds, the ones that mattered, were broken. Lee deepened the kiss anyway, and she twisted to wind her arms around his neck, her fingers threading through his hair as their bodies strained closer.

It was no good. He was about to have sex with a woman he no longer respected, and he didn't want to be that kind of man.

He released Jules so suddenly she staggered. Lee caught her by the arm, steadying her. She looked at him in bewilderment.

"I'm sorry," he said. "I guess…I'm not ready." He didn't give her a chance to respond, stumbling into the bedroom and closing the door before he did something stupid.

Like tell her the truth didn't matter.

JULES THREADED HER arms through the straps of her green tank, straightened her shorts and moved mechanically down the hall, shutting her bedroom door behind her before sinking against it. Drawing up her knees, she hugged them tight.

She'd expected mood swings, knew there'd be changes in Lee's personality—irrational anger, difficulty expressing himself—she'd prepared herself for that. But this was different. It was almost as if he was punishing himself for wanting her. Had she triggered some dark memory…held him too tight?

With a groan, she dropped her forehead to her knees. He'd been the one to call stop, but it should have been her. Only this afternoon she'd pledged to keep a lid on old emotions. *You idiot. He'll only feel more betrayed when you tell him the truth.*

But his first touch woke a craving Jules had been powerless to resist. She'd mourned him as dead for over a year and a half. To hold him was a miracle. To kiss him, a miracle.

To be wanted by him....

Even now—rejected—she wanted to go to him and say, *I have to make love to you one last time, please.*

In the months that had followed Lee's apparent death, she had grown to know Lee better through his friends and family. Had grown to love him more. And to see why their relationship would never have survived—they were inherently mismatched.

Coming from the bedrock of a loving family, Lee could never have understood Jules's almost obsessive need to prove they were solid before taking the next step.

Wearily Jules pushed to her feet, switched off the light and crawled into bed, pulling the covers tight to her chin despite the warm night. Needy and unfulfilled, she lay very quiet and concentrated on calming her breathing, relaxing her muscles and trying not to cry.

What had crying ever solved?

Laying her hand on the pillow beside her, she stared at the silhouette of the ring gleaming in the moonlight.

How often in her grief had she struggled to hold on to Lee in a dream, weeping because she knew at some point she'd have to wake up and face reality?

It had been naive to think she could help him while living a lie. And she certainly couldn't risk this situation escalating into intimacy. Love didn't conquer all—they'd proved that argument nineteen months ago and there was no point repeating history. He'd changed in ways she hadn't yet fathomed, but she couldn't rely on his resilience if she got this wrong again.

She would tell him the truth tomorrow after dinner with Nate and Claire.

CHAPTER TWELVE

THE FIRST LEE knew of Nate and Claire coming to dinner was when he found them on the front doorstep holding casserole dishes. "This is a nice surprise." He kissed Claire's cheek, clasped Nate's shoulder. "We weren't expecting you guys…were we?"

He glanced at Jules, who'd arrived home at the same time as their visitors. Dropping her house keys on the hall table, she smiled vaguely in his direction.

"Didn't I tell you? We thought it would be nice if we all had dinner together before you guys leave for the farm tomorrow." She'd already left the house by the time he rose this morning, and he'd spent the afternoon at the dentist. Lee had arrived home, steeling himself for a final confrontation, only to discover her out again. Shopping, her note had read. Clearly she wasn't in any hurry to discuss what had nearly happened last night. Was that why she'd brought in reinforcements?

"Pie, too." Nate gave Lee a pie dish. "Your favorite— rhubarb and apple."

Except this was clearly no impromptu arrangement. "Well, come on in then." That's when Lee registered the teenager hanging shyly behind Claire. "Lewis?"

"Hi, Lee."

"Holy hell, mate, you grew." Lewie had been eleven when they'd last met and Lee had swung him around in big airplane swoops on the lawn. He stuck out the hand he wasn't using to hold the pie dish. Steve's son, a lanky blond teen. Lewis had his father's firm grip—and his hazel eyes. God. Lee released his hold. "You look so different."

The teenager stared at him. "*You,* too."

"Lewis," his mother murmured, but Lee laughed.

"Like I told my nephews, you've got a month tops to beat me at arm wrestling so make the most of it." He'd been the games organizer at gatherings. Football, volleyball...hell... anything that could be made a competition.

"I can do the 'hanging man' for two full minutes," Lewis said.

"Yeah?" The hanging man involved holding a bicep curl while suspended from one of the ceiling beams at the Stingray Bay cabin. "Good for you."

In the bustle of their arrival Lee drew Nate aside. "Spill."

"I missed you," he said.

"We're going to the farm together tomorrow," Lee said drily.

"Lewis isn't and, as I told you before, he's been dying to see you," Nate said. "Plus Jules mentioned you'd taken delivery of a home gym and we wanted to check it out. So where is it?"

Ah, so that was it. "Set up the spare room, but plenty of time for that. C'mon, I'll find you a beer." Leading the way to the kitchen, Lee resolved to show Nate the equipment *after* he'd adjusted the weight load down. But when he arrived at the fridge, he realized nobody had followed him.

Dammit. Dumping the pie on the counter, he went to the spare room, where he found Lewis in front of the mirror, using his whole body to sling the dumbbell to his shoulder. The kid was built like a pipe cleaner, all his growth still in height. Lee exchanged a secret "aw, cute" grin with Nate, who sat on the weight bench. "We need a home gym at our house," the teen said.

"And keep it where?" Nate inquired.

Lewis changed sides with the dumbbell. "Mark could add a weight room to the extension plans."

Lee stiffened. "You're renovating?" he asked Nate casually.

"We need more room to live there permanently."

Lee glanced at Lewis, who was scowling. "You're not happy about that, mate?"

"We could move to Hollywood—instead we're gonna *fish*." Lewis dropped the dumbbell and moved to the lat pulldown.

"Hey, Zander Freedman's coming to the launch," Nate teased. "What more do you want?"

"The rock star who fired you as his bodyguard?" Lee said. "How does that work?"

"He'd decided to forgive me for making him fire me—and yeah, he really does think like that. So he's magnanimously coming to give his blessing since he's here visiting family anyway. Zander assures me the publicity will throw our charter business into the stratosphere. He might be right. I must tell Jules—she has a crush on him."

Lee frowned. "On Freedman? He's what, forty?"

"Guess she likes the wild ones." Nate grinned.

Then why had she dated a man who wore polo sweaters? "So the guy who drew your plans." Lee replaced the dumbbell Lewis had discarded in its holder, watching Nate carefully. "Maybe he should take a look at this place."

"Maybe...Lewie...keep your arms bent." Rising from the bed, Nate busied himself adjusting the teen's handhold on the overhead bar. Avoiding Lee's gaze.

Huh. So his buddy knew about Jules dating Mark and hadn't mentioned it. On the other hand, how *did* you break news like that?

In the cold light of day Lee was ashamed of his feelings

last night, ashamed of his continuing desire for a woman who'd deceived everybody he cared about.

"Yeah, mate, that's better." Stepping away from the other two, he watched Lewis, his attention miles away. The Pashtun had a saying, "Who has fallen from the top of a high mountain recovers. Who has fallen from the heart's anguish recovers not." Revenge wasn't sweet, it was corrosive, and he needed to rebuild his life. These games had to end. Tonight, when their friends left.

Nate moved to the barbell suspended over the weight bench. "You're lifting way too much for a convalescent."

So it was out in the open now. "You're here to check up on me."

"Have you visited the doctor yet?"

Lee folded his arms. "I suspect you already know the answer to that."

"Hey, don't get pissed at Jules. She's worried about you."

"Look, I haven't thrown up since Monday," Lee said irritably.

Nate gawked at him, then threw back his head and bellowed. "Jules!" Footsteps hurried down the hall, and she stuck her head around the door. "You didn't tell me he'd been vomiting!"

She threw Lee a look of disgust. "Blabbermouth."

One corner of his mouth lifted. "Sorry, I thought you'd squealed. You run, I'll cover."

She didn't need to be told twice. Nate put his hands on his hips. "Grab a jacket, dumb-ass. We're getting you checked out right now."

"And sit in Emergency for hours?" Lee said. "I'm a paramedic, I can self-monitor."

"When did you last take your temperature?"

"Um." Shit.

"What's your pulse rate?"

"Aggravated."

Nate didn't smile. "Lewie, please fetch the med kit out of the car."

Giving Lee a sympathetic grin, the teen obeyed.

"Interesting that you have a med kit handy." While Lee had been the team's specialist paramedic, all SAS combatants cross-trained in one another's skill set, so the mission didn't abort if the specialist was taken out.

"It's for *Heaven Sent*." The charter boat. "But to be clear, either I check out your vitals or we head to the hospital. Your choice."

"If you recall," Lee said evenly, "I've been surviving alone for the past nineteen months *without* help—"

"And you've forgotten how to let people care for you. Got that. I'm not here to ease your mind, I'm here to ease mine. And Jules's."

"Jules can take care of herself."

"Yeah?" Nate gestured to the open closet where Jules's clothes hung neatly. "Is that why she's still sleeping in the spare room?"

Double shit. And he couldn't use the excuse that he wasn't up to sex, not if he wanted to avoid the emergency room. "She and I have some things to work out."

"Mate, if you need to talk…"

"I'm good." This was between Jules and him. How his friends and family reacted to the truth came later. He felt a pang of disquiet on Jules's behalf but quelled it immediately. She'd brought this on herself.

This was his last night in Whangarei. After the weekend he figured he'd stay with Ross in Auckland for a few days while he found a rental and decided what the hell he wanted to do.

Even short-term, he couldn't live with his siblings. Their solicitude would drive him crazy.

"It took Claire coming to L.A. and dragging me home to deal with her family trust before I confronted the emotional fallout from the ambush." As he spoke, Nate removed half the weight plates from the barbell. "I do know something of what you're feeling."

I doubt that. Lee remained silent.

Nate retightened the collar around the remaining plates. "You want to be the guy you were before the ambush."

And he would be. Lying down on the weight bench, Lee lifted the adjusted bar. "These are pussy weights," he complained.

"You're hoping," Nate continued quietly, "that if you shove all the pain aside long enough, it will disappear."

"Five…six…seven… I'm not even breathing hard."

"Maybe I can help you avoid the traps I fell into."

"Ten, eleven, twelve… Seriously, Nate." Lee ignored the trembling in his biceps. "I'm not getting a workout with this."

Impassively Nate helped him guide the bar into its holder. "Fine, have it your way. For now."

Lee greeted Lewis's return with relief. "Et tu, Brute?"

"Huh?"

"You're ganging up on me, too?"

"I dunno."

"Just following orders?"

Nate came to the kid's rescue. "Quit stalling, Lee, and sit up."

Reluctantly he complied. Nate stuck an electronic thermometer in his ear, waited. "Surprise, surprise. You have a temperature."

"I've been lifting weights."

"Pussy weights," Nate reminded him.

Grabbing the thermometer, Lee checked the reading. "It's trending way down from what it was."

"Uh-huh." Nate took his pulse while Lee concentrated on lowering it.

"Remember I've been exercising."

"And said it didn't raise your heart rate... As I expected, a tad high."

"Because your bedside manner's scaring me, Dr. Jekyll."

Lewis laughed.

"Don't encourage him, Lewie." Nate pulled out a blood pressure meter.

"You're kidding, you carry a sphygmomanometer? Lewis, ten bucks if you can spell that."

Nate wound the cuff round his upper left arm and started inflating it.

"S...p...i—" Lewis began.

"Wrong...ouch...it's pinching," Lee complained. "Did I teach you nothing?"

Ignoring him, Nate used a stethoscope to listen to the brachial artery as he released the pressure. "Elevated but not drastically. You pass...but only because I can keep an eye on you over the weekend."

Lee groaned. "Can we eat now, Nurse Ratchet?"

WATCHING LEE WEAVE his old magic through dinner, charming Claire and Lewis with his self-deprecating humor, trading insults with Nate, Jules wondered numbly if anyone else realized how much he was pretending.

Across the table Claire gestured to Jules's plate. "You've barely touched your dessert."

"Guess I ate too much of the first course." Smiling, Jules rubbed her stomach and the diamond snagged on her top, a fitted short-sleeved black angora.

Lee wasn't the only one putting on an act tonight. She released the stone carefully, grimacing at the tiny rent in the wool. This damn ring had derailed her life.

No wonder Gollum had gone insane.

Jules returned her attention to Lee as he and Lewis talked Nate and Claire into doing the dishes. Wearing himself out pretending to be normal. She recognized this journey; she'd made it. So had all of those affected by the ambush. But unlike Nate, she accepted that Lee was too stubborn, too independent, to be guided by their experiences.

Was he really well enough to hear the truth? No, she couldn't waver now. Even if her stomach dropped every time she anticipated her pending confession.

Restlessly, Jules stood. "Who's for coffee? Lewis, I can make you a hot chocolate...?" Taking orders, she cleared the dessert plates and made drinks, oblivious to the conversation behind her.

A burst of laughter coincided with her return to the table. "What did I miss?"

Lewis nudged Lee's elbow. "Tell Jules the goat story. It's really funny," the teen assured her.

Dispensing drinks, Jules said politely, "I'd love to hear it."

"Last tour, we were plagued by a herd of goats in the village where we were stationed," Lee said. "They ate everything. I still can't understand how one managed to get my underwear. I swear I pegged them six feet off the ground."

Conscious of Lewis's expectant gaze, Jules contrived a chuckle as she handed him a hot chocolate. Then she thought...wait a minute. Something about this story didn't quite gel.

"You know what I think happened?" Nate cupped his mug. "It climbed on the roof and craned its scrawny neck—"

"Last tour," Jules interrupted. *"Last* last tour?"

"Yeah," said Nate, puzzled.

"But what about Lee's—"

"I'll fill you in later," her fiancé said evenly.

Amnesia. She stared at him.

Lee broke eye contact, pushed back his chair. "I'll make a start on dishes."

Jules sat down. She could be wrong. She could be. But if it was true, if Lee's amnesia was a lie— She stopped reeling and settled into a state of unholy calm. "Sugar anyone?"

It was probably better not to have witnesses.

CHAPTER THIRTEEN

SHE KNEW. THE CONVICTION grew in Lee over the next half hour. Outwardly Jules continued to play relaxed hostess: "No, leave the dishes. It's a school night and you don't want to be home too late."

But he could feel the tension building in her, like a low-pressure system before a storm.

He wanted closure—that tidy word that assumed tragedy could be neatly bookended. But after last night, cutting her out of his life would be easier than having to confront his feelings every time he saw her.

"So I'll see you tomorrow," Nate said as he left. "Pick you up around nine."

"Have a good weekend." Claire kissed his cheek. Did she know about Jules's deception? Surreptitiously, Lee studied his fiancée's best friend. Except if Claire knew, then Nate would, too. Immediately, Lee dismissed the suspicion. His army buddies would never be party to such a conspiracy.

"See you, Lewis. Next time we'll get some competition happening."

Because right now wasn't going to be fun at all.

The door finally shut behind their guests, Jules turned and leaned against it, her social smile fading. Her chest rose in a sharp breath. "Please tell me you haven't been faking amnesia."

Lee folded his arms. "You've been masquerading as my

fiancée for close to two years," he said quietly. "I deserved a confession."

"So everything since your release—the sweet talk, the proposal…" her palms flattened against the door "…last night. All of it was to *punish* me?"

"I needed time," he said defensively, brusquely, "to find out what game you were—"

"Game!" The expression in her eyes was harder than his diamond on her finger. "You think mourning you was a game?" she demanded furiously. "That I've been withholding the truth for giggles?"

He set his jaw. "You lied to my family and friends, you accepted my inheritance. I don't know *what* the hell's going on."

"You should have asked me!"

"Don't turn this on me—the pretending started with *you*. I gave you every opportunity to come clean in our first phone call."

Impatiently she pushed away from the door. "I was protecting you until you found your feet." Her brown eyes narrowed. "Or have you been scamming me about the PTSD, too?"

Lee hesitated, unwilling to acknowledge that he had a problem, even to himself.

She laughed wildly. "So you can't even claim temporary insanity."

"I don't need an excuse," he flung back. "*You* do."

In the taut silence they stared at each other. Then she swallowed. "I don't have one."

"Yeah," he said, "that's what I thought."

She lifted her chin. "I'm not denying culpability for accepting your ring. It was the stupidest thing I've ever done and I'm sorry. But I don't regret keeping the truth from your friends and family. They were so raw in their grief and this gave them hope." Her voice caught, and she cleared her throat and scowled. "And I was reeling, too."

"You're forgetting," he said, letting his bitterness show, "I remember everything."

"You may not have amnesia but you're definitely suffering from selective memory." Pushing past him, Jules went into the living room.

"'Saying yes now,'" he quoted, following her, "'would be succumbing to emotional blackmail.'" Deliberately, he sprawled on the couch opposite Jules, who sat in the armchair as straight backed as a judge. "Oh, I got the message loud and clear," he added. "You didn't love me enough to say yes."

"And you didn't love *me* enough to wait until I was ready, she retorted. "My nerves were already on edge with you leaving for Afghanistan, plus you'd already agreed we could take things slowly. Suddenly you're trying to dazzle me with this *rock*."

She leaned forward to wave it in front of his nose.

"The *rock* was to set your mind at rest," he snapped, no longer lounging. "I thought you only suggested a go-slow because you were worried *my* feelings wouldn't last a six-month separation. Turned out it was *your* feelings you had doubts about."

"All I said was that we didn't know each other enough to make a commitment."

"You were a talking Dear John letter—in full goddamned retreat."

Her eyes flashed. "Because I couldn't share your gung-ho romanticism after dating six weeks? I wasn't a challenge to be conquered like some Boys' Own Adventure—we were talking marriage, a commitment for the rest of our lives. Why did wanting more time have to be such a big deal?"

"Gee, I don't know." Shoving to his feet, he glared down

at her. "Because I invested ten thousand dollars in a diamond maybe? Got down on bended knee maybe? Got kicked to the curb by the woman I wanted to spend the rest of my life with?"

She rose, too. "I may have rejected your proposal but *you* were the one who walked away. Ironic that the *forever* you were so desperate to start couldn't survive our first fight!"

"Proposing was a very big deal for me and you shot me down in flames," he said heatedly. "It took a while to process that."

"Claire heard from Steve twice over the next two weeks and you left me hanging. That's not processing, that's punishing."

"I hadn't told the guys what happened and we didn't have privacy when we made phone calls. I couldn't risk emotional stuff messing with my head through a mission, it was too dangerous." And he'd been terrified she'd tell him they were done.

When he was first captured, he'd even had a fleeting sense of satisfaction…like some angsty adolescent fantasy. *Ha, I went and died, that'll teach you.* Her rejection had reduced him to that level of pathetic.

He gathered his outrage now and used it as armor. "When I said the commitment drives the prenup not the other way around you called me stupid."

"I said the idea was stupid!" she yelled.

He snorted. "Semantics."

"Common sense. I deal with people every day who thought they'd married their soul mate and now want to slap that person with a restraining order. People who deny custodial access out of spite and who hide accounts to prevent a fair division of assets."

He resisted the urge to tear out his hair. "I'm not like that."

"How could I be sure after six weeks? How could you be sure about me? And don't tell me you'd take me on faith because nothing you've done since you returned suggests any faith whatsoever."

What was the point of arguing? The gulf between them was unbridgeable.

"You talk about good faith," he said hollowly, sinking to the couch. "Even if I can believe the impulse that caused you to take my ring…you accepted my money after Dad died, knowing you had no right to it. Where the hell is the integrity in that, Jules?"

She didn't flinch. "There would be none if I'd accepted it from you." She reoccupied the armchair with the same judge's pose. "But I *didn't* accept it from you."

He needed a few seconds to understand. *I thought I'd talked Ian out of it,* she'd said when they'd discussed his father's will.

"Oh, my God." People talked about lightbulb moments— Lee felt like a lighthouse had just collapsed on him. "You told Dad the truth."

"It seemed the lesser of two evils. It didn't change our relationship. In fact, Ian remained adamant that had you lived, you'd have come to your senses." Her gaze narrowed but the lamplight picked up her unshed tears. "So much for that."

Lee's anger evaporated in his relief. "He was right, it wasn't over." He'd spent his entire captivity planning how to woo her. He reached for her hand but she leaned back in the chair, folding her arms across her chest.

"Ian said something that struck a chord with me. That when your mother died he got through his grief by assuming the qualities he loved about her." He swallowed. She was remorseless in her honesty.

"I figured I could carry on being burdened by guilt, regrets and self-recrimination. Or I could celebrate your life by adopting what I loved about you—your courage, your adventurousness, your enthusiasm for people."

The understanding of what his injured pride had made her suffer suffused Lee with shame. Jules's motivation since his return had been all about protecting him, and his had been exactly the same. Protecting himself. He hadn't been ashamed lying naked on a dirt floor being kicked by his captors. But he was ashamed now.

And he'd just made it bloody easy for her to get over him.

"I took the money not on your dad's advice but on yours," she said. "You said I needed to take more risks."

The phone rang. They ignored it.

"I'm sorry," he said, recognizing the apology came too little, too late.

Her gaze dropped to the diamond on her left hand. "I accepted the ring when the guys offered it because I was desperate to believe you loved me, even though you walked away. I think part of my desire for a tangible object was because I *didn't* believe it."

The phone stopped ringing.

Taking the ring off, Jules turned it over in her fingers, letting the diamond catch the light. "It never suited me," she said wryly. "I only loved it because it reflected you." Her lips tightened. "I guess that says it all."

She held it out. "Consider us quits."

He took it. Because no matter his regrets, she was right. He should have asked for the truth.

"You know what the irony is?" Jules said, delivering the final blow. "I would probably have said yes two years ago if you'd given us more time."

She studied him before asking, "How long would you have tormented me with this amnesia?"

Lee frowned. "I was going to challenge you tonight."

"Should I believe you?"

"Said the pot to the kettle…" He sighed. "I'll never lie to you again."

Her throat ached but she had to ask. "Is that what last night was about? Screwing me for revenge?"

"It started that way," he admitted. "I stopped because it wasn't fair to either of us. Even believing the worst of you, I wanted to forgive you." He took a deep breath. "I'm not over you."

She looked at him, incredulous. "What good is love without trust?" If he'd really loved her Lee would have asked for the truth, given her the benefit of the doubt. Hadn't she done that by hanging on to the conviction—despite all evidence to the contrary—that he'd died loving her?

"And if you believed me capable of conning an old man out of his money, you don't know me."

And if he didn't know her, Lee couldn't really love her.

THE PHONE RANG AGAIN, pealing loudly in the silence. Lee left the room to answer it and Jules rolled her head back against the armchair and closed her eyes. Four days after her frenzied midnight cleaning, the smell of lemony furniture polish still lingered, a reminder of how much she'd wanted to put things right. Pushing to her feet, she went to the window and opened it wide.

Lee came back in. "That was Ross. We're on *60 Minutes*." Picking up the TV remote, he flicked through the channels until the interview they'd given a couple of days ago flashed up. Lee was sitting in the window seat fielding questions.

Jules's cell beeped an incoming text and she glanced at the screen. "Dan and Jo are letting us know it's on." Tomorrow all their friends would have to take sides. Lee's actions would come in for some disapproval but when you compared transgressions she was more obviously in the wrong. His betrayal was too complex, too personal for anyone else to get.

On TV the scene changed. She'd joined Lee on the window seat. His arm was around her and she was smiling, her lipstick freshly applied, hair neatly brushed and her lawyer face on, expression neutral. "When it's right, it's right," said TV Lee.

Beneath her anger she felt hurt, as tender as a bruise, as familiar as a recurring injury. Maybe if he hadn't started this "you're the one" soul-mate business, she could have forgiven him. Maybe if he hadn't made some part of her believe they had a magical bond.

But he had. Not once but twice. And she'd let herself be swept away, let herself be *played,* twice.

"I will say one thing about my captivity," said the liar on screen. "Jules was my talis—"

Seizing the remote from Lee, she punched Mute.

"I'd say it was all true," he said quietly, "but you wouldn't believe me."

"I wouldn't." Jules tossed the remote onto the couch. "What the hell do you suggest we do about the press? Honestly, I could kill you for that."

"I have to warn you that many have tried and failed."

"Be serious."

Absently he walked to the window and closed it, drew the curtains. "I'll call a press conference and announce I've dumped you."

"What!"

"Think about it," he said. "Even if we both show up smiling to a press conference and announce the breakup is amicable, a lot of people will think you should've stuck with the poor broken war vet so close to my pledge of undying love."

Jules dropped her head in her hands. "I wish to God neither of us had started down this path."

"As you pointed out, I stirred up the hornet's nest, I deserve the stings."

Her desperation to be rid of him tussled briefly with her sense of fair play. "I'm not forgetting my culpability in this, even if you're prepared to. Since I'll be the pariah anyway with our friends and your family, I'll take the fall."

"I won't tell if you don't." Frowning, he leaned his shoulder against the mantel. "Let sleeping dogs lie."

"Even sleeping dogs are lying now?" Wearily Jules shook her head. "I have no problem evading media attention but I made a solemn vow when you were found alive. As soon as you knew the truth, so would they. This has weighed on my conscience long enough. Besides, they'll want a reason why we're breaking up."

"No one's going to be surprised it didn't work out," he said impatiently. "Look at me, I'm a changed man."

She did look and saw his exhaustion and defeat—but Lee had admitted the mental fragility had been an act. "It's not how you changed that caused this," she said defensively. "It's how you didn't."

"Hey, I was making a statement of fact, not pleading for sympathy. But thanks for the vote of confidence that I've integrated the worst of both worlds."

"Oh, you'll be beautiful again," she said darkly. "On the *outside* anyway."

He grinned and it was so unexpected Jules returned it. "There's nothing funny in this situation."

"I developed an appreciation for black humor in captivity." He sat on the couch. "As I see it, the only way to avoid adverse publicity is to keep the engagement going for a few more weeks until our novelty wears off."

"No."

"Hear me out. I figure I can spend a night or two in Auckland with Ross or my family, or down south with Dan without raising suspicion, which means I'm not living in your pocket 24/7. We only need to play the happy couple on public occasions where we're expected to be seen together. Like the boat launch, my family reunion and Ross's wedding."

"More games? No." She needed him out of her life.

Lee inspected his ruined hands, the only testament to his ordeal he couldn't hide. They both needed this tragic chapter to be over and as painlessly as possible. "You know what we skipped first time round?" he said. "Friendship."

"We have the wrong kind of history for that but...I'll consider a truce."

"I'd prefer an armistice."

"What's the difference?"

"A truce is a temporary cessation of hostilities. Under an armistice we negotiate terms and the war is over."

"I don't know." Was this another game? Jules didn't think she could yield an inch of ground.

"Hey, I get it," he said quietly. "You don't trust me. So let me clarify the terms. From here on in between you and me, it's the truth, the whole truth," Lee raised his right hand. "So help me, God. I won't pretend that I don't want you back."

"Lee—"

"Let me finish. But I swear—" he raised his hand again "—that I won't manipulate you into giving me another chance through begging, guilt or emotional blackmail of any kind. I'll do my best not to make you uncomfortable for the few weeks we need to continue the engagement. How does that sound?"

"Fair." Jules's pragmatism replaced her panic. "Let me return your honesty. There's no hope of reconciliation.

None." She met his gaze steadily. "I need you to accept that."

"Then let's tie up loose ends and do this breakup cleanly." Lee hesitated. "I appreciate that you were trying to protect me, and I'm sorrier than I can say for lying to you about the extent of my amnesia. I'd spent so much time in captivity working out how I'd win you back that hearing you'd taken the ring, my money and were lying to everyone…"

Jules squirmed uncomfortably.

"Well, I was devastated. And when guys are devastated we don't do crying jags and chocolate binges. We default to pride and anger."

Both useful shields. She was deploying them now.

"Again, I apologize for that," he added.

"I accept your apology," Jules replied, protecting herself with formality. "Please accept mine."

Lee proffered a hand. "Shake on it?"

"That won't be necessary." She didn't want him to know she was shaking. "As long as we're clear—as soon as the dust settles we go our separate ways." Which made it more imperative that she repay his money as quickly as possible.

"You're calling the shots."

"I'll tell Claire in person this weekend."

"Why didn't you ever confide in her, once things settled down?"

Jules swallowed. "I was too ashamed."

"I didn't think it was possible to feel any guiltier," Lee said gruffly, "but you keep proving me wrong."

"Don't bother. I can reliably inform you that guilt serves no purpose."

"Got any alcohol in the house?"

She dug out of a kitchen cupboard a bottle of duty-free gin her mother had brought on her last visit and splashed generous portions into tumblers. Lee topped them up from the carton of orange juice in the fridge.

Sitting at the table, still partially set from dinner, they sipped their drinks and picked over details.

"I'll tell the guys this weekend," he said. "On the way home to Whangarei I'll stop off in Auckland and put Rob and Connie in the picture."

"I can phone them," she said.

"It'll go down better from me."

"It's okay," Jules said after she finished her drink. "I'm expecting everyone to hate me."

"Not necessarily. The upside to my lousy behaviour is that it mitigates yours."

"Nice as it is to think so, I'm afraid my rap sheet is longer and affects more people than yours does." He only hurt *her*.

Lee stood and finished clearing the table of napkins and place mats. "I suggest we keep this quiet from my extended family. The more people we tell, the higher the likelihood of the press finding out."

"You do have loose lips among your relatives," she agreed, and caught him looking at her strangely. "What?"

"It's still weird that you're on first-name terms with my entire gene pool."

"Like I said, my rap sheet's longer than yours.... Good night, Lee."

"Jules."

She turned to see him holding out the ring. "I'm sorry, but you're stuck with this a little longer."

Only later, when Jules was tossing and turning in bed reviewing the minutiae of their armistice, did she realize Lee had never agreed to give up hope.

CHAPTER FOURTEEN

LEE DIDN'T WANT to think about how badly he'd screwed up, and on a five-hundred-and-fifty-hectare property running three thousand sheep and four hundred beef cattle he wouldn't have to.

He just had to get there first.

The phone woke him and a glance at the time—seven-thirty—suggested Jules had already left the house. He picked up, expecting Nate confirming a time. "Yeah."

"Hello?" A woman's voice. "Is this Juliet Browne's number?"

"Yes, but I don't think she's here. Hang on and I'll check."

Rolling out of bed, Lee, in boxers and T-shirt, wandered out to the kitchen, taking in the half-empty bottle of gin he'd consoled himself with after Jules had gone to bed. There was a note propped against it in her handwriting. "I'm relying on you to follow through on our agreement."

Lee crumpled the note in his hand. Not a bad dream he could wake up from then. And the subtext couldn't be clearer. Don't let me down *again*.

He lifted the phone. "I'm sorry, she's left for work. Can I take a message?"

"Is that Lee Davis?"

"Who's asking?"

"Her mother."

"Mrs. Browne. Hello." He dredged his memory for her

first name but came up with nothing. Every reference Jules made was to "Mum."

"Mrs. Edwards now."

That didn't help a bit. He scrambled for small talk. "Congratulations on your recent marriage."

"Heavens, it's been months now. How are *you* feeling?"

"Very well, thank you," he lied politely. *Your daughter just crushed me for the third time.*

"It's odd, but I only know you from attending your memorial service. Jules couldn't bear to discuss you, so you've got the advantage over me."

Mrs. Edwards's assumption that Jules had regaled him with anecdotes was interesting considering how often her daughter had changed the subject whenever her childhood came up. Fortunately her mother didn't wait for a reply.

"For years Jules lectured me about being a fool for love," she confided, "and yet here she is, throwing herself into an engagement with a guy she hasn't seen for nearly two years. You can't imagine how great it is to get the last word, although if you're marrying my daughter you might have a new appreciation of it in a few years." He heard her belly laugh come down the line. "Just kidding. You must come over to the Gold Coast and stay. Have you set a wedding date yet?"

Did Jules want her mother to know the truth? They hadn't discussed it so Lee played it safe. "Not yet."

"Gus is rich. We could host the wedding here. We've got a beautiful property leading down to the water… Think about it. What are you doing, staying in the military?"

"I haven't decided."

"I'm sure Gus could give you a job. He's big in property over here. Will you, sweetie?" It took Lee a moment to realize she wasn't talking to him. "He says sure, we could use you on billboards. 'Hostage to renting'…something like that."

"That's, um, very kind of you."

"Don't be silly, you're family now. And it's nice to be able to do something for my baby girl. She cleaned up my messes for years. Not that you're a mess… My tongue!" Another peal of laughter. "Take care, Lee, and I look forward to meeting you."

There was little likelihood of that now. "And you."

After an exchange of goodbyes, they hung up. Lee took two Tylenol and went to pack and was still shoving clothes into his weekender bag when Nate rang the doorbell at eight.

"You look like shit," his mate greeted him. "Didn't you get any sleep last night?"

"And hello to you, too." Slinging the bag over his shoulder, Lee pulled the front door shut behind them to lock it.

"If you were smiling," Nate commented as they strode toward his SUV, "lack of sleep would be a good thing, but that scowl…"

"Save the fishing for *Heaven Sent*. I'm not ready for the third degree." Everyone needed to be together before he spilled the beans.

Climbing into the passenger seat, Lee tossed his bag onto the backseat. "In fact, topics are strictly restricted to the vehicular."

"Suit yourself." Nate flicked the ignition and the V8 engine roared to life. "Let me tell you about the torque on this baby." His former troop mates enjoyed waxing lyrical on engines. As soldiers in a mobility troop, mechanical expertise had formed part of their stock in trade.

Discussing engines passed the two-and-a-half-hour drive to Ross's beach house on Auckland's West Coast and the second stage of the long drive south was enlivened by an argument over cravats or ties for the wedding suits.

In Hollywood, Nate said with a straight face, fedoras were popular, and metallic bow ties. By the time the ute arrived at the cattle sale where they were rendezvousing with Dan, Lee had shored up his brave face and was almost certain it would hold.

Nate pulled up outside the big corrugated shed where the auction was and Lee and Ross got out.

"So have fun, kids. I'll see you later."

"You're not staying?" Lee had planned to tell them when they met up with Dan. His only goal this weekend was to mitigate any fallout for Jules.

"Seen one cow, seen them all." Nate slung an arm along the open cab window. " I'm meeting Jo—" Dan's wife "—at a café to drink good coffee instead."

"Hair gel, good coffee." Shaking his head, Lee revised his plan. "And I thought I'd had the life-changing experience. The Taliban has nothing on L.A."

"Let's buy Nate a bumper sticker," Ross suggested. "Metrosexuals are us."

"Hey, I'm not the bore who talked wedding details for the past hour," Nate retorted. "So long, Groomzilla."

The ute's wheels spun in the dry clay of the makeshift parking lot as Nate accelerated and left them standing in a swirl of dust.

Both men breathed deep and then grinned at each other. "I love the smell of cow shit in the morning," said Ross.

"Me, too." Around them, dusty trucks and utes were angled haphazardly under shade trees or bunched as close to the auction shed as their owners could get. Farmers avoided walking if they could; their working days were physical enough.

They found Dan eying stock prospects from the labyrinth of wooden walkways above the pens, but a clatter and snort interrupted their greetings. Amidst the broad backs of the cattle, a young bull tossed his head and charged the four others in his pen. Brandishing cattle prods with the economical precision of orchestra conductors, two stockmen segregated it, aided by a border collie, which darted around the animal's heels to stop it from bolting.

"If you're buying for beef and not breeding, why get bulls instead of castrated steers?" Lee asked. "They're only more trouble." Testosterone, he thought bleakly, the bane of males everywhere.

"Bulls bulk up more quickly." Dan ran a pro's eye over the pens. "The trick to managing them is to keep the mobs small—around twenty in one paddock—and separate troublemakers like this one."

"Sounds like SAS selection," Ross said.

Dan grinned. "Except, fail here and you're shipped to the slaughterhouse. No second chances for this prima donna."

He and Ross snickered.

Lee rolled his eyes. "Really, guys? You're *still* bringing that up?"

Applying for the SAS hadn't been on his radar when he'd joined the army for adventure and a free education. But he'd become intrigued by the folklore. SAS troopers were best of the best. Only the top one percent made it through the military's toughest selection process. Yada, yada.

As someone who'd never had to exert himself beyond ninety percent, Lee figured he'd be a shoo-in. As it turned out the SAS demanded one hundred and ten percent.

"Are you kidding?" Ross said. "If you'd had a headstone we would have engraved it." He drew big air scrolls. "Here lies Lee Davis for whom it took two attempts to get into the SAS."

"Yeah, yeah," he said. "Make fun of the one-hundred-thirty-pound weakling." The unit gave Lee two things he hadn't known he lacked—a goal and an ability to learn from failure.

Dan assessed him as thoroughly as the cattle. "I expected you to look better."

"Sweet talker...when does the bidding start?"

As Lee hoped, his buddy dropped his sharp gaze to his watch. "We should think about finding seats."

"Meet you inside," Ross said. "I need caffeine."

Lee followed Dan into the sales shed, a modified barn with a unique aroma equal parts hayseed, dirt, sweat and animals, where they found seats among the tiers of wooden benches set up around the show pen. Along a walkway running above it, a row of stock agents in short-sleeved business shirts and ties pored over clipboards.

Lee started to feel uneasy. Maybe it was the glances he was getting from the few who recognized him. Or the hangover trying to override the Tylenol. It couldn't be claustrophobia in this vast building.

The first auction started for a dozen Hereford bullocks, and the lyrical yammer of the auctioneer echoed off the corrugated iron walls. The man's gaze darted among the crowd, swooping in on a laconic nod or a briefly raised hand.

Bang went the gavel.

Lee jumped.

"So-o-old to bidder number six."

"You okay?" Dan asked.

"Fine."

A second bunch of cattle were guided in and another round of bidding started. Why the hell was he sensitized here of all places, at a country stock sale?

Flashing surreptitious glances around him, he understood. The weather-beaten faces of the surrounding men—

with their stoic, patient expressions—reminded him of the
Afghani villagers who'd sheltered him for the first five
months after the ambush. Both lifestyles revolved around
animals, were attuned to the seasons and subject to the
whims of nature. And in the Afghanis' case, the vicissi-
tudes of war.

He suffered a pang for Ajmal, mule-stubborn, loyal to
his God and with a two-thousand-year-old code of honor.
By invoking Pashtunwali law, Lee had made himself the
man's tribesman, and the old man's honor, and that of all
his family and his village, depended on keeping a military
heathen alive. Or to die trying.

Ross rejoined them, carrying three paper cups. "Vend-
ing machine's only doing tea. I added extra sugar."

"Thanks." Lee accepted the hot drink and slid along the
wooden bench to make room.

Ross sat down. "What have I missed?"

"Two lots," Lee guessed.

"More like five." Dan glanced at him curiously. "The
animals I'm interested in are next."

"So is it like poker, we have to keep a straight face?"
Ross's long legs nudged a man sitting in front of him.
"Sorry, mate."

"I'm done here, anyways." The farmer stood, tucked his
purchase number into the breast pocket of a faded plaid
shirt and tipped his hat back to reveal a white strip of un-
tanned forehead. His eyes were bright in his wrinkled face.
Lee had to look away.

In hospital he'd made discreet inquiries about Ajmal.
The headman and his family were no longer in the village.
Which meant they were dead.

Ross took a casual swig of his tea, then dug in his jacket
and produced a protein bar, which he held out. "You haven't
eaten in what…five hours?"

"What are you, my babysitter?" Hemmed between his friends, he felt like he was being observed, watched. Notwithstanding their benevolent motives, Lee had to keep reminding himself they were on his side. His nerves only recognized that they were elite soldiers.

Ross waved the bar in front of his nose. "Take it."

"You're being anal." Reluctantly Lee accepted. "How the hell did you get a free spirit like Viv to say yes anyway?"

"I'm loose in bed."

"Ice," Dan growled, his gaze fixed on the cattle currently being auctioned. "No sexy talk about my sister, remember?" He used a curt nod to signal a bid.

"Look at you being all laconic and salt of the earth," Lee said admiringly.

"Screw you" was the affectionate response. "Now quit squirming in case the auctioneer thinks you're making an offer. I don't want to pay more for these bulls than I have to."

Ross raised his arms in a big stretch and pretend yawn. The auctioneer hesitated. Dan shook his head and the man's lightning gaze moved on.

"Don't make me come over there, Ice," Dan warned.

Odd, thought Lee, that bickering could be so soothing.

"I figure we'll organize the groomsman suit for you this afternoon," Ross commented to Lee. "And make allowance for weight gain over the next three weeks. How much do you reckon you've put on so far? I'll calculate an average."

"Pre-wedding jitters," Dan confided, signaling another bid. "It's just so darn cute."

"I'm marrying Hurricane Viv," Ross protested. "The more I can organize in advance, the freer I'll be to douse fires on the day."

"Uh-huh," scoffed his future brother-in-law.

Lee jumped in as peacemaker. "Viv flies in from New York when?"

"The night before the wedding, with Mum." Dan kept his eye on the auctioneer. So far no one had matched his bid.

"That's cutting things fine," Lee said.

"Going once," sang the official.

"There's some redesign needed on one of Johnny Depp's costumes." Ross scowled. In hospital Lee had learned that Viv was the chief costume designer for a Broadway remake of the musical *Kiss Me, Kate*. "I don't know why she didn't just put her foot down."

"Going twice!"

Dan glanced around, checking for late bids. "Even I couldn't say no to Depp."

Lee struggled to keep up. "So Depp's in the play?" He felt like he'd come into a movie halfway through and was still trying to work out what was going on—and how he fit into it.

"Sold to bidder number twelve," bellowed the auctioneer.

LEE'S SENSE OF dislocation only increased over the next twenty-four hours.

Dan found him plenty to do from moving the mobs of twenty bulls between the one-hectare cells made by electric fencing to checking on the recently weaned lambs. But the stillness of the countryside, the vast emptiness that amplified every occasional sound no longer felt like freedom; it felt like loneliness.

Revenge had filled the vacuum following his immediate return. But now that it was gone, desolation seemed to have taken its place. He'd lost Jules twice. If responsibility for the first could be attributed to mutual misunderstanding, bad management and bad luck, responsibility for the second rested squarely on his shoulders.

And they weren't as strong as they used to be.

Turned out the only manual job he could currently handle was tractor work—driving neat rows across the fields tilling, sowing and rolling in the brassica seed that would grow into forage for the bigger lambs in a couple of months.

Where would *he* be then? Other than out of Jules's life.

His first impulse to get the truth out there had been replaced by a desire to wait until as close to his departure as possible. Because he could only handle so much attentiveness and he was already close to his limit.

"The SAS needs instructors of your caliber," Ross said over a roast beef dinner the second night. His mates kept dropping casual suggestions like this into the conversation, thinking they were helping.

Lee considered telling Ice that sitting this close to men he considered brothers was all the military he could stand. "I'm weighing all options," he said instead.

"Don't discount a noncombat role," Ross persisted. "I never thought I'd say this but there's something incredibly satisfying about shaping young minds."

"God help them." Jo smiled at Lee at she passed the potatoes, her auburn hair glinting under the pendant lamps above the table. The baby bump might not be showing yet but she gave away her condition whenever she touched her flat stomach. Her hazel eyes were luminous. Only Jo seemed to sense his discomfort discussing a future career. She turned to Dan. "Honey, why did we ask Ice to be our baby's godfather again?"

"Because you owe me," Ross reminded her. "I helped you spin Shep into husband material in return for your firstborn. It's the Rumpelstiltskin clause."

"I did not promise that!"

"Some things don't change," Nate commented to Lee across the table. "These two still bicker like siblings."

Lee realized something. "And when Ross marries Viv you actually will be related," he said.

Jo stabbed a potato. "Viv may still come to her senses."

"Shame her brother didn't," her nemesis batted back.

The guys looked at Jo expectantly. She sighed. "Dammit, I got nothing. Blame my pregnancy brain."

"Want me to beat him up for you, honey?" Dan smiled at her from the head of the table but she returned a quick warning frown. Reminding him that someone at the table might find the comment insensitive.

Everyone concentrated on their plates. Knives and forks chinked on china. It had been like this throughout dinner, all of them second-guessing his reactions. The silence grew awkward. "I think I'm pregnant, too," Lee said, and everyone's head lifted. "I can't think of a comeback, either."

They laughed, a little too heartily.

"You could go to medical school," Nate said. "Become a doctor."

Inwardly Lee sighed. "I *could.*"

As soon as it was polite he cleared the table. "Dishes are still a novelty," he insisted when his hosts protested. "No, really, stay here, I've got this."

As he scraped plates, rinsed and loaded them into the dishwasher he noted the murmur of conversation developed more flow, got easier. The bursts of laughter came more frequently.

I don't fit in anymore. So, get over it.

He leaned on the counter and stared out the kitchen window at the stars, so much brighter away from civilization. Afghanistan had a spectacular night sky. Lee had seen it often in the early months as he was hustled from cave to cave to escape the night raids on Ajmal's village. Raids intent upon seizing him.

The headman's standoff with the rebels had worsened

when the Taliban's regional commander arrived and Ajmal could no longer rely on his son's grudging protection. It was one of the old man's great sorrows that his boy had eschewed the old ways for political power.

"The stars are beautiful, aren't they?" Jo bustled in, carrying condiments. "They're one of the things I love about living in the country."

"I'm enjoying seeing southern hemisphere stars again." He used to long for the Southern Cross, pointing the way home. Another burst of laughter came from the dining room. Lee returned to stacking the dishwasher.

"They're as giggly as schoolgirls since you've come home," Jo commented as she returned the salt and pepper shakers to the pantry. "High on happy."

Nice try. He smiled politely. "Yeah."

She hesitated. "All the career suggestions…they're only trying to help."

"And I appreciate it," he said. His friends had gotten on with their lives. And it was mean-spirited to feel resentful, left behind because he lacked direction. He'd never have with Jules what Dan had with Jo.

"They've all struggled to find their feet since the ambush. It does get better."

"Dan's enjoying this lifestyle, isn't he? Taking over the family farm."

"Very much." Nudging him away from the sink, Jo began rinsing the plates. "Particularly now that Herman's loosened the reins and is making more of his retirement." Dan's father was currently touring golf courses on Australia's Gold Coast.

Lee stacked the last of the dirty dishes. "I still can't believe his parents have separated." Pat Jansen had hightailed it to South America to learn the tango. Find herself. Maybe he should join her in Buenos Aires.

"The wedding's going to be challenging." Jo added soap to the dispenser and turned the dishwasher on. "It's the first time she and Herman will be together since she left. No doubt she'll be vocal about the changes I've made to her former home." The reception was being held here, at the family homestead.

Lee shook his head, trying not to grin.

"What!" Jo demanded, but she was already half laughing.

"You," he said. She'd been one of the guys when he'd left, Dan's best friend in civilian life. A tough cookie and astute businesswoman, she owned the local paper. "Not just married, barefoot and pregnant—" she'd kicked off her flats in the heat "—but scared of your mother-in-law."

"Not scared," she protested. "Invested... You'll have a mother-in-law soon who's way more work than mine."

He took a couple of seconds to process what she'd said. "You've met Jules's mother?"

"No, but Claire gets worked up about her on Jules's behalf." She put the kettle on, added tea bags to mugs. "You guys would have talked about this, right?"

"Oh, sure," he lied, encouraging her.

"It's not that we expected her mother to cancel her wedding because it was a week after the funeral and memorial services." Jo placed the mugs on a tray with a sugar bowl and jug of milk. "But she could have *tried* to postpone the honeymoon cruise and given her daughter emotional support. God knows Jules gave her plenty over the years." Curious, Lee waited for more, but she seemed to recollect herself. "Hey, it's none of my business."

"You've always been a crusader," he said. "Righting wrongs, fighting for the underdog."

"Like your fiancée," she replied. "It's a shame Jules had

too much work to catch up on to come with you." The kettle boiled; she filled the mugs.

Lee replied with a noncommittal murmur.

"I've never met anyone who devotes so much time to their career." Jo waited for the tea to brew. "And that's coming from someone who was back at work within weeks of a mastectomy."

"What?" he said, stunned.

"Oh, dear. I thought Dan told you my big secret. It's okay," she reassured him, removing the tea bags. "I've been clear over two years. That's why we're having this baby."

"Are you…cured?"

"Time will tell. So far so good."

"Jesus, Jo." Forgetting his own troubles, he hugged her. "Dan was with me at the hospital for five days. Why in hell didn't he tell me?"

"He's Shep, remember? You'd just been rescued. You were recovering. And like I said, we're good now." Opening a cupboard, she pulled out two packets of biscuits.

Following her lead, he kept his tone light. "So what other secrets are my friends hiding because they don't believe I can deal with them yet?"

Something close to guilt flashed in her eyes. Smiling, she held up the packets. "Choc chip or peanut brownies?"

"Both," he said, interpreting her guilt. So everyone knew about Mark. Though what the hell difference did it make now anyway?

Jo plated the biscuits. But she must have read something in his expression, because her gaze was troubled as she passed him the tray to carry.

"Wait." She stopped him as they were leaving the kitchen. "I understand what it's like to go through the motions when you're wondering if things will ever be normal again. Hang in there, because it will get better. And you've got Jules. You two have settled that future—it makes things easier."

Lee sighed. "Listen, there's something I need to tell you all…. Grab the guys, let's go sit outside on the porch."

He needed the space, and the dark might make this easier.

CHAPTER FIFTEEN

NERVOUS ADRENALINE PROPELLING her forward at a cracking pace, Jules walked her suburban neighborhood at seven-thirty Saturday night.

Her real estate agent had phoned with an eager out-of-towner on the hook, someone who could only view right now, and suggested Jules leave the house. "Instead of hovering anxiously and signaling that you'll all but give it away, like you did last time," Chloe had said with acid diplomacy.

At a major intersection, Jules stopped for the lights, jiggling from foot to foot at the delay. Nothing was happening fast enough. She desperately needed bites, not nibbles, on the house or she'd be forced to accept Nick's offer.

The Walk sign flashed, and Jules surged forward, hanging a right toward the waterfront, where she could march unimpeded by traffic.

Pinning Claire to a meeting was also proving difficult—her best friend had a fully booked weekend with Lewis at some swim meet. "Find me an hour," she'd pleaded. "It's important."

Pulling out her cell, she checked again whether she'd missed a message, wishing she and Lee had synchronized a time for their disclosures. Jules didn't want Claire getting the news secondhand from Nate. She owed her best friend the truth in person.

"She'll forgive me," Jules said aloud as she stepped out

from the shelter of the buildings onto the boardwalk. The sharp wind whipped her words away.

The sea was as turbulent as her emotions; whitecaps scudded in the harbor under a howling crosswind. Ignoring the clouds amassing overhead, Jules zipped her sweatshirt and kept walking, trying not to think about how many relationships she could lose today.

A squally shower began to blow in across the sea. She felt the first warning drops on her face and ducked under one of the waterfront pohutukawas to wait it out. How had a loner ended up invested in so many people?

Her cell chimed, Claire's name flashed on the screen and Jules answered in relief mixed with trepidation. "Hey."

"I've got a two-hour window between picking Lewis up from a swim meet and going for a late dessert at Nana's. Are you at home?"

"No—" *dammit* "—walking. And I'm miles away." Raindrops splattered through the canopy. Jules moved closer to the trunk and glanced at her immediate surroundings. This part of the waterfront was unfamiliar, but across the road the bright light of a quayside bar caught her eye.

"Meet me at a bar called Barracudas," she said. "It's somewhere on the waterfront."

"See you soon."

Swallowing hard, Jules rang off. Not long now.

BARRACUDAS PROVED TO be a seedy, dimly lit sports bar whose clientele consisted of armchair athletes drinking copious amounts of beer while yelling at various big-screen TVs. In the commercial breaks they ogled passing booty. Not the most suitable venue to unburden your soul.

Every male swiveled to check out the fresh meat when Claire arrived fifteen minutes later, pausing at the door to scan the dim interior. Seeing Jules sitting by the window, she strolled over, attracting a couple of wolf whistles en route.

"I'd hug you," she said as she stopped beside Jules's table, "but I figure these idiots would only get excited at the girl-on-girl action. Would you like to go somewhere more civilized?"

She wanted to get this over with. "It's okay, I've perfected the brush-off technique." Jules bared her teeth at a guy gawking at them from a bar stool and he swung back to the screen. "If you're rude enough they leave you alone."

Claire eyed the tumbler of Scotch in front of her. "Four in the afternoon is a little early for the hard stuff, isn't it?"

"Not where I'm sitting."

"That sounds ominous. Hang on." Crossing to the bar, Claire ordered an orange juice. Two guys watching a game-fishing show tried to chat her up and she handed them business cards. "Here, improve your catch quota."

Oh, God, she was going to miss this woman. Jules knocked back her whiskey.

Claire returned and took a seat. "I'm pretty sure I know what you want to talk about."

"Wh-what?"

"You and Lee sleeping apart. Nate saw your clothes in the spare room when we came to dinner. Lee's finding intimacy difficult."

"No...I mean, yes...but that's not it. In fact, it's not even relevant now. The engagement's been a sham for both of us."

"Excuse me?"

"Lee proposed to me before he deployed. I turned him down." Nervously swirling the ice in her empty glass, Jules said it fast. "I wanted more time. He thought it meant I didn't love him and walked out. I took the ring from the guys for so many reasons...but mainly from wishful thinking and to save everyone further misery." Jules paused to take a breath. Across the table Claire sat like a statue. "I told his dad when I discovered Ian was going to leave me Lee's money. He left it to me anyway. I know this is a terrible—"

"I need alcohol." Abruptly Claire stood and returned to the bar. Jules laid her face on the greasy tabletop. It was cool against her cheek. Night had closed in and she could see her face reflected in the window. She looked like a kid in need of a hug.

A few minutes later another glass of whiskey landed in front of her. "I take it this is what the split is about. You told Lee?"

"Oh, he knew." Wearily Jules sat up and raised the whiskey, noticing that Claire had opted for a glass of white wine. "He's been feigning amnesia. He made the airport proposal to put the squeeze on me."

"Son of a—"

Jules looked up as Claire took a swig of wine. "You two are as bad as each other."

"I'm sorry," she said.

Her best friend's stare was as merciless as a prison searchlight. "After all we've been through together, Jules. You should have *told* me."

"You were dealing with Steve's death. Did you really want to know that Lee died a bitter man or that I was riddled with guilt?"

Some of the fierceness went out of Claire's eyes. "Go on."

"The guys offered me Lee's ring at Ross's hospital bedside. He'd all but had last rites, Nate was a zombie and Dan…" She cupped her hands around the whiskey, needing even the illusion of warmth. "Dan was desperate for something good to cling to."

How could she explain the allure of the ring? "And the

diamond seemed like a symbol of a day when Lee still loved me."

She pushed the whiskey away. "And then I got so invested in being part of a group of people who cared about one another, who were good for one another. I tried to distance myself, but I'd created a myth and as far as you were all concerned I was family." She snorted in self-disgust. "And I'm making excuses."

"No, we did drag you into the tribe," Claire conceded. "I don't know what I would have done without you through those early months. But why didn't you tell me later? When our lives returned to some semblance of normalcy?"

"By the time my good reason for keeping the secret became irrelevant I'd built relationships. There was too much to lose. Instead I got busy, too busy to think." She swallowed hard. "With the passing of time you forget the desperation that drove you to it. All you're left with is shame."

"Oh, honey, I understand the corrosive power of guilt." Her friend stretched her hand across the table and Jules grasped it. "I couldn't mourn Steve because I was too angry that he'd deployed when he'd promised me he'd leave the service. Forgiving him let me love him again and opened the door to a new life with Nate."

"You're a better person than I am," Jules said.

"Then I'd best make my own confession. I might wish you'd told me earlier, but I probably would have lost you, because I didn't love you then as the sister I do now."

Tearfully, Jules bit her lip. "Thank you," she managed to say at last. "I love you, too."

Claire grinned. "These idiots are watching us hold hands."

With a watery laugh, Jules leaned forward and hugged her friend tight. "Thank you," she repeated.

"Does it have to be over?" Claire asked, twenty minutes later after Jules explained why she was still wearing the ring. "You might think differently when you're not so angry and sad."

"We're done."

"The two of you love each other," Claire persisted. "You could still work this out. Even if you make Lee suffer a while before—"

"You mean go back to game playing? No." It was important Claire understood—there was no equivocation on this. "I grew up with a mother who let her emotions overrule her judgment and I swore I'd never follow in her footsteps. Lee made me forget that vow, not once but twice. If you had our history—my childhood—would you take him back?"

Claire hesitated and then picked up the coffee she'd moved on to.

"Me, neither," Jules said sadly. "Any chance of a lift home?"

THEY'D JUST PULLED into Jules's driveway when Claire received a text. Engine idling, her best friend read it and then looked over to the passenger seat with an unreadable expression. "That was Nate. Lee's told them."

Jules ignored the swoop, like the brush of a dark-winged predator, across the pit of her stomach. Casually she undid her seat belt. "What's the reaction?" Not everyone would be as forgiving as Claire.

"They're all in shock."

"That's understandable." Jules opened the passenger door. "Give my love to Lewis and Steve's mum."

"If you don't want to be alone, come have dessert with me. Ellie makes a mean pavlova."

"I fancy an early night, but thanks for the offer. And thank you for forgiving me." A telltale quiver threaded her next words. "You're the best."

"Are you sure you don't need moral support?"

"Positive." She smiled. "Good night." Conscious that Claire was still wavering about what to do next, Jules put a jaunty spring in her step as she approached the house, turning at the front step to give her best friend a cheerful wave. She was a big girl who could handle the emotional fallout of this breakup alone.

Inside, she dragged her pajamas from under the pillow and then took a shower. With painstaking thoroughness she applied night cream and brushed her teeth. Within twenty minutes of being dropped off, she was under the covers, lights off.

And crying herself to sleep.

NATE WAS THE FIRST to recover after Lee dropped the breakup bombshell. The rattan chair squeaked as he leaned forward. Even in the moonlight, his bewilderment was easily decipherable. "What the hell did you do that was so bad, Lee, that the woman who recommitted to spending the rest of her life with you six days ago wouldn't forgive?"

Lee tipped the remains of his tea over the balustrade beside him. Even two sugars couldn't help the sour taste in his mouth. "When I proposed at the aerodrome I didn't mean it. I was punishing her for taking my ring from you guys when she'd turned me down on the eve of leaving for Afghanistan."

Sitting next to his wife on the swinging love seat, Dan cursed as he spilled his drink. "What?"

Lee looked up at the stars, finding the Southern Cross with its false promises of home. "It was my bad. She wanted more time. I got pissed and walked out on her. I didn't contact her in those first couple of weeks, remember? Let her stew."

"But…" The rattan squeaked again. Nate was clearly

struggling to get his head around it. "She accepted your ring when we offered it."

"Because she didn't want you thinking I'd died unhappy. And she needed to believe I would've come to my senses and realized she was the best thing that ever happened to me." He found Venus, the bright evening star, low on the horizon. "When I heard she'd taken the money I'd left her when my father died, I thought she was being an opportunist."

He closed his eyes briefly under a new wave of self-disgust. "Except she'd already told Dad the truth."

"She told Ian but not us?" Ross snapped. He balanced on the porch railing, his big silhouette incongruous with the ghostly white filigree edging the overhang.

"To talk Dad out of leaving her the money," Lee clarified. "Except he didn't care because he understood what I should have if I wasn't so fricking screwed up and angry." He dug his fingers into the arms of his rattan chair. "That Jules has a pure heart. Instead I believed the worst, faked amnesia and started playing mind games."

Jo found her voice. "You faked amnesia?" She and Dan had stopped swinging in the love seat and had their feet planted firmly on the deck.

"How about I start from the beginning."

Lee filled them in.

"No wonder Jules looked like a trapped possum when we offered her the ring." Dan shook his head. "I still can't believe she accepted it."

"She thought you needed to believe you were following my wishes." Lee glanced among his friends, gauging reactions. Only Ross was still scowling.

"Actually, I'm glad she didn't tell me," Nate reflected. "I was screwed up enough at the time."

"Anyway, Jules wants out as soon as possible and,

frankly, I don't blame her," Lee continued. "Unfortunately it's not that simple." He filled them in on the decision to gradually and quietly end the engagement.

"So what's your real plan?" Ross asked.

"That is the real plan. Our relationship has always been about what I wanted. Now it's about what Jules wants. And that's not me."

"Walking away work for you the first time?" Dan asked.

"This is different."

"Let me get this straight," said Nate. "The guy who swept a cynic off her feet on their first date—" he started ticking off points on his fingers "—who survived an ambush, then torture and captivity…who's been dead nineteen months, yet got a yes to his marriage proposal five minutes after the plane landed…" His dark eyes challenged Lee. "*That* guy is giving up?"

Lee started to get irritated. It was hard enough accepting Jules's decision without his friends making it harder. "She only said yes at the airport to buy time until I was well enough to hear the truth," he reminded them. "For some reason she thought I was…" he drew quote marks in the air "…fragile."

In the subsequent silence he heard crickets chirping.

"For the last time I have *not* got PTSD."

"I'll go make more tea," Jo suggested glancing around at four set male jaws. "Why don't you guys return to Lee's immediate problem."

As opposed to what, Lee thought, my long-term problem?

"Think about what Jules needs," suggested Nate.

"For me to get lost," Lee rasped. "She was very clear on that."

"Forget what she said, she's hurting," Dan said patiently. "Nate's right. Figure out what she needs and give her that."

Lee felt a familiar sense of helplessness. "What the hell does that even mean?"

"I'm glad you asked." Clearly having no clue, Dan sat back and indicated for Ross to take over.

Ice shrugged. "What Viv needs from me is faith. She's testing me with this wedding, not consciously, but she's testing my patience and trust in her. Hell, she's not even in the country and we're doing a big wedding. Can Ice the control freak see past Hurricane Viv—the woman everyone thinks is random and erratic—to the person she and I know is brilliant and creative, who can always pull a rabbit out of the hat when it's needed? And I'll pass her test. I'll have a goddamned heart attack doing it," he added. "But I'll pass."

There was a following silence. "Okay," Dan said. "You can marry my little sister."

Ross snorted. "It's so sweet how you think you could stop me...and you're up next, by the way."

"Okay." Dan thought about it. "Jo needs me to forget her cancer may come back. And that means not fussing. It means leaving her with a 'see you in a couple of days' even when I don't want to and taking each other for granted like a normal couple. It means matching my wife's courage and believing that no matter what happens in the future—" he swallowed "—we're solid."

Lee struggled to hide his emotion. He noticed he wasn't alone, either.

Ice put a hand on his future brother-in-law's shoulder.

"Claire needs loyalty," Nate said steadily. "She needs a guy who will always put her first because—and I'm not saying this with anything but love and respect—Steve didn't always."

Lee wasn't sure how to respond to that, so he said nothing. Nate sighed. "Mate, we've watched Jules grieve for close to two years. Trust me, she loves you."

"As she pointed out, what good is love without trust? I've promised her no more games and I meant it. My hands are tied."

Ross grinned. "Isn't it lucky then, that you have us."

"THERE'S A GUY here to see you," her secretary said on Monday morning, and Jules's heart walloped her rib cage before she recalled that Margie knew Lee by sight. And he'd stopped in Auckland for two nights to break the news to his family.

She didn't have to deal with him again until Wednesday.

She hadn't heard from him since he'd left Whangarei, and was beginning to regret asking for a "no contact" few days.

"Says he hasn't got an appointment but figures you'll see him." Margie glanced at her note. "Ross Coltrane."

Jules swallowed. It had been thirty-six hours since Claire told her the guys knew she'd lied to them and until now she hadn't heard a peep from any of them. And the two reactions she dreaded most were Lee's sister, Connie's—and Ross Coltrane's. Black and white were the only shades in Connie's moral palette, and Ice didn't suffer fools.

"Show him in," she said. On the bright side, she had no spirit left to crush.

Margie grinned. "If he's single, put in a good word for me."

"Sorry, he's getting married in less than three weeks." And was probably here to rescind her wedding invitation. She removed Lee's ring—no point rubbing salt into the wound—and hid it in the desk drawer.

"Corner office," she heard Margie say cheerfully. Bracing herself, Jules stood. Lot of good it would do her. Ice was six-two.

Ross limped in, still exuding a lethal grace. Without

even glancing in her direction, he selected a chair and sat down.

"Welcome," she said superfluously. Feeling awkward, she also sat.

Casually, Ice assessed his surroundings—the big desk, the Mac, her view of the park across the road through the third-story window. "So are you really this important," he asked, "or have you just borrowed this office to impress me?"

As his laser gaze swung toward her, Jules braced herself for the full glare of his accusation. There it was. Where was an SPF50 sunscreen when a girl needed it? "I'm sorry," she said simply.

"You bullshit your friends for nineteen months."

She raised her hands. "I have no excuses."

"Lee found some for you…said you wanted to save us more grief. Who needs to hear one of their best friends died with a broken heart? The fact that he's now *living* with a broken heart could lead to a robust discussion, but I don't have time to debate who wronged who the most. I have a wedding crisis." He added with a glitter in his gray eyes, "Fortunately, it's come at a time when you're predisposed to grovel to your friends."

She stared at him. "You're not concerned about what's happened between Lee and me?"

"Of course I am," he snapped, "but to paraphrase Bogart, the problems of two little people don't amount to a hill of beans compared to this crazy wedding."

"It was three little people," she corrected, unsure how to feel about this conversation. "And Bogie was referencing world problems not wedding problems."

"This wedding means the world to me. And to be blunt, I don't want you two ruining it. Not that I think either of you would do it deliberately—hell, I can appreciate that

you're both trying to get through this like grown-ups—
but it's a difficult time for me, too. Everything that can
go wrong is going wrong, including you two imploding a
few weeks out."

He paused, never taking his eyes off her. "My bride is
arriving in the country a scant six hours before the cere-
mony and Jo tells me *now* she can't be a bridesmaid because
she's likely to throw up through the service. Everyone else
gets morning sickness, but Swannie has to be different."

"Actually, afternoon sickness is quite—"

"I've got three groomsmen and only two bridesmaids.
Viv's sister and Claire. You and Jo are the same height."

"But Viv and I aren't close." The costume designer had
lived in New York for the past ten years; all their encoun-
ters had been in a group.

"Then she should be here to organize her own damn
wedding instead of checking Johnny Depp's inside leg mea-
surement. Look—" he leaned forward impatiently "—I
know it's awkward but I figured since you broke it off
you're less affected—"

"I'm not unaffected," she said. "I still have feelings for
him but—"

"But you have irreconcilable differences. Yeah, Lee said.
Whether he eventually talks you into giving him another
shot is his problem. I want to know if you'll help me with
mine."

Jules sat back. "Ross, you're not fooling me."

"I bow to your superior expertise in bullshitting people."

Her jaw dropped.

"Now, what the hell are you talking about?" he added
impatiently.

"You're…you're engineering a situation where we're
forced to continue this engagement for an extra week." At
the back of her mind Jules had a private escape clause. If

continued proximity got too hard, she could still put an end to it.

"Because I'm such an incurable romantic? Not everyone complicates his life the way you do, Jules. I'm not asking some stranger to be part of my wedding party, and Viv has approved you. You say you're sorry for lying to me." He folded his arms. "Prove it."

Jules started to doubt her instincts. But this was too damn convenient.

"No offense," she said. "But I need to corroborate your story." She punched in Jo's cell.

"I'm deeply hurt by your distrust."

Ignoring him, she swung her chair toward the window. "Jo? It's Jules."

"Jules…hang on…I'm in an editorial meeting."

The sound grew quieter as Jo obviously went in search of privacy. "How are you doing? I've been meaning to call but I wasn't sure if you were ready for a heart-to-heart."

Her throat tightened. "I'm not…but…let me apologize for deceiving everybody."

"Dan's got mixed feelings, but I think the truth would have made everything worse. You were all in a bad way."

"I guess we were," she said slowly. "Listen, I've got Ross here and—"

"Oh, good, he's asked you. Honest to God, the way he reacted you'd think I was nauseous on purpose. I'm really disappointed that I can't be part of the wedding party. But I'm like Mt. Vesuvius around two in the afternoon. And all kinds of scents set me off. I just can't risk it. I think our Iceman is in the midst of a global warming crisis so any help you can give him is appreciated."

"I'll think about it. And thanks…for forgiving me."

"I guess it's pointless asking you to pay it forward?"

"Best get back to your meeting."

Jo sighed. "That's what I thought. Bye."

"Bye."

"Well?" Ross demanded.

Jules got up and crossed to the wall cabinet, where she poured herself a glass of water from the pitcher.

"If it helps," he said, "I'm not impressed by Lee's tactics, either. The two of you deserve each other."

"Cut the bluster, Ice, and think this through. Should I even go to your wedding? I don't want to make things awkward for everybody."

"Jules, you've already made things awkward," he said drily. "Decide whether you're going to make them impossible."

"An elaborate scheme to try to get us back together won't work." She eyeballed him. "And you're only hurting Lee more if you're offering him false hope."

Ross returned a bland look. "Lee can take care of himself. Come to think of it, wasn't that why you dumped him? But let me double-check…" He pulled out his cell.

Jules spilled her water. "That's not necess—"

He held up a hand. "Lee, it's me. Jules will do it as long as you don't read it as encouragement…. Uh-huh…yep… I'll tell her." Ross cut the connection. "He said he's got the message loud and clear."

"Well, good."

"So are you going to help me make Viv Jansen the happiest woman in the world or what?"

"I can't drag this out, Ice." The words surrendered themselves. "It hurts too much."

Ross was silent a moment. "How many female friends do I have, Jules? I'll tell you," he said, not waiting for a reply. "Three. You, Claire and Jo. You're part of a very select group. Too select. I can't drop you until I find a replacement." He might have been joking; with Ice you never could tell. "If you repeat what I'm about to say I'll have to kill you. I'm scared shitless about getting this wedding right. You think I'd drive all the way up here—a four-hour round trip—otherwise?"

She had never, ever heard him admit to a weakness. Ever.

Jules sighed. "Where's the bloody dress?"

"Beacon Bay." Giving her a cherubic smile, he stood. "Jo will courier it up and my wedding planner will email you about a local fitting."

"I thought you were the wedding planner." She was already regretting this.

Ross limped to the door. "Viv's been coordinating the outfits from New York. The only expertise I have in dresses is taking them off and I'm keeping it that way." He paused before leaving, a rare warmth in his gray eyes. "Here's looking at you, kid."

Jules's resolve melted. "You're wel—"

"And get some sleep, a little sun. I need you looking good for the photos."

And he was gone.

CHAPTER SIXTEEN

"WELL, THAT WENT well," Lee murmured to his brother as they stood around the barbecue at their sister's house, staring at the sizzling meat.

Through the kitchen window, they could hear the angry chopping of a cucumber meeting its death interspersed with their brother-in-law's soothing tones.

Rob shrugged and picked up Phil's abandoned tongs. "You know Connie, she hates the idea she's been made a fool of." He turned the steaks before they'd seared, and Lee resisted the urge to confiscate the tongs. After Connie's reaction to Jules's so-called betrayal he couldn't afford to alienate a possible ally. "She'll be over it by the next Ice Age," Rob said cheerfully.

"Yeah," Lee replied glumly. "She does like to hold a grudge." She still brought up how much he'd embarrassed her with his burping rendition of "Happy Birthday" at her twenty-first. He'd been eight, for heaven's sake.

"Before I forget, with all this drama." Still clutching the tongs, Rob ducked inside the open French doors to the living room and returned with a plastic bag. He handed it over, slightly embarrassed. "A present."

Lee opened the bag and saw a couple of DVDs.

"Your porno collection?"

Rob frowned. "It's Dad's funeral and your memorial service...I said I'd make copies for you."

Now they were both embarrassed. "Right. Thanks." He closed the bag carefully. "I'm not sure if I—"

"Dad's might be hard viewing right now, but you should check out your memorial service. How many people get the chance to attend their own funeral? And we all said nice things about you."

It clearly meant something to Rob so Lee stopped arguing. "Thanks." Then he added curiously, "Did Jules speak?"

"Couldn't." His brother returned to mismanaging the barbecue. "And even if she'd wanted to, she had her hands full comforting her mother."

Lee recalled Jo's previous comments. "I never met her mother."

"Not that you'd have guessed it at your service," Rob said drily.

Their brother-in-law came back out, carrying a green salad, saw Rob turning the steaks again and winced. Plunking the bowl on the outdoor table, he firmly retrieved the tongs. "Thanks, mate, I'll take it from here."

Behind Rob's back, Phil rolled his eyes. Lee responded by refilling everyone's wineglass with more of the expensive cabernet sauvignon he'd bought to facilitate their forgiveness.

"You once mentioned that Jules was very good to Dad," he said casually to Rob. His brother hadn't voiced his opinion about her betrayal yet. Connie hadn't given him a chance to.

"Yes, she was." Rob raised his glass to the light to admire the color. "Jules was worth her weight in gold when Dad sank into depression."

"Dad was depressed?"

His brother just looked at him.

"Right," Lee said, "my horrible death." Until his rescue, he'd assumed his family believed he was alive. He hadn't known about the body swap. Or imagined why his fingertip had been cut off.

"I hope you're not discussing Jules without me," Connie hollered from the kitchen.

Lee lowered his voice. "Doesn't that count for something?"

Rob inhaled the bouquet of his replenished wine. "With me it does."

Lee glanced at to his brother-in-law and raised an eyebrow.

Phil shrugged. "I've always liked—"

"Don't go thinking you can divide and rule, Lee Davis." Connie bustled out with a bowl of potato salad and garlic bread. "And it doesn't matter how fond we *were* of Jules," she said to her husband, as she shunted the green salad aside to make room on the table. "Or how remorseful she may be. She let us down and she's still letting my baby brother down."

"C'mon, Con. Her motives stack up way better than mine."

"Defend her all you like, you won't change my mind. Boys!" She waved her arms at the pool where her three sons were playing a noisy game of water polo, oblivious to the drama. One made the mistake of looking up and she gestured for them to get out and get dressed.

"Aw!"

Lee turned to Phil, who was piling the steaks on a platter. "I love your new house. Did Jules do your legal work?"

"No, she did not." His wife answered for him.

Phil passed her the platter of meat. "But she did give us plenty of free advice, honey," he reminded her.

Appearing not to hear him, Connie found a place for it on the table and then waved at the boys, who'd resumed their game. "Now!"

Lee sat opposite Rob. "I'm guessing she helped Dad when he was checking out retirement homes, too."

"She checked out all the contracts." His brother inspected the steaks and chose one that was well cooked. "Didn't charge him a bean."

"I know what you're doing, Lee," Connie said impatiently, passing him the garlic bread. "You're trying to even the balance sheet, but the fact remains she lied to us. For nineteen months."

"Which makes forgiveness very difficult," he conceded, taking a couple of buttery rounds. Connie prided herself on her acuity.

"Almost impossible. Boys, don't make me come over there!"

"How lucky you've got Sunday sermons to remind you how it's done then." He helped himself to potato salad. There was a long pause during which both Rob and Phil concentrated on serving themselves food.

"That," Connie said with dignity, "is not fair." His sister was a stalwart of her local church.

He passed her the potato salad. "The Bible does say 'turn the other cheek.'"

"It also says 'an eye for an eye' and, as a practicing Christian, I can quote Bible verses a lot longer than you can, little brother."

Clearly the vengeful gene ran through the family. "We need to keep this between ourselves," he said, glancing to see where the boys were. Still in the pool.

"If the press get hold of it, I'll revert to Plan A, which is saying I dumped her. On national television," he added. Connie would hate that: him looking like the bad guy. "Because I forgive her, even if you can't."

His sister sniffed. "I suppose since you're still pretending to be engaged, she has to come to the family reunion."

"And Mikey's birthday party. I want to leave the kids out of this."

Frowning, Connie picked up her wineglass. "She's getting away with it, Lee. It's not fair."

"Please," he said. "For me."

Her mouth tightened in a straight line. "I won't tell the family, I won't tell the kids. I'll button my mouth for your sake."

It was the best he could hope for.

THE CADDY'S PINK rear wasn't protruding from the garage, which meant Jules wasn't home. Someone was here though. After paying the taxi driver, Lee eyed the unfamiliar Prius in the driveway.

He'd intended to stay a third night in Auckland, but his sister seemed to think that if she bitched about Jules long enough Lee would miraculously see things her way. For the sake of *their* relationship, it seemed politic to catch the next bus north.

And he'd missed Jules. Though his promise prohibited him from telling her that, he was free to acknowledge it privately. Much good it would do him, but as Ajmal's oft-quoted Pashtun proverb declared, "When he dies, then only is a man lost." Hope was hard to kill.

The front door was ajar with a key in it. Lee pushed it open. "Hello?" No response. Dumping his bag in the hallway, he followed the faint murmur of voices to the backyard.

"All it needs is an investment of energy and enthusiasm to significantly enhance the resale value." The woman's voice wasn't one he recognized. "And with the price reflecting the owner's desire for a quick sale it's a remarkable bargain for a buyer with vision… Oops!"

Three people stood in the garden, a young couple in their

early twenties, the wife juggling a fretful baby while her husband crouched to help a smartly dressed gray-haired woman ease her stiletto out of a crack in the concrete path.

"Thank you," she said, and then she caught sight of Lee. Her smile vanished. "You're a day early!" she wailed.

"Am I?" he said.

Recovering her composure, she smiled and came forward with her hand outstretched. "You're Lee Davis. I recognize you from TV, and you have no idea who I am." She pumped his hand. "Chloe Ferguson—a friend of Jules— wonderful to meet you."

Glancing between him and the couple clearly waiting for an introduction, she shrugged and handed him her card. *Chloe Ferguson, real estate agent. You dream it, I find it.* "And these are the Martins."

He gave them a cursory nod. "I'm confused. The house isn't for sale."

"It most certainly is!" Chloe flashed the Martins a reassuring smile. "This is the owner's fiancé," she explained. "You may have seen him on the news? The soldier held by the Taliban who came back from the dead."

"Oh, wow, I found your story so moving." Switching the baby to her other hip, the young woman grabbed his hand. She had big blue eyes and a dark braid down her back. "Daz, take a photo with your cell. D'ya mind?" she asked Lee.

"Well—"

"Let me take it," Chloe suggested. "Then you and your husband can both be in it."

Lee found himself between two strangers and a fretful baby. No wonder. The kid stank. Through his nose he said to Chloe, "So it went on the market today?"

"Jules will fill you in…. Smile!"

Five minutes later he watched them all leave. But not

before Chloe yanked out her cell as soon as she waved off the Martins, glancing toward the house. Warning Jules. Mr. Martin had let slip that this was their second visit in two weeks, which meant the place had been on the market before Lee got here. Why hadn't Jules told him?

He puzzled on it while he threw some protein power, a banana and frozen berries into the blender. She said she'd invested his money. Hadn't she? He tried to recall details of their first conversation but all he could bring to mind were feelings, not facts.

Frowning, he watched the fruit whiz into a pink smoothie, then switched off the machine and found the contract she'd given him. It was the reference to interest that made him assume the money was invested in a term deposit. Come to think of it, he'd asked her if that was covered by the bank and she'd answered evasively.

What the hell would she have spent one hundred and twenty thousand on in the past few...

Of course. The partnership. But if she was trying to sell the house to pay him back, why wouldn't she have told him, if not initially when she was trying to protect him, then the other night when they were supposedly laying all their cards on the table?

Lee could think of only one reason—and it annoyed the hell out of him.

"Hello?"

Arriving home after Chloe's text—one word in caps, BUSTED!—Jules felt as nervous as Inspector Clouseau waiting for Cato to leap from the shadows.

"Lee, you here?" How she got his money was none of his business and yet somehow she felt as if she'd cheated on the terms of their armistice. Jules reminded herself that she hadn't lied—she'd simply withheld personal information.

Chloe had said he was perfectly amiable, so maybe she was making too much of this. In the kitchen she peered out the window, craning her neck to check out every corner of backyard. "Looking for me?" said Lee behind her.

Jules yelped and spun around.

Across the hall, he leaned against the door to her office, fanning himself with the contract. His green eyes were as sharp as broken glass. "You led me to believe you invested my legacy."

"I did invest it. In my career." She added irritably, "Why are you here a day early, anyway?"

"We agreed to be honest with each other, Jules. Why didn't you tell me you're selling the house to pay me back?"

"What difference does it make where the money comes from as long as you're reimbursed?"

He looked at her as if she was crazy. "Because you'll end up homeless and I'm damned if I'll have that on my conscience. Take it off the market," he ordered.

Her heart sank. "How I repay you is up to me."

His jaw set. "No way am I letting you fire-sale your home. I'll be getting back pay—a lump sum—in a month or so. I'm in no hurry for the cash. I would have mentioned it the other night if I'd known how things stood."

She was an idiot. Of course he'd get back pay. But she'd been juggling too many balls.

Lee folded his arms. "You didn't admit you were struggling when we were doing true confessions because you knew I'd kick up a stink, didn't you?"

"Partly," she admitted. "But mostly I want to cut ties with you and get on with my life."

He flinched. "You detest me that much now, huh?"

"You wanted honesty," she deflected. A clean break was vital, not because she hated him, but because she loved him. And back pay didn't change that.

"Well, we have to find another way, because I won't accept any money resulting from selling the roof over your head. And that's final."

She could tell by the set of his jaw he wouldn't budge. "Fine," she said lightly. "I'll default to Plan B." *Look, Mum, I can make decisions entirely based on emotion.*

"What is it?" he demanded suspiciously.

"There were two of us in contention for the shareholding. The senior partner's happy for me to sell to the other guy—Nick—and he's expressed interest in buying."

Lee searched her eyes. "Will you lose any money?"

"Nope," she answered, determinedly cheerful. "He'll pay the same amount I bought it for."

TEN MINUTES LATE for her appointment, Jules tapped impatiently on the steering wheel as she turned left into Glenvar Close and decelerated, scanning for number twenty-four amidst the busy Friday lunchtime traffic.

Number twenty-eight flashed by. "Dammit!"

Checking her rearview mirror she pulled a U-turn and scanned the lot for a parking spot. None were sized for a pink tank, so she circled back to the street, finally parallel parking two blocks away.

Locking the car door, she checked her watch and set off at a fast clip. She really didn't have time for this bridesmaid business.

The tailor's shop where she was meeting Lee proved to be more of a walk-in wardrobe tucked between a second-hand bookstore and a motorcycle showroom. The louvered glass door rattled as Jules opened it. "Sorry, I'm a little late," she said to the middle-aged redhead, wearing a tape measure around her neck, who was chatting to Lee.

"You're Jules, I recognize you from TV." Smiling, the woman held out a hand. "I'm Maggie. And the delay isn't a problem. I measured your fiancé first." Though the grooms-men's suits were being rented, Ross wanted white dress shirts tailor-made.

Jules, still slightly awkward with her public role, turned to Lee. "Hi."

"Darling," he replied.

Funny how it didn't sound like an insult anymore.

"So!" She glanced at the fall of champagne satin on the counter beside him. "I'm guessing that's the bridesmaid dress?"

Lee touched the fabric. "The courier dropped it off this morning."

Maggie stared at his scarred fingers against the glossy satin and Jules moved to pick up the outfit before Lee no-ticed. "Let's get on with it, then. Where's your changing room?"

"You're in it." Maggie locked the door and twitched the louvers shut. "These premises are temporary while my old store is being refitted."

Jules looked at Lee.

"I'll wait outside," he said.

"Don't be silly, take a seat." Maggie cleared some fash-ion magazines off a filigree chair, and noticed that Jules hadn't moved. "There are hooks for your clothes behind you," she encouraged. "Here, I'll hold the gown."

Lee sat down.

Turning her back, Jules started unbuttoning her ruffled blouse, conscious that she was stripping in a room barely wide enough to swing a sewing machine.

"So," Maggie pulled down the side zip on the bridesmaid dress, "have you two set a wedding date yet?"

Jules let Lee answer.

"Not yet."

She hung her blouse on the hook and Maggie caught sight of the diamond.

"Your engagement ring's gorgeous. Can I take a closer look?"

Jules half turned in her lacy black bra and held out her hand.

"It's stunning!"

In her peripheral vision, Jules saw Lee studiously reading a bridal magazine.

Maggie finished admiring the ring. Relieved, Jules faced the wall again and started removing her pencil skirt, only recalling as it fell that she was wearing a G-string.

She tried not to bend too much to pick up the skirt. This was *awful*. Was it her imagination or could she hear Lee turning the pages faster?

"I love handling Wang," Maggie said cheerfully.

"Excuse me?" Lee said, clearly startled.

"Vera Wang…the designer of this dress, and the bride's I hear. If I could only match her skill."

"Quite," Lee said, and the wicked undercurrent in his reply sparked a chuckle in Jules's chest. She tried to hold it in, she really did. For heaven's sake, she was miserable, broke and lovelorn, and yet…and yet…

She began to giggle, silently at first, then snorting through her fingers and, finally, a helpless belly laugh. Shoulders shaking, she stood in her G-string and bra, clutching at her ribs, and howled.

Lee threw back his head and laughed with her. The sound soared to the ceiling, ricocheted off the narrow walls.

Maggie, smiling nervously, glanced toward the locked door.

Lee recovered first. "Sorry," he gasped. "It's just your reference to Wang."

"Oh," Maggie said politely. "Oh!" She started to laugh, too. "Good heavens, I never thought of that before."

Still grinning, Jules wiped her eyes dry and picked up the dress. "You need a guy in the room to make the joke work." As her amusement subsided, she grew self-conscious again under Lee's watchful eyes and she wiggled quickly into the thigh-length sheath.

Fully lined, the side-draped gown had an asymmetrical neckline and stylized bow detail on one side. An edging of filmy fabric at the hem kept it decent.

Maggie zipped her up. "There's not too much alteration needed at all, a couple of tucks at the waist. It's quite snug around the hips but you've got the bottom for it." She cast a mischievous look at Lee. "Wouldn't you agree?"

"She looks beautiful," he said huskily.

Jules swallowed. She should never have laughed with him. It had given him the wrong idea.

He must have sensed her discomfort because he stood and said, "I need some fresh air, I'll wait outside. Nice discussing Wang with you, Maggie."

"Don't!" Chuckling, the dressmaker unlocked the door.

Jules concentrated on her reflection in the mirror. Her desire wasn't going to go away simply because she wanted it to.

"What a lovely man," Maggie said as she began pinning adjustments. "So have you purchased your wedding dress yet?"

Jules shook her head.

"I'll give you my card so you can check out my website. My prices are very competitive with off-the-rack dresses. And I can recommend a good wedding florist, too." The dressmaker chatted on as she tucked and pinned.

Jules watched her own reflection get sadder and sadder. When she came out, ten minutes later, Lee said, "It's okay. I'm not here to make things worse than they already are by hitting on you."

"Good," Jules said sharply. She'd donned some emotional armor when she'd changed back into her own clothes.

"You're going back to the office, right?"

"Yes." She'd increased her hours again—the less time they spent together the better. Something in her balked at saying yes to Nick before the deadline. Who was she kidding? She was pinning her last hope on Saturday's lottery results.

"Then you need lunch first."

"I'll pick up a sandwich—"

"Come on," he said. "I'm hungry, too."

He ushered her into a coffee shop a few doors down. "Cappuccino with trim milk, right? What would you like to eat?"

She scanned the display. "A chicken and mango panini… thanks."

Taking a seat, her gaze followed him as he went to the counter. He seemed to have put on weight over the past week. He was looking healthier and—*not your concern anymore*. Jules counted the sugar cubes in the bowl.

"Here we go." Placing a tray on the table, Lee sat down opposite, passing Jules her order and taking his own. Two sausage rolls—ground beef rolled in savory pastry.

Her throat caught at the sight of them. "I forgot to buy you sausage rolls when you came home," she exclaimed. They were one of his favorite foods and his sister had always shipped them on his birthday, vacuum-packed, to wherever he'd been stationed.

"They were Connie's tradition, not ours," he said.

The steamy fragrance of meat, onions and herbs was making Jules's mouth water. Hungrily, she lifted her chicken panini.

"Speaking of my sister—" Lee picked up his own food "—she's still a little pissed with you. I thought I should warn you before Mikey's birthday party tomorrow."

"I suspected as much when you assured me she'd come around." Jules tried not to let the confirmation affect her appetite. "You were much more positive about Rob's and Phil's responses."

"I hoped a week's cooling-down period might do the trick," he admitted. "But cryogenic freezing might have worked better."

"I could stay home."

"You could, except we need to clear the air before the big family reunion next weekend. The local press will be taking photos."

"Okay." Jules ate her panini.

"No arguments?"

"The milk's been spilled, there's no point on crying over it. Let's get on with the cleanup."

He nodded. They ate for a few minutes in silence that was surprisingly companionable. "I checked in with HQ while I was in Auckland and started the resignation process," Lee commented.

Jules couldn't hide her delight. "You've decided then."

"My military career's over." He added more ketchup to his plate.

"Do you know what you want to do instead?"

"Not a clue." He dipped his sausage roll into the ketchup and took a reflective bite. "But after spending this morning on the phone chasing wedding RSVPs to help Ross out, I can tell you it *won't* be a wedding planner's assistant."

Jules finished her panini and wiped her fingers with a napkin. "Tell me the truth," she said. "Is the wedding some part of a dastardly plot to keep us together?"

"Not on my part...I can't speak for Ross. And without

wanting to rub salt into the wound, you're the one who wove herself into the fabric of my life. We have a lot of people we care about in common now."

"I know," she said glumly. "It's why I said yes to this bridesmaid thing."

It was easier talking in a neutral environment. At home she felt more guarded. "Where will you live?" she asked. The question that had been pricking her. "When this is all over." *When we're done.* "With Connie or Rob?"

"God, no!"

"Any of the guys would happily have you stay."

"And I'd love to play house with loved-up couples."

She grimaced. "Fair comment."

Lee eyed her over the rim of his cup. "What does it matter to you where I go?"

"We're trying to be friends," she reminded him.

He smiled. "I do have some ideas," he admitted. "I might buy another Harley and take a road trip around New Zealand for a few months. Or maybe I'll rent a place on a rugged coastline—somewhere remote and beautiful—and commune with nature."

Jules frowned. "But is isolation good for you? I mean, so soon after your release?"

Lee put down his cup. "We're strictly friends?"

"Yes."

"Then you have no say." He stood. "I'll let you get back to work."

CHAPTER SEVENTEEN

WITHIN FIVE MINUTES of arriving at Mikey's birthday party, Jules knew a thousand years of cryogenic freezing wouldn't thaw Connie's animosity toward her. Despite the polite welcome, Little Mrs. Sunshine smoldered with resentment.

Jules turned to greet Rob and Phil, who reintroduced her to his parents.

"Congratulations on your engagement. How delightful," Phil's mother said.

Connie gave a loud sniff, which she explained away as hay fever. "Mikey!" she shouted in the direction of the pool. "Come greet your uncle and his *fiancée*."

Jules was quickly surrounded by kids, the birthday boy's welcome more effusive after he glimpsed his present. As she watched him unwrap the box disguising an iTunes gift voucher, Jules was conscious of Lee having a quiet word with his sister. Connie responded with the same sulkiness she might have expected from one of her kids. Faintly, Jules caught, "I *am* trying."

Rob heard it, too, and glanced at her sympathetically.

"Hey," she murmured, "I deserve this." Whatever Lee's sister wanted to throw at her was entirely justified.

"It's because she considered you family," Rob said as they stepped out of range of some overexuberant pool splashing. "With you and Lee splitting up, it's a double blow."

Her cheeks heating, Jules stumbled through another explanation and apology, which he waved away. "Speaking for myself, I hope you'll remain part of the family."

"That's not going to happen." Her tone was gentle but firm. "I'm afraid your brother and I have burned too many bridges for that."

"It's not conditional on you and Lee reconciling," he clarified. "Under the circumstances, I think your decision not to forgive him is perfectly logical. You don't want to get hurt."

"Thanks for understanding," she said, slightly uncomfortable with the tenor of this conversation. And unsure why she felt a twinge of cowardice.

Jules ended up spending most of the afternoon by Rob's side, his acceptance of the situation exactly the right balm. Conversation naturally seemed to revolve around his passion, which was genealogy.

"Why did you never marry?" she asked curiously, after he expounded on the best research websites. To their left, Lee was dispensing sodas from a cooler, tossing each one with lazy accuracy to delighted thirteen-year-old boys. "With your interest in family trees I would have thought you'd want to add a few sprigs of your own."

He adjusted the table umbrella to shade the avocado dip that had begun browning in the sun. "I saw what Dad went through after Mum died and decided marriage wasn't for me. Watching you after Lee died only reinforced my decision."

Jules took a moment to reply. "Your mother's death had a huge impact on you guys. How lucky you were all so close to Ian."

"We weren't—then. Mum was the homemaker, Dad the provider, working long hours. He was a Sunday treat to us. But her death impacted Lee most. He was only eleven, whereas Con and I had already left home."

Jules tried to fathom the disconnect between the Ian she'd known, the loving center of this family and the workaholic Rob described. It was easier than imagining a lonely little boy left motherless. "So Ian took over?"

A shadow fell over the grass. The tingle at the nape of Jules's neck told her exactly who it was.

"Dad took six weeks' leave then went back to work with reduced hours," Lee answered, pulling up a chair and joining them. "Basically he restructured his life for me."

"He was a good man," Rob said gruffly, raising his coffee mug.

His younger brother chinked it with his own. "The best... Rob, you need sunscreen. The back of your neck is the color of an Afghani sunset."

Jules tilted her deck chair to check. "Ouch, he's right. Sorry I didn't notice."

Putting a tentative hand on his neck, Rob winced. "I think I'll move inside."

He left and they were alone for the first time since they'd arrived.

"I'm sorry about Connie," Lee said.

"She has a right to be disappointed. And thanks... You said you wouldn't make this—us—awkward at public gatherings and you haven't." She hesitated. "On the subject of Afghanistan, can I ask you something?"

"You can ask," he said cautiously.

"Who is Ajmal?"

Lee watched the kids, chattering as they fixed a volleyball net across the pool.

"Don't answer if you—"

"Ajmal was my reluctant protector and, later, my friend." Lee began talking about a creed called Pashtunwali and Jules listened, fascinated, as he described his petition for sanctuary, and the obligation the old village headman felt because Lee had once treated his grandchild.

She could barely comprehend the world he described.

"By accepting my request, Ajmal obligated his clan as well as his village to protect me. Fortunately, his family connections stretched across all the Taliban supply routes. The militants can't function without local support—and his son was a local Taliban commander—so they didn't immediately bomb his village into oblivion. Instead, they relied on a combination of threats and dawn raids. Ajmal hid me in caves while he tried to negotiate some kind of compromise."

"Why didn't he just let you go?"

"Because he couldn't be sure I wouldn't turn against him. I was the enemy, remember, Special Forces. Ajmal knew what I could bring down on them. His Taliban son would be at risk."

"He didn't accept his father's decision to offer you sanctuary?"

"To Ajmal's sorrow, no."

"Uncle Lee!" Mikey ran over, breathless. "We're set up for water volleyball and we've picked teams. You're on mine."

"Great, let's kick some ass. So are you getting wet today?" he asked Jules.

She'd bought her swimsuit; in this clan, sitting on the sidelines was frowned upon.

But now she was shy. "If you've got enough people…"

"C'mon, Jules." Mikey tugged her out of her chair. "You have to because it's my birthday and…and…"

"Giving up isn't an option," his uncle supplied.

"Yeah, what he said…go get changed." Mikey shoved her bag at her.

"Okay, okay!" Laughing, she headed to the house.

Glimpsing Connie in the master bedroom, Jules hesitated. The other woman was standing in front of the mirror in a one-piece pulling her hair into a ponytail. Their eyes met in the reflection.

"I'm sorry."

"And that's supposed to make it all right?"

"No." No one knew better than Jules. Sometimes parting ways was the only thing left to do.

"Then we understand each other." Connie turned away from the mirror. "In public I'll play nice to save my brother further distress, but in private, I refuse to engage." Recognizing the pun she'd accidentally made, the older woman grimaced. "Now hurry up and change. You're on my team."

LEE HAD WATCHED Jules walk to the house, wondering if she'd made the connection. *Giving up isn't an option.*

He already wore board shorts, but he stepped around the side of the house to strip off his good T-shirt and replace it with one he could get wet. He didn't want to scare the kids by going topless. Bundling up his good shirt, Lee returned poolside and, ignoring the moans and groans, made all the kids reapply sunscreen while they waited for the adults to reappear.

He'd told everybody he wanted no scheming or interfering, but Ross had steamed ahead anyway. In Ice's case, Lee suspected, with Jo and Dan's abetting.

But he couldn't control their actions—clearly!—so he'd adopted a "don't ask, don't tell" policy. Nate and Claire had already assured him they'd stay out of it, which he appreciated. They were closest to Jules and their loyalties were already torn.

His only plan was to give her the time she needed to get past their emotional reunion and remember she loved him.

And maybe, just maybe he'd work out the right words to convince her to give him another chance.

The tough part was working out what she needed. Because if she reconsidered, he wanted to be a man who deserved her.

An hour later, after he'd set the birthday boy up for the slam dunk that sealed the match, the kids were devouring what remained of the birthday cake and the exhausted adults were sharing a last cup of tea.

"Have you ever thought about working with kids?" Jules asked him. "You're so good with them."

There were murmurs of assent around the table.

Lee had considered it. "I don't think a classroom would suit me."

"Didn't a couple of ex SAS set up a youth charity for at-risk teens a few months ago?" Jules pulled a face. "Of course, you wouldn't know that. It's based at Tutukaka—" twenty minutes from Whangarei "—and it's an outdoor adventure facility that teaches life skills. Ask Nate about it."

"Thanks, I will."

"How did you become a lawyer?" Rob asked Jules.

"Boring story," she said.

"You listened to all his," Lee said, and earned a punch on the arm from his brother.

"I owe it all to one of my mother's boyfriends," said Jules. Absently she finger combed her damp hair. Lee wanted to take over. Jules in her red bathing suit rising to punch the volleyball over the net would haunt him tonight.

"He was a lawyer, too?" Connie asked, revealing a slight aversion in her emphasis of the word.

"No, a lazy, shiftless real estate agent," Jules replied good-humoredly. If she'd recognized the insult she wasn't acknowledging it. "Patrick did have the gift of the gab, though, because Mum never begrudged supporting him between his rare sales."

Phil sliced himself a second piece of birthday cake. "This story sounds fun."

"Not really." Jules loosened a tangle. "Patrick lived with us just long enough claim a half share in the family home when they split."

Rob was horrified. "Wasn't it in your mother's name?"

"Didn't matter. Neither did the fact that his contributions to the mortgage had been patchy. Pat made them when he could afford to. He even had the gall to say he babysat when Mum worked night shifts. As though I hadn't been looking after myself for years. He won his claim. We had to sell to pay him out and afterward moved to an apartment where we could afford the rent."

"Hey, Uncle Lee, watch this." Mikey and two friends did a simultaneous water-bomb into the pool. Every adult ducked as water sprayed the table.

"One at a time!" his father yelled.

Laughing, Jules brushed water off her bare arms. "And that's when I decided to become a lawyer. To protect people like my mother from poor decisions."

Jules noticed everyone's discomfort—even Connie looked appalled. "Did I make it sound like we ended up in the workhouse?" she said, trying to laugh it off. "We found a nice apartment and I never went hungry. Mum's always been a tireless worker. She had to be with so many dependents."

Turning her childhood into a joke again. It was probably the way she coped with it.

Connie couldn't help herself. "I hope your mother learned her lesson."

Jules's smile froze and Lee helped her out. "Helen did eventually find a prince, didn't she?"

"Yes," she answered brightly. "And I even talked her into a prenup."

So many pennies dropped for Lee, he could have collected them and opened a bank. He'd already guessed that Jules's mother wasn't going to win any parenting awards. His ex-fiancée's childhood wasn't the situation comedy she'd sold him, but until now he hadn't appreciated the ramifications her upbringing had on *their* relationship.

"I should go. I've got a ninety-minute drive ahead of me." Jules stood and started making her goodbyes.

"You're not leaving together?" Phil's dad said in surprise.

"Lee's staying on for a couple of nights," Jules explained.

"Tests," Lee added vaguely. "Military stuff." He was giving her space as per their agreement. "I'll walk you out to the car."

"I just figured out what spooked you into suggesting we slow things down," he said casually when they'd left the others and stood by the Pink Lady. "It was adding me to your five-year plan, wasn't it?"

Hunting through her bag, Jules said, "Where are my car keys?"

But this was too important to let go.

"Right from the start I was crazy about you," he said. "But, of course, you'd heard it all before—from the bullshit artists romancing your mother."

"*Here* they are." She pulled the keys out of her checkbook.

"Honesty works both ways," he reminded her.

Jules shrugged. "You used indelible ink on my planner," she accused him. "Even though there was a pencil right beside it."

"Pretty scary to fall so hard and fast into something you didn't even believe in," he guessed.

"The grand passion, soul mates… I *hate* that stuff." Jules unlocked the Pink Lady. "If I hadn't loved you I would have dumped you there and then but I talked myself down, told myself to take a deep breath and see what happened after your deployment."

"And then I blew it with an impulsive proposal. I might as well have showed up with a straitjacket."

She shifted uncomfortably. "I need to go if I'm going to beat the traffic."

"Sure." Lee opened her car door. "Safe journey. See you in a couple of days."

He watched the Pink Lady until the taillights disappeared from the end of the street. She'd given him something to work with. Lee took that as progress.

CHANGING GEARS ON Jules's road bike, Lee veered off the busy main street and down the towpath along the waterfront, grateful for the dappled shade of the trees as he rode the last few miles home.

Seagulls ripping into a bread roll rose squawking and flapping at the interruption as he whizzed through their midst. He glanced down at the discarded scraps, which not long ago would have represented a meal to him. Different worlds.

A fellow cyclist whizzed by and he nodded a greeting, grateful for the anonymity of his helmet and sunglasses. Recognition since the *60 Minutes* segment had increased, though generally people left him alone. It was the pity in their expressions that he couldn't stand.

He hit the last hill before home, dropped down a couple of gears and dug in for the climb. He hadn't yet made it to the top, but every day he'd got a little farther before his lungs and legs gave out. Today, he thought as his thigh muscles began to scream. Today.

Sucking in warm air, he dropped another gear and stood on the pedals, forcing his shaky legs to deliver. Only when he crested the hill with his lungs burning did Lee allow himself a rest stop and a celebratory fist pump.

He reached down to the holder on the chassis for his water bottle, took a swig and replaced it, automatically finding Jules's house in the valley, its lichen-streaked iron roof standing out from its neighbors.

It had been nearly a week since Mikey's party and in every area he felt he was making real progress. He was putting on weight, his fitness was improving and his strict adherence to their armistice agreement was softening Jules. Maybe in the way snow softened in daylight only to refreeze again overnight, but there was a thawing. He could feel it. Sometimes she even turned her back on him. That took trust.

Screw it, he was a romantic and whatever it took, he'd get the girl.

For now it was enough that she liked him—sometimes.

The wedding was in a week, after which he'd move out. But there would be lots of time together because of it, and watching Viv and Ross pledge their vows might...

Lee snorted.

Yeah, and Jules is such a sucker for romance.

He resumed his ride, coasting down the other side of the hill, happy to let gravity do the work.

All his life he'd been a full-speed doer. Now one of his favorite moments was standing on the back step first thing in the morning. Cupping a mug of fresh coffee and gazing across the dew-soaked lawn to the plum tree where spiderwebs sparkled like jeweled dream catchers. For now it was enough that he kept the faith.

The bike gathered speed. Enjoying the breeze on his face, Lee weaved skillfully through traffic, reluctant to apply his brakes. At the bottom of the hill he bounced the curb and squealed to a stop outside the gas station. The tires on the bike needed air.

One of his new rituals was to buy a sports drink and ingredients for dinner at the grocery store next door while enjoying a chat with the owner, Rajesh. He couldn't keep relying on friends and family to run defense. And the occasional introduction to other customers was good for his rusty social skills—the boat launch tomorrow was going to be a shindig.

As he unscrewed the cap on the tire and plugged on the air hose he glanced around, but the coast was clear. The press circus had largely moved on. Once or twice he'd still get snapped by a freelance photographer lurking for a shot. He took off his helmet and sunglasses and wiped his brow.

Lee was tightening the screw cap on the front wheel when a silver Porsche caught his attention. Nice. The guy filling it turned to slot the nozzle into the pump and Lee's enjoyment faded. The architect.

But, hey, Lee could be a grown-up. Mark had also seen him and plastered a similar "oh shit not you but let's make the best of it" smile on his face as he strolled over.

"Sergeant Davis, nice to see you again."

They shook hands and Mark looked at Jules's purple bike. "Nice wheels."

Smart arse. Lee almost liked him for it.

"Borrowed," he said, and nodded toward the Porsche. "Still paying yours off?"

The other man reddened. Guess Lee had misjudged his sense of humor.

"Nope, all mine," Mark replied. "Cars and women. I've always liked a classy ride."

Lee stiffened. The innuendo had to be coincidental. His

successor couldn't be that much of a jerk. Jules's taste was too good for that.

Mark met his stare blankly and Lee relaxed.

"How's Jules?" the architect asked.

Son of a bitch. Lee's fists curled before he understood. Mark didn't realize Lee knew about him and thought he was making a private joke. Two could play at that game. "Exhausting," he said, gesturing to the bike. "Which is why I'm working on my endurance—so I can keep up with her."

Mark's expression took on some personality at that.

Come to think of it, the jerk had played mind games with Jules in the pub. Making her extremely uncomfortable.

Lee added, "Turns out I'm not the only one who's been starved of great sex."

The architect wasn't red now, he was pale with anger. "Is that supposed to be funny?"

"No, not funny…not funny at all. Did you imagine I was too thick to put two and two together when you were playing the passive-aggressive prick with my fiancée?"

"Don't be such a jerk."

"*Me* a jerk. Hey, where do you think you're going?"

Lee's simmering anger rose to a fast boil. Catching the other man by the arm, he spun him out of sight around the corner of the building.

"What the hell are you doing?" Mark asked.

"You like bullying people don't you," Lee spit, shaking with rage. "Is it always women and weaklings? Would you be as witty and urbane with your mind games if someone fought back?"

With snakelike speed he pinned Mark against the wall of the gas station. The other man's leather jacket squeaked against the tinted plate-glass window as he tried to wriggle free. Using techniques he'd learned in Special Forces, Lee held the larger man immobile.

"Yeah," Lee said savagely, "not so much fun being the one bullied is it, asshole?"

"Please." Mark's eyes bulged as Lee dug his elbow harder into his windpipe. "Don't hurt me."

Lee recovered himself in an instant, dropped his arms and stepped away in horror.

Coughing, Mark slid down the wall clutching his throat. "What kind of monster are you?" he wheezed.

"I…" Breaking into a sweat, Lee reached out to help Mark to his feet and the man instinctively threw up his hands to shield his face.

"Get away from me!"

Grabbing the bike and his helmet, Lee stumbled around the corner of the building and cycled away. After five minutes he'd started shaking so hard he had to dismount and walk. And through his brain, the same sentence repeated over and over again.

What kind of monster are you?

CHAPTER EIGHTEEN

LEE WASN'T HOME when Jules arrived at one and the pique she felt that lunch wasn't on the table made her smile as she fixed herself a ham sandwich. Actually it was good she had to fend for herself again. In another week she'd be eating soup and salads.

Sipping her coffee, she settled at the kitchen table with her laptop. While she waited for it to boot up, she ate one of yesterday's blueberry muffins and then another. Because, dammit, Lee was right. His baking *was* tastier than hers.

Word came up and she started formatting a document. Nick's deadline about her shareholding was Monday. Jules figured the surest way of guaranteeing a lottery win tomorrow night was to begin updating her résumé.

Yeah, right.

Her cell rang. She looked at the display and hesitated. Did she want to talk to Mark? Not really, but better for everyone to keep relations civil. "This is a surprise. How are you?"

"Half-strangled," he snapped. "Your maniac fiancé attacked me at a service station two hours ago."

"But why…how?" Jules struggled to connect the incident with Lee in her imagination. "What did you do?"

"What did *I* do? I'm phoning to warn you that you're living with a madman and you ask me what—"

"I'm sorry, I don't know why I said that. Are you badly hurt? Where are you?"

"I'm at my office. My throat feels like it's had a boa constrictor wrapped around it and it hurts like hell. I'm considering laying charges. I want to know if Lee has a history of violence."

"No!" Cell to her ear, Jules went to the hall telephone and dialed Lee's cell. She should never have believed him when he denied having PTSD. Was he safe? Did he need help? Emergency counseling? "Mark, don't do anything hasty."

"The number you have called is either turned off or outside the coverage area."

"Who's that with you?" he demanded suspiciously. "Is Lee there threatening you in some way? I'll phone the police."

He was obviously still shaken and Jules tried to keep the panic out of her voice at the way the situation was escalating. "Lee's not here, Mark," she reassured him. "It's an automated message on the other line. Look, stay where you are, I'm coming over right now."

Grabbing her keys and handbag, she hurried out to the car.

"I'll be there in ten minutes."

On the drive over Jules scanned every street, hoping to glimpse Lee, feeling sick and frightened for him. What had triggered his violence? He'd never been a possessive boyfriend and had maintained friendships with a couple of ex-girlfriends. A jealous rage was out of character.

Out of character for the old Lee, but what about the new one?

She tried his cell again but it was still turned off. As soon as she'd convinced Mark not to call in the National Guard she'd trawl the streets, get Nate and Claire to help if she had to.

Pulling up outside Mark's office, Jules locked the car and hurried into the foyer of the three-story Georgian-style building. As she waited for the elevator to take her to the third floor, she caught sight of something that made her blood run cold.

Her bike lay half-hidden under the stairs.

Oh, my God. Forgetting the elevator, she took the stairs, two at a time, and wrenched open the door to Mark's office. Lee turned from his position sitting on the other side of Mark's desk. His features were drawn, his expression bleak. Ashamed.

Mark sat on the other side, his fingers steepled grave and oddly condescending. He appeared to be relieved as soon as he saw Jules.

Panting, she caught the door frame for support. "I saw your bike," she explained to Lee, and then realized that she'd basically just revealed that she'd expected to find Mark beaten to a bloody pulp.

Which wasn't true. She'd hurried to prevent Lee from beating Mark to a bloody pulp.

Pressing her fingers into a stitch under her ribs, she went to stand beside him, putting a hand on his shoulder. "Are you okay?"

"Weren't you coming here to ask me that?" Mark answered.

"Yes, of course. Tell me what happened."

"A savage and unprovoked attack," Mark told her. She let him vent, making appropriate sounds of shock and sympathy when he pulled down his collar to show her the mark on his neck, tinged the faint red of a sunburn. And all the while, with the pad of her thumb she stroked tiny reassuring circles on Lee's tense shoulder blade.

Lee gave absolutely no sign that he felt it. He listened silently to Mark, until the guy ran out of steam.

Then he cleared his throat. "As I said before Jules arrived, I completely understand if you want to press charges rather than accept an apology."

"And I'm asking you not to," Jules said. Lee shifted away from her hand and she dug her thumb into his back. "You know what he's been through."

"That's all very well, Jules, but is he getting help?"

"He's had some counseling," Lee answered. "He'll get more."

Mark looked at him. "Is Jules safe with you?"

"Yes, she is," Jules answered.

"Still choose him, huh?" Mark sighed. "Okay, I accept your apology."

Jules waited until they were in the car, her bike angled across the backseat and out the open window, before she asked again, "Are you okay?"

"I'll move out," he said. "Tonight. Go stay with Nate… no." He rubbed his face. "They've got the launch tomorrow. I'll find a hotel."

"You're staying with me for another week," she said, "as per the conditions of our armistice. Otherwise, all the effort we've put into continuing this tortuous engagement becomes a bloody waste of time."

His gaze met hers. "Jules, everything he said was true. I identified him as a bully and I lost control."

"The SAS liaison will be able to recommend someone experienced in dealing with your problem. We'll call Kyra tomorrow."

"I will," he said. "You've done enough."

"Okay." She started the car. "But under all this you're still a good man."

"I thought I was a selfish, manipulative jerk."

"That, too," she said. "In a male, they're not mutually exclusive."

Lee almost smiled.

JULES WOKE THE next morning to the chirrup of an incoming text and fumbled for her cell. Can you pick up fifty extra glasses from the party rental place en route? Claire.

Yesterday's drama had pushed *Heaven Sent*'s launch out of her mind. Jules texted back: Sure.

Shrugging on a robe, she went in search of Lee but found no sign of him. Or her bike. Had he remembered? Would he still want to go? After chewing her lip, she forwarded a reminder. Duty was a powerful motivator, and being among his friends would speed up the return to normalcy.

When she returned from her shower she found a reply. Home soon. About to delete it, she paused.

Then, leaving it in her in-box—for reasons she didn't want to examine—she got dressed.

The launch was at the boathouse on the estuary of Stingray Bay so Jules opted to wear practical glamour: a hot fuchsia halter top over navy capris and a matching cardigan in case of a sea breeze. Strappy sandals. Pink lipstick. When she was finished, she scanned herself in the mirror.

"Who are you getting dressed up for?" she asked suspiciously. She tossed her head. "The rock star, of course."

Bravado locked and loaded, Jules drove to the party rental place and collected the extra glasses.

Under a blue sky, every passing garden bloomed with the bright freshness of pending summer. Some of that promise crept into her spirit.

By the time she'd negotiated traffic and arrived home, Lee stood in front of the mirror in the living room, adjusting the collar on a shirt that bought out the green of his eyes.

She'd chosen it for him.

His gaze flicked to hers, then returned to his reflection. "Are you going to tell any of our friends what happened with Mark?"

Jules folded her arms. "What do you think?"

"Neither am I," he warned her.

"It's not the right forum. Today is a celebration."

"I'm not ever telling them, Jules."

She wanted to give him the right answer, one that would help him, so she took a few seconds to reply. "They won't judge you," she said at last. "Maybe it's time you discussed the ambush and how it affected them."

"I booked some counseling," he said abruptly. "A local guy recommended by Kyra. No one else needs to get involved."

Don't shut everybody out. What right had she to say it after telling him emphatically and repeatedly she was shutting him out? And why *now,* after he'd beaten up her ex-boyfriend and revealed himself to be troubled, was she suddenly questioning her decision not to give third chances?

Both of them needed their heads examined.

"Let's talk about this later," she said quietly. When she'd had time to untangle her thoughts.

STINGRAY BAY WAS picture-postcard paradise. Blue water mutated into a blue sky. The footbridge spanning the estuary hosted a number of hopeful anglers and, across the channel, sun glinted off the windows of the colorful old cabins.

Climbing out of the car, Lee put on his shades and wondered how soon he and Jules could politely leave. He still felt shaken by the depth and ferocity of his anger yesterday, which seemed to have come out of nowhere. Oddly, Jules's compassion only intensified his humiliation.

He didn't want her pity; he wanted her love.

He didn't want her to see him as weak; he wanted her to see him as the indomitable optimist she'd fallen for. Because no way in hell would he win another chance in his current shape.

Claire must have been watching for them, because she strolled from the boathouse to meet them.

The doors of the corrugated shed were open at both ends and framed the estuary view and the restored sixty-year-old launch sitting on the skids.

"Thank God, you're here," Claire said to Jules. "We were about to break out the plastic goblets and that is *not* the impression I want to make when we've got Zander Freedman attracting national press."

In white capris, a nautically striped top and a captain's hat, she sparkled even more than the tinsel wrapped around the railings of her forty-foot pride and joy. "And of course I'm delighted to see you, too." Laughing, she kissed Lee's cheek.

He made an effort. "It's going well then?"

"Brilliantly."

Lee opened the trunk. "I'll unload the glasses, you two go ahead."

"Thank you!" Claire tucked her arm through Jules's and started leading her away. "Dan's tending bar. He'll know where to put them."

Jules hesitated.

"Go," he said. "Have fun."

After yesterday, she deserved a break from worrying about him.

Picking up the two trays of glasses, Lee nudged the trunk closed and headed toward the boathouse, passing Claire's son, who was kicking a ball with a bunch of other teenagers.

"Want to organize a game of football later?" Lewis said hopefully. It had been one of their traditions.

"Sure, mate." Any excuse to avoid questions from grown-ups.

Inside the boathouse, he threaded his way through tables decorated with checkered tablecloths and centerpieces of spring flowers. He nodded hello to Claire's mother-in-law, Ellie, who was overseeing the cutting of a ham behind a buffet table all but sagging under the weight of food.

On the estuary side of the boat shed he found Dan dispensing drinks from a makeshift bar. Lee placed the trays of glasses on the far end to stop the white tablecloth billowing in the breezy gusts.

"Good thinking." Dan finished loading a tray with glasses of white wine and handed it to a passing waitress. "I was wondering how to anchor that. Local or imported?"

"Local, thanks."

Dan freed a can of Steinlager from an ice-filled tub and flipped the tab. "Here you go."

Lee accepted the chilled can. "Want a hand?" Because he really didn't want to stand around wringing his.

"Nah, I can cope. You can take another beer to Ross, though. His lordship is on the poop deck."

"What the hell is a poop deck?"

"No idea…just like the sound of it."

"Derives from the Latin *puppis,* meaning stern," Nate supplied, arriving with an empty tray. "Commonly the rear cabin roof on a sailing ship's main deck. Which means we don't have one."

Dan began refilling the tray with wine and beer. "Hark at the old sea dog."

"Less lip, galley slave, or it'll be the plank." Nate grinned at Lee. "Ross is inspecting the engine for the fiftieth time."

Lee delivered the beer and kicked *Heaven Sent*'s tires with Ross for ten minutes. He thought he was doing well until Ice looked up from his inspection of the Leyland 680 engine and said casually, "Everything okay? You seem edgy."

"Box of fluffy ducks." Lee collected Ross's empty glass. "I'm going to get another drink. Want one?"

"I'm good."

Heading toward the bar, he saw Jules and Claire approaching the rock star and detoured away from them.

After yesterday's attack on her ex-lover, the last thing he wanted was to make her nervous by hovering while she met her schoolgirl crush.

Instead he found Lewis and his buddies. "How about that soccer game?"

CHAPTER NINETEEN

JULES WATCHED LEE walk away and told herself not to take it personally. He needed perspective on yesterday and that probably meant avoiding the person who reminded him of it for a few hours.

"…he got a bit miffed when Nate told him he didn't need a bodyguard in li'l ol' backwater New Zealand and sent the entourage away."

With an effort, she attempted to pick up the thread of Claire's conversation.

"So we figured if we gave him an ego assistant, someone to give him drinks but not too many, listen to his stories, maybe keep him moving if he gets stuck…"

Jules's brain synapses made the connection. *Zander Freedman.*

"…and who better than someone who's had a massive crush on him since she was thirteen?"

"Wait…me?" She had too much on her mind today to appreciate a hedonistic rock star.

Her friend laughed delightedly. "I *knew* you'd be thrilled! C'mon, let's go introduce you."

Can't someone else do it? Jules swallowed the words and jollied up her expression as she followed her friend. Claire had arranged this as a special treat and she wasn't going to spoil it.

Even if Zander Freedman hadn't been chatting to Nate he would have been easy to distinguish as a rock star. In this sleepy seaside settlement he looked both incongruous and completely at home wearing a Stetson with a hatband of silver buckles, cowboy boots and a chunky collection of chains and rings.

A few respectful feet away, other guests clustered in small groups, either trying not to send him surreptitious glances or talking and laughing loudly in the hopes of attracting his attention. He looked like a matador surrounded by bulls. Any moment they might charge.

"Zander, this is Jules." Claire drew her forward. "She's your local minder."

"And she's engaged," Nate cautioned. "So no moves."

"Invitation only." The rocker's grin dazzled her. "Got it." Close up he was classic Hollywood with very white, very even teeth and a perfect tan. In his crystal-blue eyes she read wariness and a royal's expectation to be amused. But then he had been famous for a very, very long time.

There was something surreal about shaking hands with a guy whose poster had hung on her bedroom wall when she was a tween.

She told him so and his eyes glazed over. "That's great, honey."

"It's okay," she said drily. "I got over you."

"Thank God. I need to be drunk to deal with rabid fans and I'm pacing myself." He swigged from a silver hip flask. "Until I've cut the ribbon or whatever the hell Nate needs me to do."

"Smash a bottle of champagne against the hull," said Nate.

"There we go," Zander drawled. He draped a proprietary arm around Claire. "You know, Captain, I was kinda hoping you and I would become a lot better acquainted today." He grinned over at his former bodyguard like a misbehaving teenager daring a parent.

Nate just laughed.

Jules wasn't sure if she was amused or appalled by her former hero. Either way, she sensed that keeping him out of trouble would keep her busy. And with Lee avoiding her she needed to be kept busy.

Over the next hour she was both efficient and thorough. She made sure Zander's flask was filled with his favorite Grey Goose vodka; she steered him from group to group, saw that he wasn't monopolized and filled in gaps in conversation when he couldn't be bothered.

Lee still didn't come anywhere near her. It shouldn't hurt but it did.

She did get one reprieve when Zander left to smash the champagne over *Heaven Sent*'s hull and pose with Claire, Nate and Lewis for photographs. He talked to Lee afterward but, clinging to her pride, Jules kept her distance.

"Jules." Ross limped over. "Can I have a quiet word?"

Uh-oh. Jules put her game face on as they walked out of earshot of the other guests.

"Has anything happened we should know about? Something's off with Lee."

"I'm afraid you're going to have to talk to him about that, Ice."

"So I'm right?"

"I'm not confirming or denying—"

"Fine, I'll confront him."

And have Lee think she tattled on him? Jules grabbed his arm. "This is something Lee will raise with you when he's ready. In the meantime—" counterattack was the last defense of a desperate woman "—we'd both appreciate it if, *for once,* you minded your own damn business."

"Fair enough," he said mildly, then surprised her by smiling.

"What!"

Ice gestured to her ring. "You're going to keep that."

He'd limped away before she could deny it.

"How's the house sale going?" said a man beside her.

"Nick." She smiled, then glanced around for Lee. "What are you doing here?"

He raised an eyebrow at her tone. "I'm dating the manager of the marine company that supplied the new canopy." He pointed out a redhead talking to Claire. "Have you met Veronica?"

"What...no." Jules was still scanning the crowd.

"So any update on your decision to sell to me? The deadline's in two days."

"Is there any chance you'd reconsider my leaving the company as a condition of purchase?"

"None," he said cheerfully. "I don't think it's good for the firm—which is why I'll leave if you manage to sell your house—except a little birdie told me it was off the market."

"Shouldn't you be in the estuary swimming with the sharks?" she asked.

"It's your choice, Jules," he reminded her. "I'm not holding a gun to your head."

She sighed. "I know. And the lottery didn't come through for me so I guess I'm saying—"

"No," Lee said behind her. "She's saying no."

Nick turned, surprised. Needing a moment to rein in her temper, Jules did not. This wasn't Lee's call; neither was it the place for a scene.

His arm snaked around her waist. Lee jerked her against his body in a parody of affection and reached across her to shake Nick's hand. "How are you doing?" he said. "I'm Lee Davis, Jules's fiancé."

Nick had a reputation for reading judges and he clearly saw a hanging one in Lee because he absented himself within thirty seconds of exchanging pleasantries.

"Make sure you invite us to your farewell drinks," Lee called after him.

Grabbing his forearm, Jules twisted free to face him.

"How dare you?" she said through clenched teeth.

"How dare I?" His eyes glittered more than the estuary. "You said he'd buy your shareholding at the same price, you never mentioned you'd lose your job! Are you bent on bankrupting yourself over me? I just don't get it. I've said I can wait for the money."

"I pay my debts…and particularly to you. Every loose end will be tied up by the end of next week."

"What are you so afraid of? That I'll use the money to leverage myself into your life?"

"I can't give any man a hold over me," she said.

"I'm not some asshole boyfriend of your mother's who'd pull the rug out from under you when you least expect it."

"Lee," she reminded them both, "you already have."

His jaw set, but he was called away for a group photo with his former SAS buddies before he could rebut her argument. Jules would talk to Nick on Monday.

"I need a drink," she said glumly.

"Finally, you're interesting," a gravelly voiced man said from behind her, and Zander materialized holding his ubiquitous flask.

"Do you talk to everyone like this?"

"Like what?"

Jules sighed. "Never mind." Her gaze dropped to his flask.

"So, you want a drink?"

"I probably shouldn't…"

One of his fair eyebrows lifted, reminding her who she was talking to. To hell with it.

"Yes, please," she said firmly.

"Wait here." He returned with a glass half-filled with

clear liquid and crushed ice, and a half-full bottle of Grey Goose vodka. "In case we need refills." He gave her the glass. "Take the edge off before you cut yourself."

"You really have a way with words."

"I'm a genius songwriter, what can I say?"

Jules sipped her drink and gasped as it vaporized the lump in her throat.

"Neat," Zander said, "is the only way to drink vodka. Purists like me lose the ice… Let's go sit by the water."

They settled on the grassy bank overlooking the estuary, some fifty meters away from the party. The rocker tipped his flask to her glass. "Cheers."

"Cheers." Cautiously Jules took another sip. The vodka was icy as it slid down her throat but with a lovely liquid after burn that warmed the cold in the pit of her stomach.

Zander gestured to her engagement ring. "Your bling's better than mine."

"Uh-huh." Jules took another gulp.

"I met your guy. that's quite some miracle story you and Lazarus have got going." Idly, he picked a stalk of grass. The sun glinted off the silver buckles on his hat. "I love military stuff. I collect war memorabilia, have a library full of military memoirs. I guess it's the fascination of the overindulged for a life motivated by duty and sacrifice." He grinned. "Don't want that life, can't understand why any rational person would choose it, but I admire the hell out of those—like your fiancé—who do it."

He's not mine. Jules took another sip.

"So anyway, which is it?"

"Pardon?"

"Are you drinking to forget, drinking for fun or drinking to numb?"

"The last one." Jules frowned. The alcohol couldn't be

going to her head already, could it? She tried to remember if she'd eaten breakfast. She definitely hadn't eaten lunch.

Her gaze drifted to *Heaven Sent,* now bobbing at the end of the pier gangplank. On deck, Nate drew Claire into his arms, removed her captain's hat and kissed her.

Jules clutched the icy glass harder. Zander half turned to see what she was looking at. "Aw, sweet," he said. "So what's with you and Lazarus avoiding each other?"

"Wh-what do you mean?"

He turned back. "In your place, I'd be locked in a bedroom shagging my true love's brain out."

"We…we're here to support our friends." Jules gulped another sip and changed the subject. "What's it like living permanently in the spotlight? We got a lot of press interest immediately after Lee's release—I didn't like it."

"I liken it to swimming with sharks." Zander paused to take a swig from his flask. "Exhilarating, addictive and occasionally painful when the paparazzi take too big a chew. But worth it."

And yet in the bright sun he looked slightly burned around the edges as he dangled his legs over the edge of the bank and kicked away chunks of clay with the heels of his cowboy boots.

"You shouldn't do that," Jules said. "It erodes the bank. See how the council has planting agapanthus to try to stabilize the soil?"

Zander scoffed but stopped and lay back on the grass. Legs still dangling over the bank, he covered his face with his Stetson. He lifted a peremptory hand. "Flask."

Shaking her head, Jules passed it to him. "You're welcome."

"Don't mention it."

There was really no reason to like him, yet strangely she did. Tucking her legs underneath her, she sipped her vodka and watched the shadow of a stingray glide past on the outgoing tide. Numbness, she decided, was nice.

"I'm surprised we're being left in peace," Zander commented. "And more surprised I like it."

"Nate asked everyone to respect your privacy once the formal part of the day was over."

"How much would it take to get him back in L.A., d'ya think?"

"I'd say you had no chance through the fishing season, but you might tempt them in our winter. Work on Lewis, Claire's son. That kid's dying to go to Disneyland."

"Thanks, I will. Nate was the only employee I ever had who had my best interest at heart. Real friends are hard to come by."

Jules lifted her glass. "Cheers to that."

"So what do you do for a living?" He made work sound like a disease.

"I'm a lawyer." A soon-to-be-unemployed lawyer. She reached for the bottle of Grey Goose.

"Ugh," said Zander. "Some of my least favorite people."

Jules laughed as she refilled her glass. "You're mean," she said. Yet oddly restful. "Even I feel like a good person next to you."

"Even you." He chuckled under his hat. "So what have you done...pulled out an agapanther?"

"Agapahtas," Jules corrected him. "Wait...agatapus. You're right, it *is* hard to say." Putting down her glass, she picked a daisy and started picking the petals off it. She caught herself playing "he loves me, he loves me not" and stopped. "Can you keep a secret?"

"Not really, but I can do with the practice. What did you do?"

"Lied," she said. "A lot. And now it seems I've been

lying to myself, as well. If there's a flame, can you blame the moth for wanting to keep banging it?"

"I think you mean, banging *into* it, but I like your version better."

"I turned down this guy, then changed my mind, then he came back and blew it, so I turned him down again, only he's not even the same guy I loved except in a way we're more suited because the wounded part of me understands the wounded part of him, if that makes any sense."

"None at all," Zander said lazily.

"I know, right?"

Jules dropped the stripped daisy and picked up her glass. "I'm really confused."

Tipping his hat up, he turned his head. "I'm thinking that if you want to keep this secret, honey, you probably need to stop drinking."

"You're probably right." Jules lifted the glass to her lips and the rocker plucked it from her hand and replaced it with his flask. "Here."

"How's that gonna help?" She sipped it. "Ugh...water."

"I tip out the hard stuff and replace it when no one's looking. And now you have a secret of mine you can't tell. It'll keep us both honest."

Sitting up, he patted the breast pocket of his shirt and bought out a packet of cigarettes. Catching Jules's eye, he shrugged. "One vice at a time."

After a couple of puffs, he stubbed the cigarette out on the grass and tossed the butt into the estuary.

"That's pollution," Jules pointed out.

"One fish with a nicotine addiction. How can it hurt?"

In companionable silence they watched it float away.

FROM HIS POSITION leaning against the bar, Lee watched Jules laughing with the rock star and something in him relaxed.

Maybe he *hadn't* traumatized her yesterday. Now he just had to stop the bloody woman taking three steps backward in her career. Scowling, he turned to find three pairs of eyes fixed on him.

"Zander's honorable," Nate said. "In his own twisted way."

"And Jules won't take any crap," Ross added.

Dan handed him another orange juice. "Lee's never been the jealous type, have you, mate?"

But the same bloody woman was right about leaning on his buddies. Lee decided to ease his way into it. "Depends whether the architect shows up," he said.

The three men gaped at him. "Jules told you about Mark?" Dan asked.

"Not so much tell, as show-and-tell," he replied. "I've known for a while."

They looked stunned. "Why didn't you say something earlier?" Ross demanded.

"Perhaps I was waiting for one of you to."

They exchanged glances and Lee relented. As if he wouldn't have shot the messenger. "It's okay," he conceded. "In your situation I would have done the same thing." Impossible to reveal information like that without being a squealer.

"You would?" Nate asked carefully.

"Of course." He was a little peeved at the implied slur.

"I don't know what to say," Dan replied. "We've been flaying ourselves over this ever since you were found."

Lee was touched by the depth of his buddies' emotion. "It's not an easy thing to tell."

"All the women thought we should stay out of it," Ross confided. "But Jules was so damn lonely…and we knew you'd want her to be happy."

Lee looked over at Jules. "Yeah, I want her to be happy.... Wait—what?"

"Our criteria was to find someone you'd approve of," Nate said quickly.

"And Jules only went as a favor to us," added Ross. "No one was more surprised than we were when they hit it off. Turned out we're good at this shit."

"We nearly canceled that date half a dozen times," Dan offered. "Swear to God, I know how fathers feel with daughters now. Torn between letting their little girl live and threatening the guy if he so much as laid a finger on her. It was horrible."

The bottom dropped out of Lee's world.

"Of course, Mark's a hell of a nice guy," Ross added, "but if we'd believed for one moment you were still alive we would never have fixed them up."

Clearly they'd been practicing this...explanation.

"We couldn't stand the thought of some loser filling your shoes," Nate said earnestly. "It's not like Jules's judgment has been all that great lately. Grief does crazy things to a person."

One by one they ran out of steam. Or maybe it was the look in his eyes that shut them up. There was a sudden, terrible silence.

"Oh, shit." Dan rubbed his forehead. "You didn't know."

In captivity Lee had learned to step outside himself when the beatings started, retreat to a space three feet above the action and observe it like a movie...nothing to do with him. He tried to do that now but was pinned by a shaft of pain between his ribs and weighted by a dreadful sense of betrayal.

Laughter burst from a group of partygoers to his left, the estuary sparkled and the edge of the bar's tablecloth billowed playfully. Every happy sight and sound scraped across his nerves like sandpaper.

"Lee," Ross began, but he held up a hand.

"You thought I was dead," he said conversationally.

Three chins jerked assent.

"And now you're dead to me."

He started walking away but paused.

"You know why I believed *you* were dead?" he threw over his shoulder. "Because if you were alive, you would have come for me."

It was a perfectly timed lob that stopped them dead in their tracks as they moved to follow him. Coolly, Lee pulled the pin. "I never thought Steve and I would be so easily replaced."

He saw Nate's pain, heard Dan's hiss and watched Ross reel as if struck. "Now," he said in a low voice, "you really *can* relate to how I feel."

CHAPTER TWENTY

JULES WATCHED LEE stride toward her across the grass and his pallor pierced her alcohol haze. She was scrambling to her feet before she was even aware of it.

"Are you sick?" she said.

"Yes, I need to leave right now," he said unsteadily. "If you lend me your car, someone can give you a ride home later."

"I'll give her a ride," Zander drawled.

Lee's dismissive gaze raked over him. "You can try." He held out his hand. "I need the keys, Jules."

"Of course. I'm coming with you." She picked up the sweater she'd discarded along with her handbag. "I'll just tell Claire we're leaving."

"Don't bother. I've said my goodbyes." Behind him, Dan approached, his paleness matching Lee's. Seeing her attention diverted, Lee pivoted.

"Don't bother," he barked. "Jules, I'll meet you by the car." Ignoring Zander, he strode toward the road. And she understood that whatever was wrong wasn't physical.

Dan's eyes met hers in a silent telegraphing of big trouble before he forced a smile for Zander. "My wife's talking about naming our firstborn after you. I'd really appreciate you talking her out of it."

"Use my middle name, Lovell." Zander kissed Jules goodbye with a kiss on each cheek. "Drunk, I'd challenge your fiancé for you," he murmured. "Sober I'm more realistic." He pulled away. "And in answer to your earlier question, it's a woman's prerogative to keep changing her mind."

"Thank you." She pressed his hand. "Dan, I'll phone you later." She hurried to catch up to Lee. He was leaning his forehead against the roof of the car but straightened when he heard the crunch of her heels on the gravel. "I've been drinking." She held up the keys. "Are you okay to drive?"

He nodded and they got in the car.

"What happened?" Jules fastened her seat belt, as the Pink Lady's engine growled to life.

Maneuvering the Caddy out of the tight parking space, Lee didn't reply until they were on the road that twisted through the hills sheltering Stingray Bay.

"Why didn't you tell me the guys set you up with Mark?"

Multiple thoughts ran through Jules's head simultaneously. No wonder he was devastated. And what possessed them to tell him today? The timing couldn't have been worse. They should have run it by her first. "What good would it have served?"

Expertly he took a sharp corner, spinning the wheel almost immediately for another.

"They told you, didn't they?" she persisted. "That's worth something. Did you give them a chance to explain?" Jules braced herself against the door as he took a third corner. "They believed they were following your wishes." Ross had hatched the idea then talked Nate and Dan into it, but that point was moot. Once in, they were all in.

"In what loopy universe would setting you up with another guy reflect *my* wishes?"

Put like that... Jules tried again. "They thought you'd want me to be happy." Their concern had touched her, which was why she'd agreed to one introduction.

"I do want you to be happy." Lee ground the gears as he

changed down. "Haven't I backed off to make you happy? That doesn't mean I wanted my friends *pimping* for you."

She closed her eyes as the car zigzagged through the bushy hills and then opened them because the alcohol was making her dizzy. "Can you slow down please? I'm feeling queasy." Immediately Lee eased off the accelerator. Jules massaged her temples. "I'm not doing this very well. I'm sure they'll explain it better. Once you've calmed down and—"

He snorted. "You think I ever want to see them again after this?"

"All they did was arrange an introduction, Lee. I was the one who slept with him, and yesterday you apologized to Mark for reacting like a Neanderthal. This reaction doesn't make sense."

"It's about loyalty. You didn't owe me anything because you'd already dumped me. And even if you hadn't, only an idiot would expect you to give up on love, marriage and kids for the rest of your life."

Jules recoiled. "It was only sex…touch I wanted. I'd never date someone I'd have to love like I loved you. I'm not *that* much of a masochist. And if you're blaming the guys for leading me astray, don't! I'd already joined an internet dating site before they set me up with Mark."

He set his jaw. "These past days I've been telling myself to stop begrudging everyone for getting on with their lives. But I can't frickin' believe how *easily* I've been replaced."

"Easily." Jules gaped at him, sure she'd misheard. "Easily!" she repeated. Every emotion she'd been repressing for the past few weeks imploded into white-hot fury. "Stop the car!" She wrestled to undo her seat belt. "Stop this god-damned car now!"

ALARMED, LEE SKIDDED to a halt by the side of the road, under an overhang of trees. "What's wrong?"

Seizing her bag and sweater, Jules wrenched the door open, half-falling in her scramble to get out of the vehicle. "Go," she yelled. "*Be* alone! I'll walk before I listen to that bullshit!" She slammed the door before he could answer and the heavy clunk reverberated in the country quiet. Seething, she started marching down the road.

Behind her she heard the driver's door swing open. "Jules!"

She spun around and kept walking backward. "Even after our heart-to-heart you still have no appreciation of what I—or any of us—have gone through." On an angry sob, she pivoted and continued her march, too upset to consider the impracticality of a twenty-kilometer walk in strappy sandals.

Lee's footfalls only made her walk faster.

"Go away," she growled as he fell in beside her, averting her face. "I'm damned if I'll let you see me crying over you ever again." Angrily she dabbed at her eyes with the navy sweater scrunched in one fist.

An oncoming car crested the hill.

"C'mon," Lee said gently. "You'll get run over. And I'm not leaving you here...or going anywhere while you're this upset."

Jules started to argue, but the last thing she wanted was the interference of well-meaning motorists. Reluctantly, she let Lee guide her into the tract of bush beside the road, pulling away as soon as they were out of sight. She fumbled in her bag for tissues.

"You think you were the only one in chains these past two years?" The tears were falling faster than she could wipe them away. "Everyone who loved you struggled to find some meaning in your death, in Steve's."

His face was a blur through her tears.

"I started dating because I couldn't keep living a half life, couldn't keep being a victim." Every sob seemed to shake another deeply buried emotion to the surface. "I had to believe that I could get over you."

Bowing her head, Jules wept.

"Let me get over you."

"I can't," he said hoarsely. Catching her wet face between his hands, Lee rested his forehead against hers. Tears trickled onto her chin, but they weren't hers. "I can't let you get over me," he whispered. "Because I'm never going to get over you."

The dam of her long-buried grief burst its banks. "I missed you so much," she wept.

"I missed you, too." Passionately, he kissed her swollen eyelids, her wet cheeks, the corners of her trembling mouth, and his kisses were clumsy and messy and wonderful. "But I'm here now."

She kissed him back between gasps, their mingled tears salty and warm. Gradually Jules stopped crying and their kisses lengthened and deepened. Her arms tightened around his neck. She needed him closer, needed all of him.

A car honked and they broke apart, dazed, still holding hands.

"Come on." Fern fronds brushed Jules's bare legs under her dress as Lee pulled her farther into the bush, their footsteps muffled by pine needles.

"Far enough." Jules yanked him back into her arms, needing full-body contact and needing it now. Equally fervent, his mouth sought hers and she abandoned herself to sensation.

The temperature was cooler among the trees, but Lee's sun-warmed body was the only heat source she craved. With her spine pressed against the rough-barked totara, she devoured his mouth as he devoured hers, while their hands roamed restlessly over each other's bodies, unable to settle because nothing was enough. And each kiss, every caress, inflamed their desire, fed the hunger.

Nothing mattered but assuaging this burning need to reconnect, reaffirm life.

Lee untied her halter top and pulled it down to expose her breasts. His hot mouth closed over a nipple, too gently for her need. Jules wanted to be marked, she wanted to mark him. Her emotions were too raw for finesse. Impatiently, she threaded her fingers through his hair and tugged. "Harder."

Then she flung back her head and moaned as he did as he was bid.

His hot exhalation gusted over her nipples as he paused to catch his breath and Jules used the brief respite to fumble for the fastening on his jeans. Jerking the zipper down, she grasped the silky, hot length of him, her strokes clumsy with eagerness.

"Jules." Lee pressed himself against her palm with a groan. "If you want me inside you, leave that alone."

She responded with a tortured laugh to the thread of humor he brought to their dark passion. "Then give me skin!" Withdrawing her hand, she started tugging at the buttons of his shirt.

Lee caught her fingers and their eyes locked.

"No more hiding," she insisted. "I love all of you."

He let his hands fall.

The shirt opened and she saw a slash of red, the color of dried blood, slicing across the edge of one nipple to bisect a smooth pectoral. Lower, other lines curved around his lean ribs, not quite meeting in the middle of his ridged abdomen. Jules had a sudden vivid image of him curled on his side, protecting his head and heart.

Thank God she'd already seen his back and was prepared for this. Gently, she skimmed each raised scar with her fingertips.

Lee leaned forward and nipped her lower lip. "No pity," he ordered. "Not between us, and gentle isn't what I want now, either."

His eyes darkened as he spoke and Jules knew her own pupils had flared in response by the way he grinned, wolfish and wicked.

Her heartbeat escalated, as did the throbbing between her thighs. "No," she said huskily. "No gentle."

Twining one leg around his like a snake, she pressed her lips against the tendon in his neck and nipped. "In fact," she murmured, before grazing her teeth down his chest to lay an openmouthed kiss over his heart, "I don't want to be able to walk."

She gasped as he pushed himself against her, the tight ridge of his arousal pressing against her clitoris through the cotton barrier of her capris.

"Bossy," he said, and increased the friction. "Still so bossy." His jungle-green eyes reminded her of some wildcat's, predatory.

Jules leaned back against the tree trunk and lifted her arms above her head, watching his gaze drop to her outthrust breasts. "Do me," she said.

He had them both stripped naked in under a minute. She pressed her breasts against his torso, skin to skin, and rubbed herself against his heat, feeling feral. This was private farmland and their chances of discovery were small but right now Jules would have made love on the highway.

She needed to take him, needed him to take her.

His hands were warm, callused against her bare bottom as he lifted her, balancing her against the tree so she could wrap her legs around his waist. And then the press of his hot flesh against hers, already wet and yielding to his hardness.

He held back. "Tell me," he demanded.

"Tell you what?" she teased, and wiggled to torment him, but that only increased her own frantic need.

"Tell me," he whispered.

"I love you," she cried.

Lee thrust into her and she felt herself convulse around him.

Jules tightened her trembling thighs around his waist and opened her mouth to tell him to wait, to savor this shimmering moment, but she could only gasp against his throat.

But Lee did pause. Trembling as much as she was, breathing as hard, his mouth caught hers in a searing, tender kiss.

She heard a tui's bell-like call above them. Beams of sunlight pierced the canopy, spilling light onto the forest floor. The scent of pine and forest and earth filled Jules's lungs as she breathed deeply. "I love you," she whispered on the exhale.

He began moving and the only thing that mattered was his rough tenderness, the textures of his skin and the rasp of his voice murmuring endearments.

SHE WAS DRAWING him back to the light, to life before the ambush, before her devastating rejection, when all things seemed possible.

Jules's cry of release triggered his, and Lee surrendered to the most explosive orgasm he'd ever had. In the seconds that followed, he braced suddenly boneless legs to support them, waiting for his molecules to reform. Jules's ribs slammed against his as they both caught their breath. Bowing his head, he rested his cheek against hers, overcome.

He'd thought the spark that once defined him had finally been extinguished by the guys' revelation, but she'd fanned it to life. With her generosity, with her willingness to stay the course.

Her faith shored his.

Her hair tickled his nose and he nuzzled it aside and kissed the pulse point at her jaw, felt her arms tighten around his neck as she stirred.

They would get it right this time.

"I must be getting heavy." Jules turned her head and brushed her lips against his.

He returned her kiss. He would work to earn this woman's love every day. "I could cradle your ass forever, but how's your back?" She had taken the brunt of the tree bark.

Experimentally, Jules wiggled her shoulders and her breasts slid against his bare chest. Her smile suggested it was deliberate. Bending his head, he ran the tip of his tongue along the curve of that smile, savoring it.

"You heal me," he said.

Her eyes filled with tears. "Oh, Lee," she whispered.

He kissed her tears away. "No more crying. We're done with it."

Her smile wobbled. "Sounds good."

Slowly he lowered her to the ground, bereft the moment he let her go. He checked her back for scrapes. All the bark indentations were superficial. Getting dressed took a long time; they kept stopping to kiss and share endearments.

Driving home, Lee held her hand when he wasn't changing gears, lifting it to press his lips against her palm.

Within a few minutes she'd unfastened her seat belt and slid over to lean her head against his shoulder. "I don't care if it's illegal," she murmured. "I need to touch you."

"I feel the same." He released her hand to change gears and then dropped it to her knee, smoothing back the skirt to find skin. "We're going to be naked for weeks."

"Yes," she said. Her hand covered his. "What are you going to do about the guys?"

"I…don't know." There's only so much forgiveness I can muster over Mark and I need it all for you."

He only realized how that sounded when she stiffened against him. "Don't take that the wrong way," he said. "I meant he's still a sore spot. Notwithstanding that what I did yesterday was completely and totally unjustified, the guy is a bit of a wanker and you should all have had better taste if you were trying to fill my shoes."

His grip anchored her knee as she tried to slide to her side of the car. "Seriously, Jules, it was a slip of the tongue."

"I believe you," she said, loosening his hand. "But *you* need to be sure it wasn't a Freudian slip." Jules returned to her side of the car. "Imagining someone else with the person you love is tough. Maybe too tough for some people. But I'm done with guilt, Lee. If you can't get past it, we have no future."

He pulled over to the side of the road and faced her.

"I love you," he said. "I loved you within an hour of meeting you and I've loved you every minute since."

Her expression softened.

"Even when you broke my heart and I swore I'd get over you, I still loved you. And nothing—and no one— will ever change that. Now scoot back over here, because I'm missing you."

With a sigh, Jules slid over. Weak with relief, Lee checked the rearview mirror and pulled onto the road, one hand on the steering wheel, the other entwined with hers.

Jules lay her head on his shoulder. "I still want a pre-nup," said his romantic.

CHAPTER TWENTY-ONE

JULES'S CELL RANG as they were coming into Whangarei. "It's Dan," she said to him. "What am I going to tell him?"

Eyes on the road, Lee thought about what he'd accused his friends of in the flash flood of bitter disappointment and his skin crawled. "I'm surprised he even wants to talk to me."

Jules answered the cell before it went to message. "Hi, Dan. Yes, I'm with him. You guys have things you need to say? I'm sure he does, too."

"If they've got time after the launch party—"

He didn't get a chance to finish. "Yes," Jules said to Dan and hung up.

"He heard you and they'll come to the house around six," she told Lee, returning her cell to her bag.

"Okay."

"It'll work out," she reassured him. But then—thank God—she hadn't heard his vicious verbal assault. He'd made unforgivable accusations, deliberately and coldly laying waste to fourteen-year friendships. He expected equally ugly things to be said in return.

"I think you guys need to be alone for this," she commented. "I'll shower and change and head back to Claire's. I'm sure she could do with some reassurance as well as a hand with the cleanup."

Lee didn't argue. It was better she didn't hear them.

When he saw her off a few hours later, she cupped his

jaw. "Is it wrong to be so happy while you're still at odds with your friends and I'm still at odds with Connie?"

"We could always run away," he suggested. He was only half-joking. "Drive until we run out of gas and settle there."

"No man's an island," she reminded him. "I learned that lesson from you."

"That was Old Lee," he said. "New Lee would never be as arrogantly prescriptive."

Laughing, she kissed him. "Do me a favor?"

"Anything. Preferably involving servicing of a sexual nature."

"Later, Romeo. For now, watch your memorial service while you're waiting for the guys. It might give you a better understanding of your death from our perspective."

"Sure you don't want me to have a tooth pulled instead?" His army buddies weren't going to forgive him, no matter what his understanding. They were more likely to run him out of town, particularly when they heard he and Jules were a couple again.

Speaking of which. "Don't sell your stake in the law firm to repay me." Surely he had more clout now.

She looked up at him, head tilted to the side. "Admittedly, the sex was fantastic but it's not worth a rain check on one hundred and twenty thousand dollars." There was an edge to her voice he couldn't interpret.

"When you factor in forty-plus years of daily sex, then one hundred and twenty thousand dollars is ripping *you* off."

"Together or not, you need your money, Lee. I'm not taking advantage of our relationship. I will repay you what you're due. I'm still big on equity and fairness."

Order and parameters gave her security after a childhood that had offered none. He was starting to get that now. "We'll find a compromise."

"Good." She gave him a final kiss. "And good luck."

"Thanks, I'll need it."

When she'd left he found the DVDs Rob had given him shoved in a drawer in the bedroom. Reluctantly he picked one up and turned it over. His face grinned at him under a stylized font proclaiming: Memorial Service of Lee Davis.

The photograph was from his SAS graduation, a decade earlier. Trust Rob to choose a military image. His brother had cropped Lee alone but the original photograph had included the whole family.

His fingers tightened on the casing. Dad. A sudden yearning to see his late father alive was all the prompting he needed to pad into the living room and slot the disk into the machine.

Maybe from the grave Ian could tell him how to fix this.

The movie began at the start of the service. Lee fast-forwarded through the minister's homily, the hymns, and speeches by his C.O. and his sister—*Oh yeah,* he thought in disgust, *I'm such a great guy*—hunting for footage of his father.

Dan flashed up on the screen and Lee hit Play. "I speak for Ross Coltrane, who is still gravely ill in hospital, and for Nathan Wyatt as well as myself when I say—" Dan cleared his throat "—we miss you, brother."

Lee closed his eyes, then opened them and kept watching.

To his surprise, Ian didn't give a eulogy. But when he saw the footage of his father after the service, Lee understood why. Ian Davis had never been frail. But here he looked like a bewildered old man, which clearly upset the person shooting the footage as much as it did Lee because every time his father was framed in a close-up, the camera immediately retreated to crowd shots.

That's how Lee got the bigger picture.

Claire clinging to Dan's arm, her face ashen. She'd buried her husband two days earlier yet she'd attended his memorial service. Lewis, thank God, wasn't with her.

Nate at the bar knocking back shot glasses, his eyes blank.

Lee's brother-in-law, Phil, simultaneously trying to comfort Connie and his kids.

Jules, wearing sunglasses that covered half her face, shepherding out some hysterical woman who must be her mother.

Dan bringing Dad his coat as he stood removed from the crowd.

Another sequence showed Dad and Jules walking slowly through the heavily pruned rose gardens, all stalks and thorns. His throat closed, seeing his father's familiar shock of white hair. Jules's shoulders were as hunched as the old man's as she helped him navigate some steps.

You think mourning you was a game?

Dropping the remote, Lee leaned his head against the back of the couch and groaned. When Jules had flung the comment at him, he'd been throwing counter accusations and hadn't paid much attention.

Fixated on surviving his captivity, he'd given little thought to how his loved ones were coping. And discovering on release that he'd been "dead" had had enough comic quality to trivialize the impact. Little wonder Jules had lost it in the car earlier.

Oh, Dad, what have I done?

Dealing with his troop mates' supposed deaths had been different—he'd expected to join them within days. Through the darkest period of captivity Lee had even envied their quick passing. Mourning had been a luxury he couldn't afford, not when all his emotional energy had been needed to survive. And not when his captives had beat him for any signs of emotion.

Maybe his antipathy for Nate and Claire's relationship stemmed from the fact that he hadn't grieved Steve's death.

Whether or not they accepted it, he owed his army buddies a serious apology. After Mark's begrudging reaction to his other apology, he only hoped he was getting better at it.

On impulse he removed the CD, replaced it with the recording of his father's funeral and forced himself to watch it. He suffered and celebrated his father's life with all the people who'd had to do it without him. And through it all walked the woman he loved—supporting and comforting his siblings, standing arm in arm with his buddies.

She hadn't taken Lee's place; she'd taken over his responsibilities.

It was time to take them back.

NATE'S GLARE, FROM where he stood behind Ross and Dan, was the first thing Lee saw when he opened the door. "Honest to God," Nate fumed, "if I didn't understand how much you're hurting and you hadn't already been beaten to within an inch of your life a couple of times, I'd lay into you right now for the bullshit you threw at us. And if you ever, *ever*—" he stepped forward but neither of his flankers let him pass "—tell Claire that Steve was easily replaced, nothing will stop me. Are we clear?"

Lee swallowed. "Yes, and I'm—"

Nate steamrolled over Lee's attempt to apologize. "Neither of you are replaceable, you jerk. Neither of you ever will be."

"I'm—"

"You haven't got the first clue of what we went through because you haven't *asked,* dammit."

Dan put a hand on his shoulder and Nate shut up. "And

we've all been so busy protecting you we didn't tell you," Shep said in a marginally calmer voice. "With the result that you've got some bat-shit crazy idea that we've all been skipping through daisies in your absence."

"That's what I'm—"

"Jesus, Lee." Ice's eyes were two pools of anguish. "Even with the mind-warping experiences you've had, you can't seriously believe we wouldn't have moved heaven and earth to find you if we'd had any hint you were still alive. I mean—"

"Will you let me speak, goddammit!" he hollered.

Silence.

He opened his hands helplessly. "I've been stuck in my own private pity party and I'm sorry."

Nate folded his arms. "How sorry?"

There was only one thing to do. Stepping forward, he hauled three angry men into a clumsy hug. "*This* sorry."

"How much are you hating this?" Ross asked a few seconds later. "On a scale of one to ten."

"Eleven," Lee muttered.

"Good." Nate tightened his grip. "Hold for five more seconds, asshole."

"Ten," Dan amended. "Let's give the neighbors something to talk about."

When they broke apart, Dan kept a hand on Lee's arm. "What you said," he began, "had some merit. Ross and Nate weren't in any fit state after the ambush, but I wasn't in the firefight. I should have asked more questions. I—"

"Stop!" Lee faced his friend head-on. "It was all self-pitying bullshit. It was easier pointing a finger than admitting I was screwed up. Mate, I just watched my memorial service. You carried everybody."

"It's true," Ross said. "In hospital Shep wouldn't let me die."

"Neither of us would be here without Dan," Nate agreed, then hesitated. "He stopped me doing myself in."

Lee's mouth fell open. *"What?"*

Ross swore. "Wait, how the hell do I not know that?"

"Because at the time you were dying, dickhead," Nate told him. "And later, if you recall, we all went off to our own corners, thinking we could fix ourselves."

Three pairs of eyes swung back to Lee. "Any of this resonating with you yet?" Dan asked.

"None of you screwed up as badly as I have," Lee said, leading the way into the house.

"Always so competitive." Dan plunked himself onto the couch. "We've all been there, mate."

Nate and Ross made themselves comfortable in armchairs.

"I can't believe that." Lee remained in the doorway. "You're the sanest people I know."

"Now," said Dan. Shadows crossed his face. "But I was riddled with guilt for not being with you guys in the ambush. I tried to browbeat my best friend into marrying me without acknowledging how much she really meant to me." He grinned. "If that's not crazy I don't know what is."

"I got hung up on revenge, too," Ice said. "All I cared about was getting back to combat and dealing with the bastards who killed you and Steve." Absently, he massaged his injured leg. "Even though the C.O. wouldn't have let me near a weapon. Even though I could barely walk, let alone run. That's how delusional *I* was."

"I walked away from everyone I cared about to punish myself for not dying with Steve," Nate said. His dark eyes narrowed. "Your issues, mate, are positively girlie in comparison."

Lee could have kicked himself. Why hadn't he asked

questions before? "I'm sorry," he said, vowing to remedy that error right now. "What exactly happened in the ambush?"

Glancing at Nate, Ross and Dan stood. "We'll go buy beers." As they passed, Ross said, "You might want to sit down for this."

Lee sat on the armchair. Nate took a few minutes to gather himself and then he lifted his head to look Lee in the eye. "When the roadside bomb detonated you were thrown clear," he said in a clipped tone. Clearly this was difficult for him. "Ross took an artery hit, was unconscious. Steve and I stabilized him in the middle of a firefight. At the same time, Steve was also trapped. His leg was caught. He ordered me to take Ross to safety. Said we weren't all going to die that day."

He stopped. Swallowed.

"I took Ross and left Steve. When the Humvee exploded and he was engulfed in fire, I shot him."

Unable to speak, Lee pulled up his chair beside Nate's. They sat there for a long time. "Claire knows," Nate finally said.

"I'm sorry," Lee rasped. "For being such an asshole, for doubting you and Dan and Ross. For giving you a hard time about Claire…. I've been so self-absorbed. Stuck in my own little nightmare for so long that I forgot about anyone else's. Hell, mate." He put one arm around Nate's shoulders, then two.

"You don't do this stuff anymore," Nate reminded him.

"Shut up and hug me back."

Nate did.

"One thing puzzles me," Lee said later when Dan and Ross had rejoined them and they were sitting around the dining table with Steinlagers and plates of nachos. "Ajmal, my protector, told me you were all killed. Why would he have lied to me?"

"Maybe he didn't know," Nate suggested. "Our vehicle was blown up and there was a lot of smoke and confusion. It would have been easy to assume we were all inside. Ross and I were flown to the military hospital in Germany, and Dan followed as soon as your supposed remains were found. None of us ever returned."

And he'd wondered why they hadn't come to find him. "I'll make it up to you. I swear," he said.

To their credit, none of them tried to make him feel better.

"There wasn't a day we didn't think of you and Steve," Ross said.

"Not a day we don't still miss him," said Nate. "And to be clear—" he pinned Lee's gaze "—I haven't replaced Steve in Claire's life, or Lewis's. He meant too much to me for that. Love is expansive, there's enough room for everybody. And I know this sounds corny but I even feel like I have Steve's blessing." Embarrassed, he cleared his throat. "And holy shit I'm sounding all new age and none of you guys are stopping me."

"Because we think you have Steve's blessing, too," Dan said quietly.

"Thank you." Nate looked cautiously at Lee.

Lee chinked bottles with him. "Amen."

"We had this pact to live big to honor your memory." Dan leaned his forearms on the table. "To live well for those no longer with us. You in?"

'I've made a good start." Lee decided it was time to lighten the mood. "Ms. Browne, she says yes."

"I am so good at this matchmaking shit," Ross said with obvious satisfaction.

There was a moment's silence. Incredulous, Lee looked

at Ice until the penny dropped. "Except for the Mark thing," he added casually.

They all burst into laughter.

MIRRORS, LEE DECIDED as he stared at his reflection, were still not his friends. Restrooms, on the other hand, were his refuge.

Someone rattled the handle and he turned on the faucet and washed his hands though all he'd done in this community hall washroom was wish that Scotty would beam him up.

Beyond the door came the muted babble and laughter of his relatives.

Connie had invited so many offshoots of the family tree it was like hacking through a jungle of Davises all repeating the same exclamations.

"I wouldn't have recognized you!"

"Such a pity your father isn't alive to see this."

"I can't imagine what you went through." The last delivered with speculative compassion.

The expectation that he'd share his experiences had driven Lee in here. That and a growing claustrophobia that frightened him. He should be getting over this, dammit. The woman he loved loved him. He'd reconciled with his buddies....

Tough it out. He dried his hands, straightening his shoulders, and left his tiny refuge, pausing at the entrance to the cavernous hall, echoing with conversation.

He missed his father terribly here amongst *whanau*— family. He recognized him in the smile of an uncle, a gesture from his nephew or a quaint phrase.

Across the room Jules's eyes met his and he smiled. She'd dealt with enough of his angst. From here on in, all he cared about was making her happy.

She returned to charming the out-of-town rellies, who'd come up especially to gawk at him. Lee frowned at his pettiness. *C'mon, man, these are good people, kind people, people you care about.* Not their fault he was overly sensitive to the furtive looks and double takes. Trying not to watch for their reactions, he was unable to stop himself. Two uncles were reacting in surprise right now.

His friends, Jules, even his siblings treated him as normal. He didn't like the reminder that he still had a ways to go.

"Nephew," his aunt said imperiously.

"Aunt Philly." Lee bent to kiss her dry cheek, trying not to inhale her trademark clash of sultry oriental perfume and mothballs from her "company coat."

Clutching his arm, Aunt Philly said, "I understand you don't want to talk about it."

And then she waited.

"You're looking well," he replied.

She frowned. "I can see why you don't want the whole country knowing your business, but you're among family now."

"And how are your azaleas?"

"It's a mistake to hold things in."

"And your cat?"

"You should be proud you survived. You're a hero."

"Not much opportunity for heroism chained to a wall, Auntie. All you have to do is take a breath and then another one." Because life was that simple. And that complicated. "Hell, we're both doing it now. In, out, in, out." He heard how sharp his voice had become and stopped speaking, aghast.

"In, out. In, out." She smiled. "It gets pretty special when you're my age."

"I'm sorry, I don't know—"

"It's okay." She patted his arm. "My father was in the war and he had little moments, too."

"Did he ever get over it?"

Her smile broadened to a grimace. "You take care," she said, and tottered away.

Guess that was a no. As he stared after her, a boy ran over. "Can I stand on your hand?"

Lee tried to imagine the towheaded kid in front of him two years younger and came up with a name. "You're too big now, Jack."

"Aw…" Glancing around, the boy grabbed a tiny girl playing chase through the adults. "Do my sister then. Eliza's only two."

The tot he'd captured took one look at Lee and started squirming to escape. Her brother tightened his grip. "You'll like it," he cooed.

Eliza started to wail, and gently Lee loosened Jack's grip on her. "Let her go, mate, she doesn't know me." Another chain broken.

"Well, can you do an airplane with me?"

"Next time, when I've built up more stamina and can do all the kids."

"And then you'll be fun again?"

Lee froze, unable to breathe.

"Jack, stop pestering Lee." His cousin put a hand on his son's shoulder. "Sorry, mate," he said when the boy ran off. "It's all about him, y'know?"

In, out. In, out. "Hey, no problem." Seeing a question forming, he added quickly, "So how are things with you, Frank?"

"Same old, same old." Rocking back on his heels, Frank folded his arms and settled in. Lee listened to a litany of woes about his sales job, which included his ass of a boss promoting a new twenty-something over him—after he'd been working for the company for eleven years—and that he was getting carpal tunnel syndrome because who made sales calls in person anymore? It was all texts and emails....

His cousin paused, waiting for a response.

Lee looked at Frank. Words trembled on his tongue. *Don't you realize how ephemeral life is? And you're wasting it whining about carpal tunnel syndrome? Then make a change! I lived in a room the size of a parking space for months. I didn't have a choice.*

He smiled weakly. "Your kids are terrific."

"There you are." Rob materialized in front of them. "Excuse us, Frank, I need to take him away."

Yeah, Lee thought, *take me away.* "Congratulations." Rob shook his hand. "Jules just told me you two have worked things out."

Lee looked around for her, surprised she'd said anything. "Did she mention we're keeping it quiet from Connie until after this party?"

Her reaction was anyone's guess.

"Mum's the word."

"What are you two talking about?" With an organizer's bustle Connie joined them, glass of wine in hand. Her flushed face suggested it wasn't her first. "Rob looks surreptitious, which suggests it's interesting."

"I was telling Lee," Rob commented, "that I asked Jules once what her secret was with Dad and she said, 'Ian needs to talk about Lee and I need to hear about him.'"

Connie's cheeks reddened even more. Lee finally found Jules. She was picking up one of the kids too short to reach the dessert table, and together they checked out the sweets. *You,* he thought.

"And how very much," his older brother continued acerbically, "I appreciated Jules making his last months so much better than they would have been without her."

Lee stole his sister's wine and gulped a sip.

"It's time to get over it, Connie," Rob said gently.

She opened her mouth to reply, but Lee got in first. "Rob, thank you for championing Jules. And I'd love you to keep doing it. But if you keep talking about Dad here—" his voice cracked and he took another swig of Connie's wine "—I'm going to break down and cry."

Instantly Connie's hostility dissipated and she put her arm around him. "I forgot this is your first family get-together without him. How can I make this easier?"

"Don't expect me to make a speech." He'd laid down the law earlier but the cake suggested she had other ideas.

Her lips tightened and then she sighed. "Okay, but I'll say a few words. Some of the family traveled a long way to be here today. In fact, the Hamilton cousins haven't seen you yet—go mingle." Plucking her empty wineglass from his hand, she began steering him toward some recent arrivals, pausing to glare over her shoulder at Rob. "I'll think about it," she said.

Like everyone else, the Hamiltons greeted him with hugs and handshakes and an expectation that he'd be the life and soul of the party.

He tried. God knows he tried, as the afternoon progressed, to be the old Lee. The joker, the charmer, the teller of tall tales.

But on face after face, he saw the same progression of emotion: excitement became confusion, compassion and then embarrassment as he struck one wrong note after another. "Before you used the bucket they called the toilet you had to thump it on the ground a couple of times to scare off the cockroaches. Otherwise you'd have them tickling your ass."

Like a stand-up comedian in trouble, he couldn't connect with his audience.

In the midst of family he felt more profoundly alone than he'd been as a captive. He felt almost as if he'd disappeared.

"Having a good time?" Jules said in one of their brief interactions.

He looked at the woman he loved, glowing with happiness. "Fantastic," he lied. "You?"

"It's fun catching up with everyone but I miss you. Want to sneak out for a snog behind the hall later?"

"Hell, yeah." He lifted her hand and kissed it to avoid her eyes, afraid of what she might see in his—a hollow man.

By the time the speeches started Lee was anesthetizing himself with more alcohol. Enough to loosen his tongue and give the punters what they wanted…fun reflections on the mother of all homestay vacations.

Except he couldn't resist correcting their misconceptions. "Most of the Taliban aren't Afghans, they're dispossessed young Muslims from neighboring states fighting for a cause greater than themselves."

"You sound like you're defending them," Frank said.

"The man who gave me sanctuary risked not just his life, but the lives of his family and fellow villagers."

"If he was so great then how did you end up in Taliban hands?"

"That," Lee said carefully, "is none of your—"

"Mind if I borrow this guy?" Jules tucked her arm in his and steered him away. "I could hear your voice across the other side of the hall. Are you okay?"

"I need to get out of here," he muttered, incapable of pretending any longer.

"Hang in there for five more minutes, Connie's just about to—"

Over by the buffet table, his sister clapped her hands. "Can I have your attention, please?"

Lee couldn't stop himself from groaning, which echoed audibly in the silence Connie's request had created. Shit.

Connie's smile grew fixed. "I promised Lee no speeches," she said. "I just wanted to thank you all for joining us to celebrate his return. It's been a tough couple of years for the Davis clan and we're so happy to have you home, Lee." She paused to compose herself.

"Speech!" someone yelled.

Connie sent him a plaintive look.

Lee stayed where he was but raised his glass. "Thanks for all your support. Great to see you all again." It was the best he could manage.

"And of course, he and Jules are engaged, so it's a double celebration," Connie continued woodenly. She hesitated. "She's become part of our family over the past year or so and was a great comfort to Dad. And on his behalf, I'd like to say thank you. It's not forgotten."

Cheers reverberated through the hall. Jules squeezed his arm and Lee grinned on cue. He felt like a balloon slowly losing air.

Out came the cake, carried by two of his nephews, slightly lopsided on the cake stand. The heat of the kitchen had softened the frosting…the red lettering of Welcome Home bled into the surrounding white.

Connie beckoned them over. "Come cut it, you two."

"I think you're getting confused with a wedding, Con," he managed to say.

Everyone laughed. Finally, he'd nailed a punch line.

But it came too late. Lee could no longer pretend Jules's love was enough to make him magically A-frickin'-okay. Or make the difficulty he was having connecting with others everybody else's fault.

The fault was his.

CHAPTER TWENTY-TWO

"It's only been two weeks, don't be so hard on yourself," Jules said as she pulled away from the community hall for the two-hour drive home.

Lee dug deep to call up the detachment he'd relied on to get him through captivity. "You're right." One last wave to his siblings, one last fake smile and finally he could lean back against the Pink Lady's passenger seat and close his eyes.

"The question that guy asked," she said, "about how you ended up a captive of the Taliban when you'd been given sanctuary. Did the militants scare him into handing you over?"

"No," he said shortly.

There was a moment's silence. "Was he killed?" she said in a low voice.

"No." *But he may have been since.* "Mind if we don't talk right now? I'm beat."

"Of course."

As soon as they got home Lee changed into workout clothes and started lifting weights. Five minutes later, Jules came to stand in the doorway, apparently unaware that he could see her reflection in the mirror as he ground through some lat pull-downs. She was chewing her lower lip. "I thought you were tired," she said.

"Mentally. Exercise will sort me out."

Ten minutes later she returned in a tee and stretchy yoga

pants. Climbing onto the rowing machine, she strapped her feet into the angled footrest and grabbed the handle.

Set up for him, it barely moved.

"How do you change this thing?"

"Lever on the magnetic wheel...right-hand side."

She peered at the control panel. "Now what?"

"You hate gym equipment."

"Do I?" She punched a few buttons.

"You better not be keeping an eye on me."

"I'm not." She started to row, settling into a rhythm.

Lee trained long after Jules had left, trained until he was drenched with sweat, until the pain in his body was all he felt. Then he took a long shower. When he left the bathroom, the smell of spicy chili wafted from the kitchen.

"Dinner's nearly ready," Jules called.

He shrugged a light sweater over his T-shirt. "Smells delicious—" that was true, but somehow the smell nauseated him "—but I ate so much at the party, I couldn't eat another bite. You go ahead. I'm all talked out so I might watch some television."

Dumping his workout clothes in the washing machine, he went to the living room and switched on the sports channel before settling on the couch.

What was left of his former self? The fearless optimist, the golden boy?

The old Lee *had* died on the day of the ambush.

For a long time he sat there, his eyes tracking movement and color but not seeing anything. He'd withdrawn to a place of numbness, a place he knew well. Where he didn't think. Didn't feel.

A light flicked on and he blinked, abruptly aware that he'd been sitting in the dark. Jules came in, ready for bed in her summer pj's and a light robe. Two mugs clinked together in her free hand.

"I made you a hot chocolate."

It was an effort to speak. "Thanks." He put it on the table.

Jules curled up beside him on the sofa, her knee touching his thigh. "Who's winning?"

Edging his leg away, Lee tuned into the game—basketball—and checked the score line at the top left of the screen. "Breakers."

"Okay." Cupping her mug, Jules sat back, somehow managing to nudge up against him again. He tried to shift away but he was already at the end of the couch. Irritation pierced his Zen-like calm. He quashed it.

Minutes passed. The warm pressure of her leg radiated into his, forcing him into a wider awareness of his surroundings—the flicker of the screen, the excitable commentary, the thud and squeak of the basketball shoes on the gym floor, the smell of the hot chocolate and honeysuckle.

Finally he caught her nodding off in his peripheral vision.

"Go to bed," he rasped. "I'll be in soon."

Her head jerked up. "I'm enjoying this." Another five minutes and her chin dropped again. Slowly she toppled to rest her head on his shoulder.

"Jules, go to bed." No response. Goddammit.

For the rest of the game he sat with her sleeping body a warm weight against his shoulder. The Breakers won, 105–103. Lee switched off the remote and uncrossed his arms, feeling the blood return to his stiff joints. Strands of her hair tickled his bicep. He brushed them off, one by one, twining the last strand around his thumb. Soft and silky, so delicate against his roughened hands.

"Ow." Rubbing her scalp, she sat up and glanced sleepily at the dead screen. "Is the game over?"

"Yeah."

She looked at him and her eyes widened. "Lee," she said helplessly.

He had no idea what the problem was.

Her fingers touched his cheek. "You've been crying."

"That's crazy." Pushing her hand away, he felt his face, and fiercely rubbed it dry. "Guess I was really invested in the Breakers winning." Humiliated, he pushed to his feet.

She followed, catching him around the waist and pressing her face to his chest. "Tell me how to help you."

"I'm fine."

"Fine?" she said. "You're obsessive about exercise, you treat offers of support from those who love you as attempts to manage you. You exhaust yourself trying to be the same guy you were before deployment then beat yourself up when you can't sustain it. We're all on your side and you don't have to do this alone."

His anger flared and he couldn't contain it. "Maybe I want to."

"You need to talk to someone," she persisted. "It doesn't have to be me. An army therapist…the guys. People who can relate to your experience."

"Don't you get it? *No one* can relate to *my* experience. No one can understand what it was like."

"Try me."

"You want to understand," he sneered. "You want to know what it was like? Really?"

She nodded, her gaze unwavering on his.

"Then come with me." Catching her hand, he half pulled, half marched her outside, across the damp grass. A light drizzle fell so softly Lee only registered it on the back of his neck, his cheeks above the stubble. It was very dark. No moon could get through these clouds. Only the yellow light through a neighbor's curtains illuminated the uneven slabs leading to the garden shed.

At the door he paused. "Stop me anytime you like."

Jules shook her head, her face an indistinct blur.

"You think I'll go easy on you," he said harshly. "You think this is a game?"

"No."

The aluminum door rattled as Lee jerked it open, steered Jules inside and slammed it shut with a clang of finality. "Magnify that sound," he told her shadow. "Imagine an echo. Every day you'll hear it when the guard opens or closes it. Maybe once, maybe half a dozen times depending on how bored they are—or how angry."

There weren't any windows in the shed, that's why he'd chosen it. After long hours spent working in the garden, he knew where every tool was. And he had long practice existing in the dark. He felt for and found the bike chain and looped it around her ankles. "Is that okay?" he asked.

"Yes."

"Then it's too loose." He yanked it tighter, felt her wince. "*Stop* is your safe word," he barked. "Say it and we're done here."

"I want to understand." He could hear the determination in her voice but also the fear... Yes...there was fear.

He threaded the ends of the chain through the exposed wooden framework of the shed and spun the combination lock. Some rags lay on the workbench; he used one as a blindfold. "Every time a guard enters, it goes on. Put it on." She did, he checked and tightened it. "If they think you're peeking..."

Lee slammed his palm against the aluminum siding beside her and Jules gasped. "They would use the butt of a Kalashnikov against my throat, pushing until I choked." He laid his forearm against her neck and exerted the lightest of pressure, felt her swallow hard. "One liked to stroke my face with it." Picking up a garden trowel, he laid the cold metal against her cheek.

"Blindfolded, you can't prepare for the blows, you can only wait for them. Here." His hand tapped her thigh. She jumped. "Here." He rested a fist against her belly. "Or their particular favorite, here." He flattened his palm over her pubic bone, struggling not to cry.

"And then they leave," he said, "taking the light with them. And you know what happens after that?"

She cleared her throat. "What?"

"Nothing. You take off the blindfold but it doesn't matter because you can't see anything anyway. Go ahead." The bike chain rattled. "You strain to accustom your eyes to the dark. On either side of you, just within reach, are a bucket and a bottle. The bucket's your toilet, the bottle holds your drinking water. Rolled up against the wall behind you is a blanket, thin, flea-ridden, it smells of decay and mold and the last man trapped here. If you had light you'd probably see bloodstains.

"You smell the dirt, the damp, the sourness of your body, your excrement in the bucket. You protect your food because in the dark, mice, cockroaches and ants will take it. Sometimes you rattle your chains, simply to remind yourself you still exist. You do squats, push-ups and sit-ups because the shackles limit your movement to a few feet.

"You have no control over any aspect of your life…when you're fed, taken for a shower, even over light or dark. You're helpless. Every time the door crashes open, you don't know if you'll be killed or fed, exercised or beaten."

He heard her choke back a sob in the dark.

"You have a safe word. Use it."

"No," she whispered.

He paused before continuing. "When they let you have light you mark time by how long it takes your bruises to heal. Your days become cycles of interminable boredom punctuated by intermittent terror. Your clothes rot on you. And you wait. You wait for your unit to burst through the door like the bloody cavalry. Even though you believe your brothers are dead...the SAS is a family that won't leave a man behind."

He heard another muffled sob from her but ignored it, caught up in telling the story.

"You thought you had inner resources...instead you're at the mercy of mood swings, delusions and hallucinations. You're unable to separate past from present, fiction from reality."

Lee started to sweat. "You start to welcome the beatings because they mean human contact. Eventually even the lies you comfort yourself with...that someone's coming for you...don't work anymore."

Jules moved and the chain rattled, startling him. She didn't say anything.

"You consider taking your own life," he said hoarsely. "Except you haven't got the means. Until you realize that you do and you stop eating. They try to force you, but they can't make you, not effectively."

He started breathing hard, his lungs full of the earthy dankness of the shed. "Dying in the dark you hear a voice say that giving up isn't an option. And it gets louder, more annoying. It won't stop. Finally you...you start eating again. You've made a choice, to try to live. You expect to feel at peace now that you've come to a decision, but all you've done is open yourself to pain again, the pain of hope."

He scrambled to find a point of reference in the dark, which closed around him in a dense suffocating mass. His skin clammy, his breathing shallow, Lee started to spiral into panic.

A touch on his cheek made him jump. Fingertips, feminine and reassuring, stroked his face. His breathing eased. Jules. He closed his hand convulsively over hers, holding it against his clenched jaw for one weak moment before releasing it.

"The Americans burst in and you think you're hallucinating, that this is another dream. And then you come home and people call you a hero and all you did was survive. Even when you didn't want to."

The bike chain rattled as she drew him closer and then her arms closed around him, like two tight bands, only they didn't feel constricting; they felt like the only things holding him together, holding him upright. With a shuddering breath, he bowed his head and buried his nose in her fragrant hair.

"It was your voice, Jules," he whispered.

Her soft lips trailed across his cheek and pressed a kiss against the corner of his mouth. At some point she'd taken off the blindfold. He turned his head, their lips touched, blood warm. Her hands closed around his biceps, holding him there. As though he had the power or will to move away.

The kiss became charged with desire. Lee needed to lose himself in her, to turn the dark into their shared refuge. How many times had he tried to summon her in captivity? How many times had he failed?

Deeper and deeper they spiraled into the kiss, until she was everything—her arms tight around his neck, her body with its narrow waist and flare of hips pressed the length of his, her scent in his nostrils.

They broke apart for a breath, then kissed again. He slid his hand up to cup her breast, found the peak through her thin robe. She wanted him. It was in her breathing, in the restlessness of her fingers, in the fervency of her response. "Jules."

"Don't stop."

He slid his palms over the silk of her housecoat, tugging the tie free, pushing it off her shoulders. He fumbled with the buttons of her pajama top, baring her skin, tasting each nipple.

Her arms were tangled in her sleeves. With a murmur of impatience she wiggled free, careless of where her clothing fell. Her hand worked at his zipper, exposing him to the cool air and her warm grasp.

"Jules." He pulled down her shorts and found her wet, swollen and ready.

"Now," she whispered hoarsely.

Lee lifted her, but the shackle around her ankle caught against something and she was stuck.

Reality returned so fast he felt dizzy.

What had he done? "You're chained," he said numbly. Hunkering down, he tried to figure out the lock, but his fingers were shaking. "What's the combination?"

"Four, nine, eight, six. But it's okay." He felt her touch his hair. "I'm okay."

Still in a blind panic, he wrestled with the numbers.

"Let me." Jules crouched beside him and took over.

Lee dropped his face in his hands. "What the hell was I thinking?"

"Lee, I'm okay…really."

"This screwed-up shit is mine to deal with, not yours." He yanked open the shed door to give her more light and saw the glint of chain around her ankle. Shame overwhelmed him.

"You don't deserve this," he rasped. "I'm so sorry." He watched her line up the rotating numbers and then helped her pull the length of chain apart.

"Nothing happened here without my consent." Her compassionate gaze lifted. "Nothing."

It was the last straw. "I'm sorry," he blurted again, and stumbled out of the shed at a run.

HE NEEDED HER.

It was all Jules could think of as she fumbled to unwind the chain from her ankle. Impatiently she did up her pajamas and then felt around the floor for her robe. It took more precious seconds to find the tie but she didn't want to spook Lee further by appearing mistreated. Judging by his stricken expression and the way he'd run, he was feeling guilty enough.

She tripped on the uneven path in her haste to reach the house, falling heavily on her hands and knees and scraping her left palm. Jules swore.

The neighbor's porch light flicked on before she could scramble to her feet. "Who's out there?" quavered the older woman.

"It's okay, Rosemary, it's only me."

"Jules, you gave me such a fright. Are you all right?" Brandishing a can of hair spray in one hand, and a leprechaun doorstop in the other, her elderly neighbor peered over from her porch in her nightgown. "I've been hearing bangs and rattles to wake the dead."

"I was looking for something in the shed and tripped." Getting to her feet, Jules brushed off her palms, ignoring the sting. "I'm sorry I woke you."

"Well, I'm relieved I won't have to fight anyone tonight." Rosemary replaced the leprechaun on the doorstep and straightened, one hand on her heart. "Ooh, I've gone all light-headed. Silly old woman getting frightened like that. I must stop watching so much *CSI*."

Jules looked anxiously toward her own porch and then stepped through the low hedge between the two properties. "Let me help you inside."

"Sweetie, your hand is bleeding," Rosemary exclaimed as Jules came into the light.

"It's nothing."

"And you've smeared blood on your pretty robe."

"It'll wash out." Jules settled Rosemary on her La-Z-Boy rocker in her living room. "How are you doing?"

"Better...perhaps a glass of water?"

Jules hurried into the kitchen and filled a glass, craning for a glimpse of Lee through the window. The lights were still on but she couldn't see his silhouette anywhere. She hurried back to Rosemary. "Here you go."

"Thank you. You go home and attend to that nasty graze." A clock on the mantel chimed. "Goodness, I didn't realize it was so late. Midnight!"

Jules caught the sounds of the Pink Lady's engine firing. "Good night." Rushing to Rosemary's front door, she eyed the dead bolt, then swiveled and raced through the house, past the startled woman and out the back door again. Hurdling the hedge, she tore down the side of her house and out to the curb, by which time the sound of the Caddy had faded to a distant rumble.

He was driving too fast.

She stared down the empty street.

Maybe he'd left a note. Jogging into the house, Jules finally found one on her pillow in the spare room.

"I can't deal with this right now. I'm deeply sorry, Jules." He'd underscored *deeply.* "You don't deserve this."

"Don't tell me what I deserve!" No point phoning his cell—he wouldn't answer it until he calmed down. Constitutionally incapable of doing nothing, she called and left a message anyway.

Where would he go? If it was Nate and Claire's she could try phoning him in forty minutes. And if he didn't answer his cell, she'd try their landline. Except if he *wasn't* there, she'd only worry them.

Maybe he'd gone to a motel. Maybe he'd already arrived. She grabbed her cell again.

"The mobile device you are calling is either turned off or outside the coverage area."

"Don't *do* this to me!" Jules sat down and tried to think but found herself crying instead, her emotions a cathartic soup after what he'd shared. Picking up her cell she sent a text. Do NOT feel guilty. No, she needed to evoke a response. Deleting it, she sobbed and tried again. I won't sleep unless I know you're safe.

Tears streaming down her face, she lowered her cell and stared at the blood on her robe.

Wiping her nose on her sleeve—what the hell, it was ruined anyway—she pulled herself together and rose to doctor her graze with antiseptic and a bandage. Then she changed into a clean pair of pajamas and hunted for one of Lee's sweatshirts to pull over it.

Crawling into bed, Jules laid her head in the indent he'd left in the pillow. Staring up at the ceiling, she prepared herself for a long night.

The beep of an incoming text sent her scrambling to the nightstand for her cell.

One word. Safe.

She let out a shaky breath. It was a start.

CHAPTER TWENTY-THREE

JULES WAS IN the garden hanging out the washing when she heard Lee arrive home the next morning at eight.

Her pulse picked up and she took a couple of deep breaths to compose herself before she called, "I'm outside."

She'd already decided that she wasn't going to make a fuss so she returned to hanging out the bedsheets. She would remain calm and follow Lee's lead. It was the perfect day for drying laundry, sunny and warm with a sporadic breeze that wafted the white cotton sheets.

His shadow loomed behind the sheet. "I apologize for what I put you through last night."

So they were starting formally then.

Picking up a blue plastic peg, Jules finished attaching a pillowcase. "As I said last night, you have nothing to apologize for."

The clothesline was an old-fashioned one, a four-sided umbrella shape. She swung it round and he came into view. He didn't look as though he'd slept, either. His stubble was almost a beard and his green eyes were bloodshot, but he was still the most beautiful sight in the world. "Where did you go?"

"I drove mostly...went out to the coast and sat on a beach. Found a twenty-four-hour McDonald's." His mouth twisted. "The usual haunts of the angst-ridden."

If he could find a sense of humor, they were going to be

okay. She smiled but he didn't smile back, instead bending to pick up a wet sheet from the clothes basket between them.

"I managed to clarify a lot of things." Pegging one corner of the sheet to the line, he added awkwardly, "If that's any consolation for scaring you half to death."

"I'm glad," she said simply. "But I was never afraid of you. Only…" *Hurting with you.* Words couldn't express her sadness for what he'd suffered.

"Yeah," Lee said gruffly and disappeared behind the sheet as he pegged the second corner.

"No one could come through what you did unscathed, but you'll eventually recover because you're…" Jules hunted for the right word.

"A bullheaded arrogant jerk?" his shadow supplied.

Jules swung the clothesline another turn. "Irrepressible." She tried to smile again, but he was looking beyond her. Turning to follow his gaze, she saw only the garden and the plum tree, both heavy with morning dew.

"I was once," he said. "And I hope to be again." His gaze returned to her. "This isn't going to work, Jules—not yet."

His tone was so even it took a moment for her to realize what he was saying.

She dropped the peg she was holding. "You want to break off the engagement?"

"Short-term. I'm not stable yet and I won't let you share the burden of my recovery."

"You're not a burden, you're my love. And that's my choice to make."

It was amazing how steady her voice sounded considering the sky had just fallen in.

"You must be having second thoughts after what happened last night."

"None. You would never hurt me."

"How can you know that when I don't?" Picking up her

hand, he examined the graze on her palm. "I hurt you last night," he said harshly.

"No, I fell on the path."

"I chained and blindfolded you, I terrorized you—"

"I wasn't afraid of you."

"But I'm terrified for you. Scared of myself and what I might do. For God's sake, I beat up your ex-boyfriend in the gas station. I didn't know I was going to do it until I had him pinned against a wall and was choking off his air supply."

"I had a safe word."

"At a certain point I don't know if I was capable of hearing it. I'm not risking your safety. You have to let me protect you."

He'd talked about not burdening her, but this was the greater burden. She thought he was wrong, but she couldn't be sure. She had no experience with PTSD. "When will you come back?" she whispered.

"When I've got more to offer than the man I am now."

She remembered her resolve to follow his lead and remain calm. "I want to do what's best for you."

She took off the ring and offered it to him, but he closed her hand around it. "Keep it safe for us."

"Where will you live?"

"At Rob's initially, in Auckland." He rubbed a hand wearily over his eyes. "There's a therapist there who specializes in post-hostage trauma."

"You said you couldn't live with your family," Numbly Jules struggled to come to grips with how quickly things had changed for them.

"I managed to share digs with the Taliban for fourteen months. I can always go back there if Rob proves too much."

She tried to smile.

"Thank you," he rasped. "For understanding."

But she didn't understand, not really. *Don't go.* "What about Ross and Viv's wedding?"

"Oh, God, I hadn't thought of that."

He really wanted to leave; he really wanted to get away from her. Jules hugged herself. "I won't go," she offered.

"No…that's not fair to anybody. And I can't pull out, either." Lee dragged a hand through his dark blond hair. "I've let my friends down too often."

What about me? she wanted to cry. *Aren't I your friend, too?*

"We'll just have to make the best of it."

She struggled to hold back tears.

"Don't cry," Lee said hoarsely. "Please don't cry. We're done with it, remember. It'll turn out okay…I swear I'll come back."

"You'd better." The joke rang hollow. Would he? Or would she lose him again, this time for good.

"That's settled then." He cleared his throat. "I'll go pack."

He didn't offer an embrace and she didn't want one. It was the only way either of them could get through it.

"YOU KNOW YOU'RE getting old—" Dan laid his golf club on the pristine green of Beacon Bay Golf Club's eighteen hole to line up his final putt "—when you stay sober at a stag because winning a game of golf the next morning is more important."

He finished gauging the distance and picked up his club. Angling his body over it, he reconfirmed the angle with two quick glances between ball and cup. The putter kissed the ball and it glided into the hole. "But, by God, it's worth it." He straightened with a grin. "Pay up, whippersnappers."

From the shade of a golf cart, Ross and Nate groaned. Slumped in their seats, their caps pulled so low the brims touched the top of their sunglasses, they looked like a couple of sulky teens on a family day trip. "Lee, make him stop," said Nate.

"Are you kidding?" Lee offered Dan his hand. "Put it there, partner."

"I hate them both," Ross said. "And the worst thing is I'm going to be related to one of them tomorrow."

"It's Dan's local course," Nate grumbled. "Of course, he's going to win."

They both revived after a big breakfast at the clubhouse and a couple of gallons of black coffee. "Okay." Ross pushed his mug aside. "I'm human again. Since this is the first and only chance the four of us have to be alone this weekend, let's get down to business."

It was Lee's turn to groan. "Haven't we covered off every detail yet?"

"I'm talking about *your* business."

"You all know why I left." He'd told them about his violent outbursts. "I didn't do it lightly."

Five days after he'd chained Jules in the shed, he still felt every nerve ending twitch and jump every time he thought about it.

"You've had a couple of appointments with the military shrink this week. What does she say about it?"

"Mark triggered a rage because I perceived him as a bully."

"*Our* Mark?" Ross said, shocked.

"Stow it, Ice," said Dan. "More important, does your therapist agree that you might be a threat to Jules?"

"Therapists don't give categorical answers." But she had suggested the incident with Jules might have had a therapeutic effect for him. And told him to focus on the positive in the experience. The moment when Jules reached out in the dark and touched his face.

Nate sat back. "Without question you did the right thing, stepping back to seek expert counsel—we don't charge for ours, incidentally—to reassess the situation. Ending the engagement on the other hand...not so smart. If Jules wants to be involved in your recovery, let her. It's not like either of you is happy apart."

Lee swallowed. "We both agreed—"

"What else could Jules say when you've asked her to release you from your engagement?" Nate interrupted impatiently. "She has her pride. And she's still unsure about the best way to handle your PTSD."

"It's short-term pain for long-term gain," Lee argued. "This is the best thing for our future. In a couple of months I'll have a job, I'll be further along in therapy—"

Dan took his turn. "So you'll do some kind of makeover and then sweep back on a white horse saying, 'Look, Jules, I'm superglued into perfection'? This is where we think your reasoning is flawed."

Lee was silent.

"You're missing an important part of the process," Dan continued. "Jules needs to see the groveling, the trying, the failing, the trying again...and she needs to see you doing it for *her*."

"And for the record—" Ice took off his cap and ran a hand through his new wedding buzz cut "—you weren't so perfect in the old days. In fact, you were a cocky son of a bitch." He replaced his cap. "Now you have my humility."

Catching the waitress's eye, Nate gestured for the check. "We only hung out with you because your Greek God looks attracted women we then picked off with intelligence and wit."

"Come to think of it," said Dan, taking out his wallet and putting some notes on the table. "Now that we're married or about to be, why do we even need him anymore?"

"Because," Ross explained patiently, favoring his leg as he stood, "hanging out with a pathetic loser makes us look like good guys, which gets us laid more often."

"Ice," Dan began.

"Yeah, yeah, no sexy talk. Okay, Lee, you're still on the team."

Lee added some bills to the pile on the table. "I think I liked it better when you were trying to protect my feelings."

THE AFTERNOON WEDDING rehearsal took place in the same tiny Beacon Bay church Dan and Jo had got married in. Jules hadn't been able to attend, but wild horses wouldn't have kept her away from this one.

Giving up is not an option. She wished she'd recalled Lee's argument when she'd needed it earlier in the week, but he'd blindsided her into agreeing to let him go.

She was much better prepared now. Patting the pocket of her red jacket to make sure she had her notes, she took a moment to admire the setting and strengthen her resolve.

On a small headland jutting into the sea, the church was a poster child for early colonial architecture with its white clapboard, steep-pitched roof and arched, stained-glass windows. Hedges of wind-twisted magnolias and camellias protected it from the prevailing nor'westerlies.

Every night she got the same text. Loving you. Every night sent one in return. Me, too. Sucking in a bracing lungful of sea air, Jules entered the church.

She'd practiced what she was going to say a thousand times and as soon as the rehearsal was over she would take Lee aside and tell him very calmly, very quietly and reasonably, why he was coming home with her after the wedding. If that didn't sway him, she'd show him the tattoo. Or not. She still couldn't quite believe she'd gotten the tattoo. Guess she wasn't as together as she thought.

The first person she saw was Ross, who stood at the altar, talking to the priest. He paused to give her a wave.

Nate and Claire sat in the front pew. Nervously, she smiled over them to Dan, who stood in the aisle chatting with the rest of his family: his dad, Herman, Viv's identical twin sister, Merry, and a little girl Jules recognized as Merry's daughter.

She scanned the church again, all her bravado leaving her. There was no sign of Lee the second time, either.

What if he'd decided he couldn't face her yet and wasn't coming?

Her heels tapped on the wooden floorboards as she approached Dan and his family but, after exchanging greetings, she couldn't bring herself to ask about Lee, overcome by a sudden shyness.

She'd presented the facts of their separation, that it was mutual, temporary but open-ended, and had backed herself into an emotionally repressed corner. Revealing herself now as a needy and scared would be—

"Hi, everyone," said Lee.

Jules closed her eyes. Thank God.

"You're late," Ross barked, making the minister jump.

Jules turned as Lee's gaze shifted away from her to the altar.

"Actually, I'm dead on time," Lee replied. No one got the joke but Jules chuckled. Lee's attention returned to her and she lost her courage and crouched to talk to the little girl. "Hello, Tilly, I'm Jules. I guess you're really excited to be a flower girl, huh?"

Simultaneously, Jo and Merry shook their heads.

Tilly scowled. "No, I hate mushy stuff."

"Me, too," Jules confided. "But sometimes we have to do it."

Ice clapped his hands. "Okay, everyone, here's what's

happening. Jo…you're standing in for the bride with Herman." Viv and her mother were flying in at dawn the following day.

The pregnant woman saluted. "Yes, sir."

Ross ignored the teasing by glancing at his copious notes. "Groomsmen, with me, and the best man here at the right of the altar…. Do you know where you're supposed to be, Father?"

"I think so, son," said the priest.

In her peripheral vision, Jules saw Lee start toward her and told herself to remain calm.

"Bridesmaids, come in from the back shortest to tallest—that's you, Jules." She tried to concentrate on what he was saying, acutely conscious of Lee's approach. "Then Merry, then Claire. Oh, shit—sorry, Father—the matron of honor's supposed to be the last attendant down the aisle. Claire and Merry, swap places."

He flipped over the first sheet on his clipboard and some loose notes fell out.

Scrambling to pick them up, he kept talking. "We're scrubbing a ring bearer. I don't even trust the best man with the rings." Lee paused, frowning toward his friend. "Then Tilly, honey—" Ross found his niece "—you come in just before the bride."

"I know," she said, bored. "I've done this before."

Ross tried to repeg his notes on the clipboard but somehow the bulldog clip kept slipping. More papers dropped onto the floor. Everyone watched in astonishment as the Iceman transformed into a dithering idiot.

"Last to come down the aisle is the bride, on her father's left arm. Or should that be right arm?" He raked a hand through his hair. "I can't remember."

Lee stepped forward, along with Dan and Nate, taking the clipboard out of Ice's trembling hands, before Nate turned him to face the stained window at the back of the church.

Dan said to the priest, "May we have a couple of minutes?"

"Of course."

Jules realized her mouth was open and closed it. If she hadn't seen it she wouldn't have believed it.

"Can we have some music for the bridesmaids and flower girl to practice to, please?" Jo called to the organist. A classical rendition of the "Wedding March" struck up behind them. "We pace ourselves five rows apart, ladies."

"What's wrong with Uncle Ross?"

"He's checking the stained glass for cracks," said Jules. "You know how he likes things to be perfect. So I go first as the shortest?"

"And walk slooooowly," the little girl advised.

"Look at me," she heard Ross say, as she slow-timed her walk down the aisle. "My hands are shaking. You made the marriage thing look so easy," he accused Dan.

"What the hell are you talking about? I was soaked in mud and ditch water after fighting my way out of the bush to my wedding."

But Ross wasn't listening. "What if Viv's plane is delayed?"

"There's six hours' grace in there, mate," Nate pointed out.

"Oh, God, what if her plane goes down?"

Jules tried to concentrate on her timing but her attention was riveted by the drama unfolding at the altar. Ross's meltdown wasn't doing anything for her own jangled nerves.

"I'd love to say this is payback for aiding and abetting Jo at our wedding," Dan said, "but I can't, you're too pathetic."

"Not helping, Dan," Nate said, taking over. "She'll be here. Remember your 'keep the faith' speech?"

"There's still another twelve hours for her to change her mind."

Jules had reached the halfway point when she heard Tilly order the next bridesmaid to follow her.

"Take a deep breath." Lee put a reassuring arm around Ross's shoulder. "Do what I did in captivity. Break time down to manageable chunks and concentrate on surviving that. Thirty minutes, ten minutes…" Ross looked at him, wild-eyed. "Five minutes…thirty seconds?" Lee exchanged worried glances with the other guys.

"Oh, for the love of…" Jo strode past Jules. "I'll sort this out."

She spun Ross around, snapping her fingers in his face. "You're the Iceman, where's your pride? Harden up!"

Jules covered her mouth to hide a smile.

Ross's panic subsided. He focused on Jo's face and then his expression solidified into horror. "I had…a girlie moment."

"You did, but it's over." Jo started back up the aisle. Winking at Jules, she called over her shoulder, "Though I'll still be bringing it up at your golden wedding anniversary."

Jules grinned. As she restarted her stately walk, timing it with the "Wedding March," her eyes met Lee's. After five lonely nights without him, the impact jolted through her like an electric current. She faltered.

"She's getting it all wrong," said Tilly gleefully. Tearing her eyes away from Lee, Jules concentrated on the steps, but her staccato heartbeat made it difficult to get the timing right, particularly as Lee stood watching her from the front of the church. Almost like a bridegroom. What if he said no? How would she cope? She had to deliver her impassioned speech before she ended up in a worse state than Ross.

"We need to talk," she said, too loudly. All the guys

looked up. "Now," she said to Lee. Heat flaming her cheeks, Jules pivoted and walked out of the church, not waiting to see if he followed her or not. Ross made some protest; she heard Lee reply. Trying to recall her speech before the words rearranged themselves into dyslexic gibberish, Jules didn't hear what either of them said.

Outside, her relief at seeing Lee behind her scattered her thoughts and she couldn't recall her opening line. Thank God she had notes in her jacket pocket. She fumbled for them.

"I have something to say first," he said.

"You had your turn," she replied, bossy when she wanted desperately to be persuasive. "Now it's mine."

He swallowed. "Okay." Why was he nervous? Oh God, it had to be bad.

The wind gusted across the steps and caught her dark hair, whipping strands across her face and billowing the skirt of her green floral dress. Flattening her skirt, Jules gestured to a wooden bench. "Sit…please."

Unclenching the fisted hold on her notes, she smoothed out the paper. "I've been doing research on PTSD. It's very bad for you to cut yourself off from your significant other."

"Jules."

"I don't want you to say anything before I've finished." She had a host of good arguments and he was going to hear all of them. "I have some stats here." Another gust caught her dress and, making a grab for the skirt, she lost her notes across the grass. They blew in all directions. She started after them before she saw the futility in it and stopped.

"Dammit," she said brokenly.

"Jules."

"No, I can wing it." She started to pace, three steps in each direction, palms pressed against her skirt.

"I'll listen," he said, "but let's get out of the wind."

He drew her to the sheltered side of the church to an ornate bench overlooking an ancient-looking graveyard. As he sat, she resumed her pacing on the gravel path. "You said you're afraid you'll hurt me, but this separation hurts me. And you won't anyway—hurt me—and you're just going to have to take my word for it."

The words tumbled out, not in anything like the order she'd rehearsed. Raw. Disjointed. Real. The gravel crunched like sugar underfoot.

"You expected me to marry you on faith after six weeks of dating and now it's your turn to trust me. Keep listening to my voice telling you that giving up isn't an option—no, don't answer yet, I haven't finished."

Unconsciously she steadied herself against an old headstone. His green eyes were starting to distract her.

"I got a tattoo," she blurted, "on my back. Because I wanted to show you how serious I am about this. From the day I met you you've been under my skin, so I figured I'd make it official." It still felt like a bruise on the inside of her left shoulder blade when her cotton bodice tightened across it.

His eyes seemed to grow warmer and warmer. She found herself drawing nearer. "The tattoo says, *Semper et pepetuum,* which is Latin for 'always and forever.'" She stood in front of him. "So in conclusion…"

Her voice trailed off as he stood. She lifted her gaze until she was looking up into his eyes, their bodies all but touching.

"In conclusion," she repeated, and then her voice dropped to a whisper. "Come home."

"Be sure," he said. "While my therapist seems to think what happened with Mark will prove the exception rather than the rule, I can be so much closer to normal in a few more months. I have a job prospect with that kids' camp you got me onto and—"

"Stop making this complicated," she interrupted, quoting words he'd spoken so many, many months ago. "Do you believe in us or not?"

He cupped her face in his roughened hands. "I believe," he said, then scooped her up and spun her around. And then they were kissing to the point where they either had to stop or get naked in a church graveyard.

Five minutes later, Jules was sitting in Lee's lap, her head on his shoulder, when Tilly poked her nose around the building. "Uncle Ross says you have to come back now." She frowned as she took in Jules's position.

"Two more minutes," Lee promised, stopping Jules from rising by tightening his hold. "I don't suppose you brought the ring with you," he said, and Jules laughed.

"No more proposals," she said. "Except mine." She buried her face in his neck. "Marry me," she whispered. "As soon as we can arrange it."

"You spontaneous romantic types never think things through." His lips curved into a smile against her neck. "Not without a prenup… In fact…I've already started working on it."

Jules sat up. "You're kidding."

Shifting her off his lap, Lee pulled an envelope out of his jacket and gave it to her. "Why I was late to rehearsal. I went to see a lawyer."

She opened it and started scanning the document.

"That money you owe me," he said. "I thought of a compromise. Sign over an equivalent share in your house. Once I'm earning again I'll keep investing until I hit forty-eight percent."

"That's brilliant." Jules stared at him. "But don't you mean fifty percent?"

"No," he said seriously, "because it needs to stay your house."

And she fell in love with him all over again.

"Are you two trying to drive me crazy?" Ross, irate, stormed around the corner. "Did I not send my best lieutenant to fetch you ten minutes ago?"

He scanned their faces and his scowl deepened. "Great that you're happy, but can we make this about me?"

Laughing, Jules stood and pulled Lee to his feet. Fingers intertwined, they followed the groom into the church.

"I didn't see any mention in this document of your conditions," Jules said as they entered the vestibule.

"Other than sighting that tattoo, I don't have any." He caught her around the waist, spun her into his arms and kissed her again, to a burst of applause from their friends. "All I ever wanted was you."

CHAPTER TWENTY-FOUR

THE BRIDE WORE BLACK.

Her groom took no offense. Ice's eyes gleamed when he saw his flamboyant love in the strapless mermaid gown, black Chantilly lace over champagne satin. From her position up front with the other bridesmaids Jules heard him murmur, "Worth it."

Dark hair loose around her shoulders in contrast to her bridesmaids' upswept styles, Vivien Jansen was fearless and beautiful. The perfect mate for Ice.

Jules caught the middle groomsman's eye and read Lee's expression perfectly. *Get a dress like that for our wedding.* She looked forward to telling him it was another Vera Wang—Viv having been too busy to design her own. "It was either the dress or some honeymoon lingerie," she'd confided at the hairdresser's. "Unsurprisingly, the lingerie got Ross's vote."

Lee's gaze brushed like a kiss over the champagne-satin sheath hugging Jules, the expanse of thigh and stiletto heels. She shivered, her fingers tightening on the bouquet of blue hydrangeas, white roses and lilacs.

Like the groom, he wore a silver-gray tuxedo and a white dress shirt under a lavender vest and tie. The effect could have been effeminate; that it wasn't testified to Viv's flair and men comfortable enough in their masculinity not to wear it self-consciously. The result was magnificent; every woman got a little fluttery around them.

Jules pressed her stomach as her own butterflies took flight. Lee's weight gain over the past month had filled in the hollows in his face and fleshed out his frame. His charisma was fast regaining its former wattage and, today, the glow of newfound happiness made him as handsome as his buddies.

I did that for him, she thought, giddy as a newlywed herself after last night. They'd left the wedding rehearsal and gone back to her hotel room, reaffirming their own vows by making love. This morning she'd been woken by Lee's tuneless shower rendition of Johnny Farnham's "When the War is Over."

Viv's father kissed his daughter and retired. Radiant, she took Ross's arm.

"Dearly beloved," intoned the priest, "we are gathered here…"

Ice was dripping happiness all over the place and Jules didn't dare to stand too close in case together they created a small lake.

"…if anyone present knows of any reason why the couple should not be married speak now or forever hold your peace."

"I'm sorry but…" From the second pew, Jo rose, her face white.

Jules snapped out of her reverie. Everyone gaped at Jo.

Slapping both hands over her mouth, Jo stumbled into the aisle and ran for the exit.

Dan strode after his wife, realized he was the best man and stopped, glancing over his shoulder at the bridal couple.

Ross was being supported by his laughing bride. "Talk to your wife about her timing," he said weakly.

Viv waved her brother away. "We'll wait…chat amongst yourselves for ten minutes," she told the congregation cheerfully and started fanning her groom.

"Remind me to apologize to Ross later," Jules murmured to Claire. "I thought that was a setup."

Viv heard her. "Oh, it was," she said. "But Jo's afternoon sickness gave us a real excuse."

"Wait, you were in on this, too?"

Everyone within earshot laughed, including the priest and the bride's parents and her twin, who was disconcerting enough just by being identical to the bride. "I needed that," Ross said, chuckling. "Jules, this woman taught me everything I know about returning things to their rightful places. Why do you think she's called Hurricane?"

That made no sense but apparently the bride understood because she said, "God, I adore you," and kissed him.

"Slightly out of sequence," said the priest, "but your groomsmen said you need the practice." He'd clearly been a family friend a long time.

Five minutes later, Jo returned on the arm of her husband, her pallor replaced by a blush of mortification. "I'm so sorry," she began again, and was drawn into a bear hug by the groom.

"Let's put it this way," he said fondly, "now neither of us gets to tell cute anecdotes about this wedding."

"Deal," Jo agreed with a sigh and returned to her pew.

The bride pricked up her ears. "What's this?"

Ross turned her toward the altar. "Vows," he said firmly. "Now, Father, if you please."

The congregation hushed as the clergyman found his place. "I, Ross Coltrane," he began.

"I, Ross Coltrane."

"Take you, Vivien Jansen…"

"Take you, Vivien Jansen."

As she listened to the sincerity in Ross's voice, Jules felt strangely moved. That was crazy because she was a cynic. This stuff didn't affect her.

"Promise to be true to you in good times and in bad…"

Instinctively her gaze sought Lee's. She found him already watching her.

"In good times and in bad…" Lee mouthed the words silently. "I will love and honor you all the days of my life."

Tears pricked her eyes and she blinked rapidly.

"I, Vivien Jansen, take thee, Ross Coltrane."

Jules looked at her feet, in satin shoes that matched her dress. She frowned fiercely. The glossy tip of one shoe darkened where a tear had fallen.

Honestly, she never cried at weddings. This was ridiculous. Her nose started to run. With no handkerchief, she tried to sniff quietly, conscious that she stood exposed in front of the congregation. Maybe it was an allergy to the bouquet?

"Vivien, take this ring," said Ross, "as a sign of my love and fidelity."

A sob escaped Jules and she tried to turn it into a cough, darting a glance at the bride and groom to see if they'd noticed.

Fortunately they were lost in each other. She did see a row of grinning groomsmen, which should have been enough to…

"Ross, take this ring," Viv began.

Another sob escaped her. It was just so damn beautiful.

Dimly she was aware of Claire and Lee swapping places. A neatly folded lavender handkerchief was pressed into her palm. She took it gratefully, fumbling with her free hand for Lee's. His fingers intertwined with hers, strong, solid and warm.

The priest said, "I now pronounce you man and wife."

And Jules started blubbering in earnest.

BOTH SHE AND Jo came in for a lot of ribbing later, after the wine had flowed freely. With the cake cut, the speeches made and the first dance over, a band was rocking the silk-lined marquee that took up most of the paddock in front of the farmhouse. The wedding party had congregated outside for a brief respite from the noise and dancing. Overhead the stars were beginning to appear as the sky faded from pale blue to a velvety deep violet.

"Actually," Viv confided from her position sitting on her new husband's knee, "I would have been perfectly happy getting married in a registry office, but a wedding forces Mum and Dad together. I have high hopes of a reconciliation."

Everyone's attention swung to Ross. Viv noticed. "What?"

"We didn't need to do the big wedding?" Ice said hoarsely. "I went through all this torture for nothing?"

"No," his bride returned serenely. "You went through it for me.... Let me tell you about my honeymoon lingerie."

Ross brightened. "Is it—"

"No sexy talk with my sister," Dan cut in. "I don't care if you're married."

Lifting Viv off his lap, Ross stood, a little unsteadily. "We need a toast since we're all together, and I hid a bottle of vintage champagne in the kitchen. "Swannie—" he pulled Jo out of her chair "—I need someone sober to carry a tray of glasses."

"Lead on, Ice-cream." Bickering fondly over nicknames, the two of them headed toward the house.

"There's one thing I don't understand," Jules said quietly to Nate, Claire and Dan while Lee traded banter with the bride. "Why he wasn't killed by his captors." This was probably her best opportunity to ask them.

"Alive he had value as a negotiating tool if they needed it," Nate said. "They still had seven fingers."

Jules and Claire shuddered.

"And many of his captors would have been highly superstitious," Dan added. "Murdering a guy who's done the honorable thing who'd been given sanctuary is bad karma in any culture."

Lee tuned in and added, "I suspect Ajmal made his own threats."

Jules nestled against him. "What happened to Ajmal? Do you know?"

Nate answered. "He and his immediate family are no longer at the village. That's all the SAS were able to discover."

"I think he supplied the allies with my location," Lee said. "My fear is that he was killed for it."

Jules tightened her grip around Lee's waist. "What would prompt him to tip them off after all those months?"

"His militant son was killed two weeks before Lee's release," Dan answered. "Perhaps that freed him to save his foster son."

Jules frowned. "If he's as smart as Lee says," she wondered aloud, "wouldn't it make sense to relocate *before* making your tip-off?"

Everyone stared at her. Then a slow smile curved Lee's mouth.

"Yeah," he said. "It would."

"Why the hell didn't we think of that?" Nate said.

"You forget," Jules said modestly, "I'm trained to look for loopholes."

A champagne cork smacked the tent wall behind them. Everyone ducked.

"Oops." Grinning, Ross carried a foaming bottle of Krug Grand Cuvée. Ignoring the flurry of good-natured curses from the guys, he bent to kiss his bride. "I missed you," he said.

Jules sighed.

"Closet romantic," Lee whispered in her ear and she feigned a scowl.

"Your fault!"

Jo passed out champagne flutes then swiped the bottle from a distracted Ross and filled them while there was still liquid in it. "What's the toast, Ice-cream?"

"There are a few." Ross gestured everyone to their feet and toasted his bride. Then his expression sobered, "We all know who comes next." He nodded to Nate, who raised his glass.

"To Steve," Nate said, looping his free arm around Claire.

"May you rest in peace, my darling." With a dignity that brought a lump to Jules's throat, Claire toasted her late husband.

Solemnly everyone clinked glasses and drank.

Ross raised his glass again. "And to new beginnings," he said to Claire and Nate.

"To new beginnings." Lee was the first to toast and it made Jules glad to see it.

"Speaking of new beginnings," Jo said carefully to Dan. "I just saw your parents making out on the love seat on our porch."

Viv whooped, but Dan groaned. "Isn't it enough that my sister's making out with my buddy?" He plucked the glass of orange juice from his laughing wife's fingers. "If I can't beat 'em."

Passing Jo's flute to Ross, he swept his pregnant wife into a passionate embrace that made everyone turn away laughing.

"Are they done yet?" Ice uncovered his eyes. "C'mon, Shep, it's your turn for a toast."

"That's easy." One hand fanned over his wife's belly, Dan held up his glass. "To a new life," he said.

Jules smiled at Lee. "We'll drink to that…and on behalf of the women, here's to a few good men."

Four glasses rang together. "To good men."

"And, in particular—" Jules raised her flute "—to a guy so selfless that he released an old man from his pledge and gave himself over to the Taliban, rather than continue to risk the lives of women and children. And so unassuming he didn't tell his friends about it."

Slowly everyone turned to stare at Lee.

"Is this true?" the bridegroom demanded.

But Lee was staring at her. "Who told you…my C.O.?"

"I worked it out." She clinked her flute against his. "Remember? We're soul mates."

His grin was like the sun coming out.

"To soul mates," he said.

* * * * *

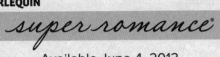

SPECIAL EXCERPT FROM

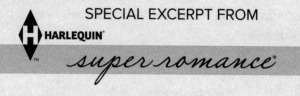

HARLEQUIN

super romance

His Uptown Girl
By Liz Talley

It's time for Eleanor Theriot to get back into the
dating scene. And now a friend has dared her
to chat up the gorgeous guy who's standing
across the street! How can she resist that dare?
Read on for an exciting excerpt
of the upcoming book

She could do this. Taking a deep breath, Eleanor Theriot
stepped out of her shop onto Magazine Street. She shut the
door behind her, gave it a little tug, then slapped a hand to her
forehead and patted her pockets.

Damn, she was a good actress. Anyone watching would
definitely think she'd locked herself out.

Hopefully that included Mr. Hunky Painter Dude, whom
she intended to ask out. Like on a date.

She started toward him. The closer she got, the hotter—and
younger—the guy looked.

This was stupid. He was out of her league.

Too hot for her.

Too young for her.

She needed to abandon this whole ruse. It was dumb to

pretend to be locked out simply to talk to the man. Then he lifted his head and caught her gaze.

Oh, dear Lord. Eyes the color of smoke swept over her. That look wasn't casual or dismissive. Oddly enough, his gaze felt…profound.

Or maybe she needed to drink less coffee. She had to be imagining a connection between them.

Now that she was standing in front of him, though, she had to see this ridiculous plan through. She licked her lips, wishing she'd put on the lip gloss. Not only did she feel stupid, but her lips were bare. Eleanor the Daring was appalled by Eleanor the Unprepared who had shown up in her stead.

"Hey, I'm Dez. Can I help you?" he asked.

You can if you toss me over your shoulder, and…

She didn't say that, of course.

"I'm looking for a screw." Eleanor cringed at what she did say. *So* much worse! "I mean, a *screwdriver.*" *Please let this nightmare end.* "I'm locked out."

Turns out Dez is *not* just a random guy and there's more than attraction pulling these two together! Find out what those connections are in HIS UPTOWN GIRL by Liz Talley, available June 2013 from Harlequin® Superromance®.

REQUEST YOUR FREE BOOKS!
2 FREE NOVELS PLUS 2 FREE GIFTS!

HARLEQUIN

super romance

More Story...More Romance

YES! Please send me 2 FREE Harlequin® Superromance® novels and my 2 FREE gifts (gifts are worth about $10). After receiving them, if I don't wish to receive any more books, I can return the shipping statement marked "cancel." If I don't cancel, I will receive 6 brand-new novels every month and be billed just $4.94 per book in the U.S. or $5.24 per book in Canada. That's a savings of at least 14% off the cover price! It's quite a bargain! Shipping and handling is just 50¢ per book in the U.S. and 75¢ per book in Canada.* I understand that accepting the 2 free books and gifts places me under no obligation to buy anything. I can always return a shipment and cancel at any time. Even if I never buy another book, the two free books and gifts are mine to keep forever.

135/336 HDN F46N

Name _____ (PLEASE PRINT) _____

Address _____ Apt. #

City _____ State/Prov. _____ Zip/Postal Code

Signature (if under 18, a parent or guardian must sign)

Mail to the Harlequin® Reader Service:
IN U.S.A.: P.O. Box 1867, Buffalo, NY 14240-1867
IN CANADA: P.O. Box 609, Fort Erie, Ontario L2A 5X3

**Are you a current subscriber to Harlequin Superromance books
and want to receive the larger-print edition?
Call 1-800-873-8635 or visit www.ReaderService.com.**

* Terms and prices subject to change without notice. Prices do not include applicable taxes. Sales tax applicable in N.Y. Canadian residents will be charged applicable taxes. Offer not valid in Quebec. This offer is limited to one order per household. Not valid for current subscribers to Harlequin Superromance books. All orders subject to credit approval. Credit or debit balances in a customer's account(s) may be offset by any other outstanding balance owed by or to the customer. Please allow 4 to 6 weeks for delivery. Offer available while quantities last.

Your Privacy—The Harlequin® Reader Service is committed to protecting your privacy. Our Privacy Policy is available online at www.ReaderService.com or upon request from the Harlequin Reader Service.

We make a portion of our mailing list available to reputable third parties that offer products we believe may interest you. If you prefer that we not exchange your name with third parties, or if you wish to clarify or modify your communication preferences, please visit us at www.ReaderService.com/consumerchoice or write to us at Harlequin Reader Service Preference Service, P.O. Box 9062, Buffalo, NY 14269. Include your complete name and address.

HSR13R

Wild hearts are hard to tame....

Matt Montoya longs to be a champion again. Not only has the tie-down roper suffered a crippling knee injury, he can't reclaim his former glory without his best rope horse. But Liv Bailey, who tutored Matt in high school, is Beckett's new owner—and when their tempers clash over who stakes claim, sparks fly in more ways than one!

Enjoy the latest story in The Montana Way series!

Once a Champion
by Jeannie Watt

AVAILABLE IN JUNE